Sam(uel)

COLLEEN GAREAU

"Great read! Keeps you hooked till the very end!"

"Lizzie and Sam find their worlds collide. Two people from two totally different walks of life, both have one thing in common – they are survivors. This book was really excellent and one of the best books I have read recently."

"This book… kept me hooked from beginning to end. There were some twists in the story that I didn't expect- at all. The author… had me convinced the story was going one way and then something would happen that sometimes made me go back and re-read as I was so speechless."

"Sam(uel) is a story of escaping unjust boundaries, self-discovery, learning to trust when life gives all too few reasons, and allowing yourself to love… If there's a heart beating in that chest of yours, you'll love this book"

"This book drew me in from the very beginning and I had a hard time putting it down. I had looked at the "Look Inside" feature and the story interested me but I definitely didn't expect to be drawn into the lives of the characters that way I was."

"I definitely recommend this book."

"Amazing! I could not put it down. The character development is so well done you feel like Lizzie is a close friend, and you come to love Sam as well. I cheered for their successes and cried with them at their setbacks."

To Heidi and Liam
with love

Chapter One

The waves of pain surge through her, gripping deeper than she had imagined possible. Her muscles and ligaments entwine like fisherman's knots, twisting, twisting. Pulling tight.

A trough arrives, bringing a minute or two of rest. Lizzie walks with care, a novice skater on hard ice afraid of falling through. She pauses when her insides seize then continues through the building. She locks the door to the women's room and spreads layer upon layer of hand towel on the floor then strips out of her clothes, stepping on the legs of her pants to pull them off when she cannot bend. Mentally reviewing the next steps, she opens a canvas bag and sets out the items she will need, trying to maintain her wits.

Girls do this everyday, she reminds herself. Give birth alone. Babies born in toilets, at schools, in alleyways, even in their own beds with parents sleeping in the next room.

This soothes her until a contraction grabs her in its fist and squeezes. Reading about a thing and doing it are as closely related as are painting a portrait and digging a ditch. There is no escaping the pain now. There is just breathing to get past the next crest.

If only she'd gotten farther away.

She closes her eyes and glimpses snippets from her life that flicker at random as though she is dying. The green tree line as seen from a spot on the cliff overlooking the river, the curl of Rue's lip as he crooned into a microphone, the stain of wild blueberries on her fingertips. Life playing out in your mind is supposed to happen before death.

Is that what birth is? she wonders. The death of something? Of what? Childhood? Being cared for? She snorts at this. Who has ever cared for her?

The next contraction erases the bitterness from her mind. A moan surges inside her and carries the enormity of her effort from her womb to the rough north country beyond the door. She isn't Lizzie now – just an animal squatting on the ground, her feet in her own fluids. The smell of iron and sweat and something wild surrounds her. Saliva fills her mouth and she retches, vomiting into the toilet.

Her legs quiver from exhaustion and the next contraction drops her onto all fours. A rib, newly healed, feels as though it might break anew as it is pushed to its limits against the pressure of her straining muscles.

Her neck and face and back are slick with sweat. She pants, trying to remember the rhythm she is supposed to use but fails and can do no more than grunt. Her mouth hangs open, her nostrils flare. She feels the cold hardness of the bathroom tiles through the paper that lies underneath the palms of her hands splayed out on either side of her to balance her weight.

As if from above, she envisions herself hunched over and straining, each vertebra in her spine outlined in relief, her long braid hanging toward the floor. Her nerve falters. What if something goes wrong?

Another contraction hits and thoughts of anything other than this task flee. Her primal body memory takes over, helping her bear down so hard she feels blood might explode through her eyes. A mournful lowing fills her ears and some part of her consciousness registers that the sound is hers.

Here, at the end, she is afraid. Frightened of what is about to happen, frightened of the pain of ripping. Frightened she might die. She is seventeen, alone, and as she labours, she cries for the one who is no longer there.

Granny Gee, Granny Gee. Help me, help me, please.

The idea that she might be running out of time flits past, but she ignores it. In her state, time is meaningless, changeless. She knows neither how long she has been here nor how much longer her work will last. She is in a middle world, her resolve stretched thin.

There is a contraction, then another and another. They come with no space between. She pushes though, truthfully, doing so is beyond her will. She can't not push. Tears course along her hot face. Her body works without her and she cries out in fear. The urge to push is more powerful than anything she's ever known.

She bears down, grinding her teeth and feeling every muscle from her face to her feet clench. And then there is nothing. The pain stops. Just like that.

She feels between her legs. A small, round head.

She gives a gentle push and a little body slides into her waiting hands.

Lizzie pulls her child forward. Her fatigue falls away as adrenaline pumps into her veins.

She looks at the tiny infant – a girl – and smiles.

"My baby," she whispers, wriggling away from the wet and into a sitting position on the floor. She lays the child onto her shaking legs and reaches for the dental floss on the counter to tie off the umbilical cord. Her hands are trembling, so it takes a few tries before she gets the knot tight enough. She cuts the cord and struggles to her feet with her new baby in her arms. With a grunt, she pushes herself to her feet; the effort forces out the afterbirth.

The blood and other fluid on her legs are inconsequential as she washes her daughter in the small bathroom sink. She pulls a doll-sized diaper from her supplies along with a fleece sleeper and pram suit.

There isn't much time, but she doesn't hurry. She wants – no, must – do everything just right.

Lizzie glances at her naked self in the mirror. The smile on her face surprises her. Her eyes sparkle against her sweaty skin.

She nestles her daughter on a bed of carry-alls so she can clean herself and the room. The last thing she needs to leave behind is evidence of a birth. While she wipes and mops, she tries to avoid looking at the effluent she has created.

By the time she has finished bathing and cleaning the room, her throat burns and she guzzles a bottle of water. She drinks so quickly the liquid spills from her mouth yet she cannot quench her incredible thirst. It is like throwing a cupful of water onto a desert floor, like swallowing dust. Suffocating, she is too hot and can't pull the suddenly stagnant air quickly enough into her lungs. She empties the bottle then lowers her head and slurps directly from a faucet. She splashes water onto the back of her neck to cool the blood-flow to her head.

In a moment, she is better. She dresses herself and places her baby in a carrier strapped to her chest, astonished that there is no pain, no soreness. It should hurt, shouldn't it? She gathers the reams of wet paper towel into a garbage bag and peeks outside. They are alone. Of course they are. A glance at the clock on a wall tells her no one should arrive for another hour or two.

She is full of energy, euphoria even, and feels like she can do anything. As though, even in the inadequate light given by the moon and stars that shine through a veil of clouds, her feet will skim over the few remaining patches of ice and still-dead grass to locate safe purchase. She walks beyond the clearing into the trees where she heaves the plastic bag as far as she can. Away from any light with brush and branches poking out everywhere, she can't see where it has landed, but it won't have been far. She can only hope animals will destroy it before humans take note.

She retraces her steps to the bathroom and slings her heavy bags onto her strong shoulders. A self-satisfied ripple runs through her. Things are working out – so far.

The crunch, crunch, crunch of her sneakers on the gravel parking lot is the only sound to crack the chilly morning air that soothes her hot face. A lamppost, a beacon standing at the edge of the tarmac opens the pre-dawn darkness with a golden slit. Just enough to let her pick the right plane – one of three Cessnas and the only one that's scheduled for an early-morning take-off.

There is no time to dawdle, to admire her newborn. Lizzie adjusts the boxes located behind the second row of seats where there is more room than in the tightly packed tail. She crams her bags among the cargo then nestles in the area she's cleared for herself. She rubs her nipples with whiskey from a one-ounce bottle stolen from a friend's house and nurses her child for the first time. Using liquor is a trick Mama told her she'd once used to get Lizzie to sleep during a long bout of colic. Although they aren't travelling far, Lizzie can't take any chances that her baby might wake during their escape.

The power of the baby's suction comes as a surprise. Who would have thought one so small could exert this type of pull? It feels as though Lizzie's skin might be sucked off.

She looks around their temporary quarters, trying to take her mind off the pain. There is little to see with boxes surrounding her. Not that it matters.

Lizzie knows a thing or two about planes and small airports, having worked behind the desk at the Black River Airport after school. Calling the single, squat building and mowed field "airport" implied undue optimism on the owners' part, yet the operation had been enough to teach Lizzie what she had to learn. She'd known what to look for in the open log books when she'd wandered in to this one three days ago pretending to be interested in flight lessons for an imaginary fiancé.

Though she'd never planned to give birth here, having thought she'd be at the end of her journey beforehand, she had intended to be on this plane, and here she is. Lizzie blows a kiss to the sky.

As her daughter nurses, Lizzie watches the delicate face with its hungry, tugging lips. She is only just visible in the meagre light from the lamppost. Lizzie marvels at the roundness of her baby's cheek, the strong grip of the miniature fingers.

"You're beautiful," she whispers to the little head. It occurs to her that she has not thought of a name for this child and instant worry over what this oversight might say about her mothering skills alarms her. "How could I forget to give you a name?" Her eyes brim with tears. Despite her best efforts to hold her distress inside, she cries. "I never even thought about it. You were just 'Baby.' For all those months."

She composes herself and wipes her face in disgust. Hormones, she thinks. It must be hormones. She searches without success for a pocket to find a tissue. Her hand runs over the large elastic panel that stretches across her stomach and she remembers these maternity jeans don't have pockets. She wipes her nose on her sleeve and says: "In my defence, I've had a lot to figure out."

Lizzie bites her bottom lip, fighting rising anxiousness over what might have happened to her had she not left when she did. Thinking she had another two weeks, she might have waited and then what? She shudders. She doesn't want to think about that now.

She watches her daughter, impatient at the length of time nursing requires. Their nestling, however, brings to mind the comfort of Granny Gee's large breasts – the way she would pull Lizzie into their billowy softness. Granny Gee said they were the only two things Grandpa had ever liked about her. "Don't say that in front of Lizzie," Mama admonished and Granny Gee hissed back at her. "I've been quieted and held back my whole life. I'll damn well say whatever I please and you won't shush me."

The memory makes Lizzie smile in spite of the discomfort of her cramped position. Her bottom is no longer anaesthetised by endorphins and soon her shoulders ache also. She squirms, trying without success for a better position, but every movement makes her ache. Her thirst grows as her own bodily fluids are suctioned from her. She reaches inside a backpack with one hand, searching for a bottle of water.

"Sarah Jane, that's what I'm going to name you. Sarah Jane. After your great-grandmother." Lizzie glances heavenward. "Stay with me, Granny Gee. Keep us safe."

The energy that had propelled her earlier, now ebbs like a cold tide, leaving her drained and shivering. When Sarah Jane is finished, Lizzie pulls the flaps of her coat around them both. The cold of the tin floor spreads through her. She rubs her legs against each other and strokes Sarah Jane's back and limbs to warm them. To take her mind off the temperature, she focuses on what is to come, hoping the noise of the twin engines will be enough to cover any sound she and her baby might make.

Tiredness overtakes her and she surrenders to fate. For the moment, she has done all she can. She squirms again in an attempt to rest her head against a box for a few moments of rest.

Her sleep is broken by the sound of a door opening. It is lighter now and her eyes roam over the boxes around her. Is she hidden well enough? The plane dips as the pilot hops into his seat.

"Be back before supper," he calls to someone Lizzie neither sees nor hears.

The small door of the plane clicks shut and she prays to her dead grandmother as fervently as any human has ever prayed to any god since the dawn of time. She prays for Sarah Jane to stay asleep, for the flight to go according to her plan, for her to be able to slip away unseen at the other end of the journey, and for a job and money and a home and finally to be a competent, loving parent. Not like hers. No, definitely not like them at all.

The engines roar to life, the vibration fills the cabin and Lizzie until she can't differentiate their thrumming from the pounding of her own heart.

Fear grabs her at what might happen next. She places her hands over the baby's head. Please don't cry. Please don't cry. Please don't cry. Please don't cry. Her thoughts run together as, over and over, she wills Sarah Jane to stay sleeping.

The plane advances down the grassy, rut-filled runway, gaining speed. Lizzie bounces, hitting the back of her head on a box. Sarah Jane begins to fuss.

"Shh, shh," Lizzie whispers into her baby's ear as she struggles to unleash a breast from her too-tight bra. A century, no, an eon, passes before Sarah settles in to nurse and Lizzie has the first inkling that her escape plan might succeed.

In seconds, the bumps of the runway disappear as the plane takes to the air. It angles sharply upward and Lizzie is pushed hard against the cargo beside her. She is glad of the close quarters that save her from injury.

After the plane levels off, Sarah Jane settles and Lizzie feels her eyelids grow heavy. She's had so little sleep in the past day and the adrenaline that had pushed her forward is gone. She exercises her face to stay awake, forcing her eyes open again and again, but it's no use. Sarah Jane is sleeping and Lizzie feels the fight to stay conscious drain away from her.

Chapter Two

It is a sunny day. The kind of day offered by late winter that its grip on Earth is weakening. When the sun offers the first hint of warmth against skin even though snow still clings to the ground, deepest in areas of shade, and at least one more storm is expected by all but the most optimistic.

It is the kind of day, arriving at the right time of year, that gives locals reason to entertain themselves with stories of bad weather. Not that much of an excuse is ever needed.

The storm in 2006 that brought everything Mother Nature had to offer — snow, freezing rain, flash freezing, whiteouts and wind – and the Deep Winter Storm of 1996 that exhausted the town's snow removal budget before December had even begun. The old-timers try to outdo each other with reminiscences of severe weather, real or invented, near or afar. The one thing the Northerners agree on is that the carcass of this winter has only a few gasps left in it, however mighty or weak they may be.

Lizzie arrives home from school to a still house. Mama is at work and Papa is sleeping. He's on nightshift and won't rise till dinnertime.

She reads a note from Mama about making meatloaf and mashed potatoes for supper and smiles in anticipation. Meatloaf is one of her favourites.

She mixes the minced beef with onions and seasoning, adds breadcrumbs and a cup of tomato sauce and slips the pan into the oven. She scrubs the potatoes, dices them and drops them into a pot of water with a bit of salt, skins on. Fresh vegetables are too expensive at this time of year so Lizzie pokes around the cupboards until she locates a can of corn. It will do just fine.

Satisfied that her task is well underway, Lizzie bends to lift her backpack filled to bursting with schoolbooks. There is a flutter inside her – nothing more than a hiccup, the gentle touch of gossamer wings, but Lizzie realizes she is feeling her baby's first hello. She presses a hand to her stomach, trying to find a lump, perhaps a little foot. The baby is too small for that.

She straightens, pushing a wide strap over her shoulder and glimpses herself in the long kitchen mirror. She has dark circles under her eyes and her usually pale skin has taken on the colour of putty. She tucks her dark blond hair behind her ears and turns to see her outline in the glass. Running her fingertips along the bottom edge of her baggy sweatshirt, she wonders how much longer it might cover her secret.

Sunlight reflects off the mirror and Lizzie turns toward the window to see it dance on the hard-packed snow in the backyard. She listens to the ice that has melted in the rain gutters gurgle down the drain spout. A cardinal flits by, its red plumage in bright contrast against the dull black-green of the trees. Moments later, a single honk and then a hundred herald the arrival of a flock of Canada geese travelling farther north. They are ahead of schedule by one or two weeks, possibly foretelling an early spring. They fly low in the sky in preparation for landing in the partially thawed lake ahead. She cranes her neck to watch how their wings carry them forward, beating like canoe paddles in a swift current, answering the call of their traditional breeding grounds.

The dread of passing time steals upon her.

She thinks of Rue and tastes the puke at the back of her throat. She closes her eyes and breathes deeply, trying to dispel her revulsion as well as her fear about the future.

What had gotten into her head that made her crazy for him?

Lust. That was all. Blind as dirt; magnetic as true north.

Goddamn. How she had wanted him. She inhales, remembering his scent, the feel of him inside her. Her eyes spring open in shock at her wetness.

She's in it now. No mistake. No escape.

Her hand travels to her belly as though to protect her baby from such thoughts.

She feels her tautness and smiles. Someone to love, to love her, isn't so bad. Not so bad at all.

She turns to the mirror to examine her profile and runs her hands in circles over her expanding bulge. The baby moves again and Lizzie imagines she can feel a ripple under her hand. Smiling, she cocks her head, lifting her top to get a proper look.

"Whore!"

Lizzie snaps her head around. Her father's frame fills the hall entranceway. His flannel shirt is buttoned to the neck, meeting his crimson face as though the collar of his shirt is choking him.

"Whore!" he roars again.

Lizzie drops her shirt and steps back.

Papa advances, trembling, boiling. He clenches and unclenches his working hands. "Gott damn it to hell!" He grabs a ladder-back chair by a leg and swings it into the air, crashing it against the solid kitchen table. The chair splinters and shards of wood fly about the room like shattered glass. Papa brandishes the length of a rounded leg in his hand.

"What have you done to our family?"

Lizzie cowers against a wall. Her mind is blank, frozen except for the knowledge that today she will die.

"You opened your legs to him?"

"Papa. Please…" She inches along the wall toward the door; her hands held out before her, palms open in supplication.

"Filthy pig." Papa lurches toward her and Lizzie darts to the side. Papa grabs a handful of her hair and jerks her head backward, pulling her toward him. "You have shamed me." The words spit from between clenched lips; saliva sprays on Lizzie's face.

He reaches high and brings his weapon down as though to crush Lizzie's skull, but she spins to the side, ripping hair from her scalp. The leg of the chair catches her ribcage and Lizzie hears the snap of a bone before she feels it. She screams and crumples against the wall, holding her hands in front of her face. Lizzie's mind breaks free from her body and floats. There is no pain. This isn't really happening. Survival is all there is.

Like all the other times: to survive is victory.

Papa smashes the piece of wood against the wall, once, twice, three times, leaving holes in the drywall.

He swings the broken leg like a hammer, but pulls up short at the last moment. The tip of the wood catches the bridge of her nose and splits open the skin. The sound of the tear is gentle, the pain – an explosion. Lizzie falls to the floor shrieking.

He throws the chair leg across the room and turns away, chest heaving, the worst of his anger spent. He stands with his back to her, not even concerned that Lizzie might attempt to retaliate. She never has.

"You will be married before your bastard is born or you will be cast out. You will be no daughter of mine. Und I will kill that Schweinhund."

Papa steps into his unlaced work boots and reaches for his thick plaid jacket that hangs on a hook next to the mirror. He glances at his hand and clomps to the sink to wash off what must be Lizzie's blood. He wipes his hands as though he were brushing off nothing more important than a bit of dirt.

Hate, as fierce and immediate as the pain, burns through Lizzie as she stares at him. She wants to claw at his face with her nails. She wants to humiliate him until he begs for forgiveness that she will never give him.

He doesn't even look her way as he stomps out, slamming the door closed with such force that it springs from its latch and smashes into the wall before snapping shut. He is letting her know – as if there was any possibility she didn't – who was in control.

Lizzie doesn't move until she hears the truck backing out of the drive. She tries to raise herself but cannot. She lies panting, wishing for inspiration to extricate herself from her life. When she hears the sound of the door opening, she peers through blood and tears to find Mama crouching over her. Mama reaches to pull Lizzie into a hug, but Lizzie shrieks and grabs her side.

When she tells Mama what has happened there is no surprise on the aging face. None at all. About any of it.

"You knew?"

Mama nods.

"That I was pregnant? You knew? And you didn't say anything?" Lizzie is confounded. How could Mama have left her to fend for herself? Surely, it is an unlikely thing for a parent to do. A caring parent.

Lizzie wants to cry as Mama blinks, her sad face betraying the inevitability of their twinned fates.

"Why didn't you help me?"

"And do what? What could I do? It was too late to change anything." Mama is tired. Her voice is flat, detached. It is the sound of defeat. Her narrow shoulders sag under her hotel maid's uniform.

"Help me. Somehow. Help me decide what to do." Lizzie again attempts to rise to a sitting position and gasps at the piercing pain. "I think my ribs are broken."

"Come." Mama holds out her arm for Lizzie to leverage her weight against as she comes to her knees and then to her feet. "Go to your room. I'll get the comfrey."

Lizzie takes a step and gasps at the stabbing in her side. "I don't think I can walk by myself."

There is a moment, as Mama helps Lizzie to her room and into a night-gown, when Lizzie considers going to a hospital. Just as quickly the thought is extinguished. It isn't what they do. People would know. Things that are now only rumours would be rumours no more.

Bruises are already growing from the welts on her torso and face. She cannot lie flat so Mama props her up with cushions she brings from the front room. They are from a set Mama made years ago to brighten the old brown sofa. Their covers have backgrounds of creamy white cotton and are covered in worn green leaves and pink roses that were once red. The old fabric is soft from use and many washings. They match the sun-faded curtains in the parlour window.

Mama places the last cushion under Lizzie's knees to take the strain off her spine. "When are you due?" she asks as she rolls the nightie to Lizzie's hip.

"Early June," Lizzie says.

"Does Rue know?"

Lizzie nods. He knows all right. He's thrilled that his little virgin will be his forever. "No one will want you now," he said when she told him.

"Are you going to marry him?"

"Papa says I am."

Mama remains expressionless and Lizzie is infuriated by her calm. She would demand her mother's outrage and wants to scream at her. Scream till her throat bleeds, till her lungs collapse. She wants to scream until Mama wakes from the safe harbour of half-sleep and denial and surrender. She wants this terrible news to spark something dead in Mama.

Instead, she swallows her anger, burying it where strong emotions hide, and says nothing as Mama sponges the blood from her face and tapes butterfly bandages to her nose. She rubs comfrey ointment onto Lizzie's skin to help with bruising.

"It's not a bad break." She says as though assessing a damaged tchotchke. "Might just leave a small bump."

How sad that you know this. Lizzie clenches her teeth, fighting back, hopelessness as Mama examines her torso, chewing her cheek in concentration.

"Your rib is going to be more difficult. Guess we should have put this nightgown on last. Here, lift your bum and I'll pull it up."

Moving is agony and Lizzie grinds her teeth together as she lifts herself by pushing down on her hands. Mama rubs ointment over the purple line that indents Lizzie's skin. "Some call this knit bone. I don't think it'll do that, but it can't hurt." She pauses. "You're going to carry one heck of a bruise there." She winds an elastic bandage around Lizzie's torso. "Not much to be done for a broken rib. It should start feeling better in a couple of days when the bone begins to heal."

Such dispassion.

Lizzie's head hurts and she touches the back of her head for the source. She locates a bald spot and her hand comes away with blood. She holds her red fingers out to Mama who applies the salve with the assurance of a nurse. She's had practice at this sort of thing.

Yet there is something about her no-nonsense approach that makes Lizzie want to strike her. To tell her to smarten up. But it's no use. This is Mama's life. She's only thirty-nine yet her greying hair and lined face say she's older. She's never been anywhere outside of Black River, doesn't know any life other than this. In few words, Mama has let Lizzie know she doesn't figure there's anywhere for her to go.

She pulls Lizzie's nightclothes down, covers her with a sheet and fleece blanket, and retreats to the kitchen to revive, as best she can, their overcooked supper. She brings Lizzie a plate and two extra-strength acetaminophen.

The meatloaf is overcooked and drier than it ought to be. Lizzie dips a piece into ketchup. It's a mistake. The ketchup looks like blood, blood on darkened flesh. She wipes her fork on a piece of paper towel and turns her plate so the meat faces away. She eats her mashed potatoes and kernel corn.

Papa's going to make her marry Rue. Wincing, she shifts her plate onto her bedside table and a sour taste fills her mouth.

The ceremony that would have thrilled her only months ago, now fills her with despair. With Rue, she'll have a carbon copy of Mama's life except it will be a degree worse, for, in addition to being a bully, Rue is a cheat. Although she's never said anything about it, never caused a scene, she's pretty sure she's right. The irony being that by the time she had it sorted out in her own head, she no longer cared, and by the time she no longer cared, she was pregnant.

If that isn't the definition of an ironic dilemma, Lizzie doesn't know what is.

As she had feared, once her secret was discovered, her problem would be made worse. And it is. Infinitely worse.

There is no way Lizzie can spend her life in this town with Rue.

She has to get away.

Before the wedding.

Before the baby.

Before she turns into Mama.

Chapter Three

Lizzie is jerked back to wakefulness as the pilot drops the flaps on the wings of the plane, slowing it quickly for landing. Her body is tense against what is sure to be a hard landing on a short runway. She wraps her hand around Sarah Jane's head to hold her still against bumps and bouncing. So many things can go wrong in these last minutes before freedom.

She strains to hear the conversation between the pilot and air control.

"… alpha, foxtrot, echo…"

"… runway… "

"… wind's…"

It is useless; the plane's engines are too loud, a fact for which she is thankful.

Her ears are blocked and the ambient sound is muted as the plane loses altitude. She provides her breast to the waking baby hoping to cut short any fussing that might result from the building pressure.

The plane touches down, jostling Lizzie and Sarah Jane as it taxies to a stop. Lizzie clutches her newborn close and recommences praying. Please don't cry. Please don't cry.

Static from the radio overtakes the roar of the engines as they wind down and Lizzie mouths a new plea to her grandma, hoping the pilot leaves the plane without realizing he has stowaways.

Lizzie rocks her body as much as she dares, comforting the now alert Sarah Jane. Their futures rely on the outcome of the next few minutes. Her stomach knots, her throat dries until it feels like sandpaper grating against itself. She fights the urge to vomit and squeezes her eyes shut as she wills the pilot to leave. If she is caught and charged with whatever it is stowaways are charged with, it would certainly make the local news, or worse, regional, alerting Papa and Rue to her whereabouts. It is a possibility she doesn't want to consider.

Whistling and the sound of paper rustling come from the front of the plane. A door swings open, allowing a welcoming breeze to enter the cramped interior, and the side of the plane dips as the pilot hops to the ground from his seat. Lizzie hears the door close, the insubstantial sound of tin on tin, and she weeps in relief, only now realizing how tense her muscles are.

She waits to feel the bump of anchors being wedged against the wheels then slowly lifts her head to examine the view from one of the passenger windows. She sees the back of the pilot's head and then his back as he strides toward the airstrip's office.

"C'mon, Baby," she coos, batting away her rising panic. "We're almost home free."

Lizzie swings her possessions onto one of the rear passenger seats and, keeping her body as low as she is able with her daughter against her chest, steps onto the grassy runway. She takes a moment to roll the stiffness from her shoulders before flipping the straps of her bags over them. Holding her daughter and all her possessions, she trots to the tree-line, keeping the cargo and commuter planes between herself and the office windows, expecting with each step to hear the shout of pursuit behind her.

Once hidden in the cover of trees and scrub brush, she drops her burden onto the ground and unbuckles the baby carrier, settling Sarah Jane on the bags. She squats for a pee then gulps the contents of another bottle of water, drinking till she runs out of breath. Her stomach grumbles. She wolfs down two granola bars, wishing for something more substantial like pancakes loaded with butter and maple syrup. Bacon. A cheese omelette. Her stomach growls and she pushes such thoughts away.

She changes Sarah Jane's diaper then scratches at the soil, trying to dig a shallow hole to bury the soiled one, but cannot. In the shade, the ground is still frozen. Spring arrives at the top of the trees before it manages to warm the roots of the boreal forest. She rolls the used diaper tightly using the sticky tabs to hold it together and grimaces as she sticks it into one of her bags.

Finding a comfortable, if chilly, seat against a large pine, she nurses her daughter, enjoying the minutes to stretch her legs and relax. For the first time, she can take in the wrinkles and folds of her daughter's hands and wrists, the delicacy of her fingernails, the lusciousness of her face.

"We made it," she whispers and kisses the top of the pale-blue, knitted cap that covers the little head. "Now, to the bus."

Lizzie has planned her escape with the aplomb of a paperback spy. Only a few more legs in this journey till she can make it to the bus station in town where she'll buy a ticket for someplace new.

"There's promise in new, isn't there?" she says as though Sarah Jane might answer. Hope finds her in the solitude of the forest and pries a giggle free. "We made it." She throws back her head and inhales the scent of green and ground – the smell of freedom, she is sure.

Map Quest had shown a bus stop near the laneway to the airfield. She picks her way out of the woods, heading in that direction, her bundles once more strung over her shoulders. She keeps deep within the trees, avoiding as best she can the pockets of crystallized snow that remain in the shadows.

When she breaks through the trees at the road into town, fatigue hits her with the force of a demolition ball. She shuffles along the road barely able to lift her feet from the damp ground. Her arms tremble from exertion. Her back feels like it's stretched to its breaking point

A signpost rises from the horizon. The bus route number 132 is printed in black letters on a dirty white background.

"Thank you," Lizzie says to no one in particular.

There is no bench, no shelter so she stands at the roadside squinting at the sign to read the tiny letters of the schedule printed there. The next bus is due at the top of the hour. She checks her watch.

"I don't have forty minutes worth of standing left in me."

Dropping the bags to the ground, she stacks them to create a stool that she sits, gratefully, upon.

"I'm tired, Miss Sarah Jane. How about you?"

Sarah Jane's head bobs on her tiny neck and she blinks seriously at her mother, her top lip pinched into a peak like the mouth of a turtle.

"I hear ya. Being born's exhausting, isn't it?"

Lizzie chatters to her daughter as a means of lifting her own spirits that a short time ago had soared, but were now sinking along with her energy.

Lizzie slips her wet sneakers off and flexes her feet. Every part of her body aches, her eyelids droop and she feels like she might cry if she doesn't find a bed soon.

Sarah Jane makes sucking motions with her lips.

"Hungry again?" Lizzie unbuckles the baby carrier and brings Sarah Jane to her tender breast. "For someone so small, you sure drink a lot. I guess there's not much to fill you before my milk comes in."

She takes her baby's hand in hers, wrapping the dainty fingers around one of her own. "You're so small. I can't believe you're mine." She kisses the miniature fingers as Sarah Jane drifts off to sleep.

When the bus arrives, ten minutes late, Lizzie hauls herself on board and asks the driver for the name of a cheap place to stay. Somewhere close to the bus terminal.

"There's the Lucky 8 right across the street from the station, but it's pretty noisy," she says motioning toward Sarah Jane. "Not a place for a child. You'd be better off staying at the Overnight Inn. It's only about four blocks. People there're less scuzzy too. More likely to leave you alone."

Lizzie nods her thanks before closing her eyes. Once again, exhaustion has won.

Chapter Four

Lizzie towels herself dry, staring at the crack that runs the length of the fogged mirror. It feels good to be clean although she is aching down there and her nipples are raw and sore. She wishes she had thought to bring something for pain.

She studies herself for signs of change, wondering if others might detect new motherhood on her.

As always, she sees a sturdier, taller version of Mama. She has her father's Teutonic complexion, but it is her mother's oval face and high cheekbones that give foundation to Lizzie's pale skin. She has her mother's straight nose and clear blue eyes. Where her mother is dark, Black Irish she would say, Lizzie is fair and come summer, her lashes and brows will lighten until they are nearly invisible. Freckles that disappear in winter will dot her nose.

Her wet, ash-coloured hair sticks to her back. Her breasts are hard and swollen. They are deeply veined and their areolas are dark and knobbly – foreign to their owner who stares at them with aversion. They used to be pink and delicate. These warty things are anything but.

Under inspection, her broad hips and strong thighs seem not to have changed at all. At her belly, the skin is loose over a layer of fat that jiggles when she pokes it. Red stretch marks branch out from below her underwear. They aren't so deep, she thinks, and hopes they fade.

This is the new me. Elizabeth Mathilda Valor. She shakes her head. That's not right. She's just Lizzie.

It was Mama who began calling her that. Elizabeth was too long and she hated Beth. Sounded too much like breath, like you mightn't really exist. To Papa though, she was Elizabeth – Elis-e-bet was how he said it – or, when feeling especially sentimental, he would use her middle name, Mathilda, his battle maiden.

Lizzie pictures herself carrying a broad shield and brandishing a long sword masterfully as she marches into war, her long hair streaming behind her in a bitter wind. Flexing her knees and bending her arms, she feels the heft of her imaginary weapon. She twirls it over her head, to smash the offending vanity. She miscalculates and hits the side of her hand on the melamine corner.

"Ahh!" She jumps back, alternatively shaking her hand and rubbing the sore spot. "Goof."

After she pulls on a clean T-shirt, she washes her dirty clothes in the motel's tub and hangs them to dry. She tackles the surface of her running shoes using the plastic nailbrush provided by the motel along with a tray of cheaply perfumed soaps and shampoos. She adds the mini sewing kit to her meagre possessions.

She crawls into bed with the napping Sarah Jane and, in an instant, is asleep.

During the night, she nurses her daughter and changes diapers every two to three hours. How does any mother manage to survive? she wonders, so tired her bones cry for rest. Travel, she decides, is out of the question for at least a day or two.

She sleeps when Sarah Jane sleeps, eats take-out from the diner across the street, watches old movies on television, reads her parenting book – stolen from the Black River Library before her escape – and works hard not to worry herself sick as her modest pile of money dwindles.

She knows she should find a grocery store instead of buying food from a restaurant, but her exhaustion is so complete that she can't imagine making a trek longer than the width of the street out front.

"That's okay, sweets," she says more to herself than to her child. "I'll get a job in no time once we get to Toronto."

On the third day, Lizzie manages the walk to the nearest corner store to load up on diapers and other provisions. Back at the motel, she prepares a loaf's worth of peanut butter sandwiches, washes two apples, and fills the empty drink bottles she's been saving with water from the bathroom tap. As long as her stomach is full with something nutritious for the baby, it doesn't matter what's in it.

She arrives at the bus terminal mid-afternoon. The chipped green paint on the cinderblock exterior and worn linoleum floors inside are disheartening.

She approaches the counter to buy a ticket to her final destination. The attendant squints at her and then at Sarah Jane, puckering his mouth in disapproval. Thankfully, he remains silent and Lizzie flees to the far side of the room as soon as the transaction is complete.

Her bus leaves in twenty minutes and butterflies swirl in her stomach in terror and excitement.

This town is the farthest she's ever been from Black River yet it isn't strange to her. Small towns often share common elements. A main street lined with shops, a large department and grocery store on a side street. A Tim Horton's near a highway off ramp. Elementary and high schools, a single hospital. A few pubs. A strip club. Maybe a movie theatre. As she prepares to leave this familiar world for the unknown, she might as well be heading to the Kalahari, the city will be that foreign to her.

Her life and Sarah Jane's depends on her getting this right.

In her jittery state, she tries to forget the little bit of money that remains in her purse, money from her savings and cash stolen from Mama's secret stash.

When boarding is announced, she hands her largest bags to the driver to store in the baggage compartment and wrestles the others onto the bus to keep with her. She catches sight of herself in the driver's mirror and notices that the few days rest has done her some good. Her eyes sparkle in spite of the dark circles under them and she isn't as sore as she was. Her spirit feels, if not replenished, at least bolstered. She has made it this far without detection, though this success could be due more to lack of pursuit than to her cleverness.

She should be relieved if this is the case, yet she ponders the possibility nevertheless and is saddened that she should be worth so little. Mary, Mary, quite contrary.

She locates a seat in the front section and, since the bus isn't full, has a double seat to herself. She raises the middle armrest and, with a blanket, builds a nest on the seat beside her for Sarah Jane.

The bus sways and rumbles down the highway and within minutes, Sarah Jane is rocked to sleep. With one hand on her daughter, Lizzie sends a silent apology to the library and pulls out the parenting book.

Two women sitting ahead of Lizzie open paper bags filled with hamburgers and fries. The smell is intoxicating and Lizzie's stomach rumbles, reminding her that she hasn't eaten lunch. She retrieves two sandwiches and a bottle of water from her bag.

She glances down at her baby and sees the outline of Rue's lips. Is it possible he isn't looking for her? Neither he nor her father? She'd been sure that wounded pride, if nothing else, would have spurred them to search for her. Could she have been that wrong about them? Could it be that she doesn't even merit a missing person's report?

Although their indifference means that she can be truly free of them, some part of her still yearns for the care and love of the men who, in another girl's world, would be her protectors. Her father and the father of her child: two men who should walk through fire and brave terrible dangers for her.

She thinks of Rue, wishing that he'd stayed the boy she'd thought he was when they first met. He'd been sweet then, handsome too. Sang in a country band that played at one of the local bars every week from Wednesday to Saturday. He was a charmer, probably just like Papa had been when he wooed her mother. Before he transformed into the snake he'd become.

Funny how some things were passed down through families that had nothing to do with the colour of eyes, the curl of hair, or the tilt of nose.

She'd tried leaving Rue before, telling him she was too young to be serious, that she wanted to try for a scholarship to university. At first, he'd just laughed at her. "When was the last time a girl from the middle of bum-fuck nowhere made it to university?" He must have figured she wasn't smart enough for him to have anything to worry about. She'd give up or fail and things would go on as they had been.

It must have been quite a surprise to him when her grades had picked up and it looked like she might succeed. He'd stopped laughing and had told her the dream of school was for none like her. When she refused to give up her extra studying, he'd hit her. No goddamned girl was going to leave him behind, making him a fool.

The thing of it was, his cruelty had not been a surprise to her. In time, Lizzie realized she'd been expecting it, waiting for it.

She'd promised to be good to him after that. What choice did she have? Hadn't her parents set her course before she'd had any say?

Who did she have to run to for help? Her papa would have told her she was just another female out to ruin another man's potential, she was pretty sure of that. And Mama, poor Mama. She could barely keep herself afloat.

Afterwards, Rue paid close attention to her comings and goings after that. There were no more trips to the library or visiting her girlfriends from school. She had to plan her outings to coincide with his gigs at the bar to be sure he wouldn't know when she was out.

She'd slipped up once when one of his friends saw her coming from the library. She'd told Rue that she'd just gone out for ice cream, but he was furious. That bruise didn't disappear for weeks.

And then she discovered she was pregnant.

She didn't tell anyone at first, trying, without success, to sort out a plan. She considered an abortion. It would have gone easier on her. Doing something in secret. No one would have had to know. She thought long and hard about it, but the promise of having that little thing growing inside her – someone to love and to love her – that glimmered in her mind like a jewel.

She knew that before too long, letting out the seam of her pants and wearing baggy tops weren't going to hide the swell of her belly. She hoped inspiration would strike and she'd find a way to survive both her father's reaction and the life she'd surely have after the baby's birth.

Rue figured her secret out soon enough – her hard rounding stomach and enlarging breasts had given her away – and was happier than she'd seen him in a while. He knew he had her all to himself then. In time, pregnancy became her personal godsend, allowing her more freedom from his watchful eyes than she'd had in ages. The way he saw it, "No one in his right mind would want to fuck a pregnant girl." Neither would "a girl with a baby on her tit be off to some snotty university."

To think she'd ever found him irresistible! It was a mistake that only the thrill of having a child – this child – would provide her with any self-forgiveness.

Although Lizzie had worried Rue might tell, her fear was groundless. Rue had been almost as afraid of Papa's reaction as she – Papa being the larger of the two. When Papa found out what Lizzie had been hiding and insisted on their marriage, Rue was relieved he would face no bigger punishment. He presented Lizzie with a ring and only Lizzie's broken rib had held them up from an unceremonious town hall wedding.

For five months, Lizzie managed to keep her secret from all but Rue. While she got bigger, she worked toward finishing her school year, hoping for high honours and a scholarship to the University of Toronto. She'd been offered that scholarship pending her final marks and added the letter from admissions to her growing list of secrets. She carried the offer with her, although none of that mattered now. She'd dropped out of school following Papa's attack. By the time she'd healed enough to attend classes, it was too late to complete her year.

Lizzie bends her head forward till her nose touches Sarah Jane's head. She inhales the clean smell from her baby's skin. It's the smell of innocence and is like a balm to her spirit. Nothing can be more perfect than a baby.

Lizzie stretches her legs, smacking her shins against the metal edge of the seat in front of her and winces. Wiggling her backside to get some circulation, she looks at the people around her wondering where they are going, what their stories are. What if, she thinks, they are a busload of people on the run – each with a tale like mine?

She glances at the young man across the aisle. He is handsome and appears to be in his mid-twenties. He has dark skin and blue-black hair and wears glasses. Lizzie leans low trying to read the title on the cover of the book he's reading. He notices her and makes a sour face.

"Title?" Lizzie asks, embarrassed.

He holds the book upright. Zen and the Art of Motorcycle Maintenance.

Lizzie mouths, "thank you" and turns away from him toward the window on her side. She can tell what he's thinking, that she made a pass. Just a girl with a kid picking up strange men on a bus. Her ears grow hot with indignation. She drinks from her water bottle to cool her irritation and picks up a thread of conversation from a middle-aged couple sitting behind the young man.

They each read a different newspaper, talking over their reading, sharing news items.

"What's with those vegetarians?" the man asks. He sounds put out.

"They don't eat meat. There's different kinds," the woman answers.

"Some eat fish. Fish is a meat as far as I'm concerned."

"That's one kind. Some don't eat anything with eyes."

"Hmmm. Black-eyed peas have eyes. Or is it black-eyed Susans?"

"Black-eyed Susans," the woman confirms.

What wild flowers have to do with vegetarians, Lizzie holds onto the belly laugh that threatens to make her look like a fool, laughing all by herself.

She grins, glad they can't see her, and settles into her seat and ignoring her book, stares out the window at the passing scenery. She marvels at how ugly it is. Train tracks and hydro lines run along the side of the highway. Construction sites dot the route, men and women working large machinery to build god knows what. She is aware of the beauty that lays beyond what is visible from the road and is disheartened at what has been created that hides it.

Towns and truck stops come and go. They all look the same. Concrete buildings surrounded by asphalt parking lots covered in large vehicles, four-by-fours, trucks, old American-built cars. The North is a world of men. Burly men wearing insulated checked jackets and ball caps with the names of truck manufacturers or beer companies. Or the Leafs. There are wiry, small men in sleeveless vests. Men whose metabolisms don't allow them to pack on weight, but everyone knew could handle themselves in a fight. It didn't matter that Lizzie didn't know them, she knew of them. She knew that those who were different moved away just as soon as they could.

Women had to be tougher here too. They had to bear, admire even, the coarse give-and-take of their men, had to be content with fashions that arrived a decade late, had to be happy with limited career choices or put up with the harassment that came with the higher-paying blue-collar jobs.

Despite her generalizations that are both true and false, Lizzie is happy to be leaving. She is escaping a miserable life. So, why are her eyes welling with tears? She recalls the lakes and wild green spaces. People like her Granny Gee who made sure neighbours didn't go hungry. Women who would just as soon swat you for cursing as they would hug you if you were hurting. Men who could live from the land and protect their families from harm. She wipes her eyes and turns to her book.

The bus travels over a sharp crest and, as it angles downward over the south side of the hump, a bucolic vista spreads wide. A river runs under the highway to a lake fringed by evergreens and the graceful lines of birch trees. The water matches the cerulean blue of the sky. A memory darts in and out of Lizzie's head with the speed of a hummingbird and she holds back an exclamation of recognition.

The image of this place is somehow tied strongly to Mama is strong. It is tied also to a feeling of terrible despair and Lizzie whimpers, wanting to pull Mama close. She closes her eyes both willing memories to emerge and afraid that they might. There is nothing. Just that one landscape and Mama's face and something awful.

Had she been here with Mama? Had they made a similar trip, trying to escape together? Had Papa found them? The thought of what Mama's punishment would have been is too horrible to contemplate. Lizzie fights the lump in her throat and swallows more water to calm the acid in her stomach.

Could it have happened?

Could it explain why Mama had so thoroughly given up?

Lizzie is filled with guilt at the unkind judgments she has made against her and wishes Mama were here.

Sarah Jane wakes, her greedy mouth searching for food, and Lizzie attends to her. Later, when Sarah Jane is ready to nap, Lizzie straps her into the carrier and they both sleep.

The ride takes twelve hours from northern Ontario to downtown Toronto. Lizzie eats her sandwiches and gets out to stretch whenever the bus stops. Her baby is a good traveller and doesn't fuss much as long as her belly is full.

It's two in the morning when Lizzie gets her first glimpse of the city and the lights that seem to go on forever. Her hand flies to her face to hold back a gasp. All the information on the Internet hadn't prepared her for the reality of anything so large. She picks out the CN Tower as the bus rumbles toward it. Her heart is racing by the time they arrive at the bus depot.

Lizzie has no option but to spend the rest of the night here. Registration at the closest youth hostel – the only accommodation she can afford – isn't till afternoon.

The night is a miserable one. Lizzie stores her belongings in a locker for two dollars and hunkers down on an uncomfortable chair with her daughter curled against her. Harsh fluorescent lighting glares overhead. She dozes off and on throughout the night and by morning the black smudges under her eyes are puffy and her arms are numb from clutching her daughter close.

Their day begins at six. Once the pair are finished with nursing and washing up in the public restroom – and that only after Lizzie has scrubbed the sink with hand soap and paper towel, she is so revolted by the thought of what might have been put in the sink before they use it – they head outside to meet their new city and find somewhere cheap to eat. She can't stomach another peanut butter sandwich.

She makes her way out of the station with no idea of which direction to take. The traffic is already building despite the early hour and the smell of exhaust is suffocating. Everything is grey. The buildings, the sky, even the people lack colour as they march to wherever they're going.

Feeling daunted, Lizzie heads south and is rewarded with a diner offering breakfast for four dollars. She savours the bacon and eggs, her first meal in her new city, and sneaks some leftover toast and jam from an empty table for her lunch. Stealing is becoming second nature. Another simple act of survival.

After a leisurely meal, Lizzie examines her Google map and checks directions with the waitress before setting out for the hostel. She walks to Bay and then south to Adelaide where she turns onto Church. Standing before her, as the waitress had promised, is the youth hostel. She reserves a spot for herself in the dormitory for two nights and is told to return after four. At thirty dollars a day, she has enough money to last a week at most.

Fear claws at her.

She must find work.

Taking the map of the city that is offered to her, she asks the woman at the registration desk to mark off the locations of the nearest fast-food restaurants and hotels. These would be the easiest places to find work, she believes.

Finding her way around isn't easy, even with the map. She spends the day walking up and down street after street, lugging Sarah Jane, looking for places to apply for work and getting lost. People bear down on her from every angle. She nods and says "excuse me" as she struggles to make her way through the crowds. No one acknowledges her. It's like she isn't there.

She fills out job applications. A dozen feels like a hundred. She loses count and by four o'clock, her legs and back ache, and a large blister has swelled and burst on one of her heels. Every step is agony, her heel is on fire.

When she limps back to the bus station to retrieve her belongings, she is ready to buy a ticket north; she is that tired.

Instead, she drags herself and her daughter the many blocks to the hostel and collapses onto a bed in a corner. She sleeps so deeply that she doesn't hear other travellers arrive and depart, waking hours later when Sarah Jane cries for supper. It is almost ten o'clock and it's the longest Lizzie has slept at one go in days. If only her calves and feet weren't in such torment.

As Sarah Jane nurses, Lizzie's stomach growls. She has a few sandwiches left although the thought of more peanut butter is sickening. She gropes around in one of her bags for her last apple. It's bruised, but she eats it anyway.

"I'm lucky you're not a crier," she tells her daughter who stares back as though in contemplation. "You've got your doubts about me, don't you?"

She grins at her daughter then sobers at the thought that someone so new to the world might be worried about her mother's ability to care for her. This idea strikes Lizzie as both comical and tragic.

Who are you? What are you doing with me? Sarah Jane's eyes seem to ask. Lizzie wishes she had an answer.

When Sarah Jane has had her fill, Lizzie bathes her in the co-ed bathroom then dresses her against the chill of a spring evening and heads outside to find another cheap meal.

She ponders the possibility of locating a place that gives food to the indigent, but is unsure of the rules about babies. If the powers-that-be discover she is underage and homeless, would they take Sarah Jane away? Could they? Lizzie is unsure of the answer and doesn't want to test it.

She buys a box of bandages for her blister at a corner store and wanders north; her inner compass pulls her onward in search of supper. Through Chinatown she makes her way, wary of the crowded sidewalks and unfamiliar voices. Everyone is rushing and when a man charges into her shoulder, he doesn't pause to offer an apology. She passes Dundas Street and glances down College. It seems calmer in that direction.

Her legs are sore and she's so tired, she could cry. All she wants this second, is somewhere to eat that's quiet and not too expensive. She soldiers on. After a few blocks, the street signs tell her she is in Little Italy. There are coffee shops and restaurants. A bookstore, a drugstore, a bank. The area is tidy. The businesses are well kept and, glancing up the block to the residential area that sits behind College, she sees garden stakes standing in yards ready for summer vegetables. Her pace slows in relief at finding something that looks like a neighbourhood. She comes upon an Italian restaurant that offers late-night specials.

She enters and orders a plate of spaghetti, the cheapest thing on the menu. A woman brings her oven-warmed buns and seasoned oil for dipping. While Lizzie bolts it down, her stomach growls at the smells around her. The woman brings her another basketful. Lizzie gobbles this too. Her hunger only begins to subside as she tucks into her pasta. It comes with a plate of garlic bread. She moans as she licks the butter that runs down her fingers. She is in heaven and soon finishes the large serving.

The waitress hands her the bill. "Boy or girl?" she asks.

"Girl."

"E così bella. She is beautiful. How old is she?" The woman's Italian accent rolls from her like a hilly countryside. She is of indefinite age, her dark hair is streaked with silver and is pulled off her face and clipped into a loose knot at the nape of her neck. A few curls trail down her shoulders. There is a knowing glint in her eyes that makes Lizzie nervous.

Finding no polite way to avoid an answer, Lizzie drops her gaze. "Almost a week."

"Why you eating here instead of home?"

Lizzie stands and edges her way around the woman. "I'll pay for my meal now."

"Tsk. Don't be foolish. You think I wasn't young once?" The woman purses her lips. She waves a finger in Lizzie's direction. "I know what trouble look like. You go now, but you hungry, you come see me. I don't let no little mama go hungry. You hear me? You come see Maria, you need a meal."

Lizzie drops a few dollars onto the table, mumbles her thanks and races into the street. She is so frightened of being noticed and of losing her child that even potential kindness feels like a threat.

Halfway down the block, she stops abruptly to orient herself, searching for the path that will lead her to her bed. Fortunately, this time, it isn't difficult. The CN Tower is lighted and looming in the distance, indicating south and her destination.

Sarah Jane whimpers.

"Shhhh, sweetie. Everything's going to be okay." Lizzie says, wishing more than anything that she were certain it was the truth.

She returns to the hostel and sleeps between breast feedings throughout the night. Other travelers arrive over the next few hours, their day's festivities at an end. Lizzie barely registers their intrusions.

In the morning, she stores her things in the lockers provided by the hostel then slips into the kitchen to help herself to whatever food she can lay her hands on. She stuffs granola bars, juice boxes, and fruit into the diaper bag then flees back to her dorm room, mouthing an apology to those whose food she has taken. She applies additional bandages strategically around her feet to protect against more blisters then straps Sarah Jane into her carrier.

"Off we go, Baby. Mama's gotta find a job."

Mama. Her use of the word brings her to a standstill. Until now, She has made a conscious attempt not to refer to herself as such. She wants no parallels or reminders that she may not be able to escape.

Enough! Focus on getting work.

She wonders what she'll do with Sarah Jane if she is successful, but flicks it away. One problem at a time is all she can manage.

For the remainder of that day and the next and the two after that, Lizzie looks for work. She covers fast-food outlets, retail shops, and gas stations further out from the downtown core. She tries to get work as a maid at nearby hotels.

By the end of each day, she is weeping with fatigue. By the end of her fifth day in the city, her knees are so sore they need icing and she has a hole in one of her shoes. Four blisters have joined the first that has re-closed and is leaking pus.

Lizzie makes a cradle of towels on the bathroom counter and lays Sarah Jane upon it. Filling a sink with hot water, she adds salt from packets taken from McDonalds and immerses her infected foot. The hot water stings and, in reflex, she yanks her foot out of the water. Exhaling, she forces her foot back.

She cannot afford to fill a prescription for antibiotics. She has to take care of this the old-fashioned way. With a pin from the hotel sewing kit, she lances the resealed blister and presses against the swelling to release the yellowish discharge. She pats her foot dry and dabs an antibiotic ointment over the area, covering it once more with a clean bandage. Her blisters have now cost her ten dollars at the drug store. What if something really serious were to happen? She has less than one hundred dollars left.

Feeling the extent of her vulnerability, she curls up in bed with Sarah Jane tucked inside her arm. She is frightened and feeling more alone than she has since the first time Rue beat her.

What had she been thinking to come here? That she'd walk into a business and the manager would be standing there with open arms, waiting for her? That she could strap her baby to her back while dusting a motel room, or better yet — that she could find an affordable daycare around the corner that would lovingly tend Sarah Jane? Had she thought she'd be recognized for her unique special-ness by a significant somebody and be mentored to a position of importance while earning a degree?

Yes. Yes, she had romanticized just such things for herself. Foolish schoolgirl daydreams meant to make her audacious enough to dare this adventure.

And they'd helped then, but they aren't going to help her now, are they?

She turns her face into the pillow and begs, "Granny Gee, if you're going to help me, please help me now."

Chapter Five

Lizzie recalls a book she once read about a girl who lived at a Wal-Mart and wonders if she might do the same.

She flops onto the bed and stares at the arched ceiling. A crack begins in the corner and runs to the centre where it branches off like a skinny sapling reaching for the sun.

It is homely, yet there is something disquieting about it as well. Her bedroom back home had cracks in the ceiling because of the old horsehair plaster used when the house was last refinished, many, many years ago. Her parents had worked on tearing the plaster down as they could afford the sheet rock to install in its place. One room was completed at a time. It was exciting to come home from school and see Mama standing on a stool with a crowbar in hand, ripping the plaster from the walls. It fell in pieces that filled the room with dust. In a vain attempt to contain the fine powder, Mama would tape sheets of plastic to doorways. As she worked, the entire house grew a grey coat.

Mama tied a bandana around her face to keep the plaster from her lungs. At the end of the day, she'd blow her nose and the tissue would come away black.

During those days, Papa would come home with a truck full of drywall and the three of them installed it together. It was hard work. Ridiculously hard. Lizzie however, didn't mind. She loved going with Mama to the store to pick paint colors and she found pleasure in the new walls. Straight, or nearly so, and smooth. Walls without the old ripples.

Her bedroom was one that hadn't been finished. Neither of the bedrooms had been. Money and energy ran out before that could happen. Lizzie used to lie on her bed, just like she is now, and stare at the cracks and think how nasty they were. Like the fissures in her family, the cracks grew until they joined and loosed a piece of plaster. The hole exposed the narrow laths behind it. The skeleton of the house, rising bone by bone.

She pulls herself from the past to the present, empties her money onto the bed, and counts the bills and loose change. There remains slightly more than thirty dollars. If she pays for another night at the hostel, she won't have money for anything else.

Lizzie pulls herself off the bed and tucks Sarah Jane into the carrier then heads to the streets for another day of job-hunting, leaving her belongings in the day locker. Although staying at the hostel is now out of the question, she cannot cart her things with her and has to trust that they will not be thrown away.

Lizzie nears panic. She can't live on the street. Not with a baby. She is torn between calling social services and calling home. Rue or her papa would come and get her. There'd be hell to pay, but they'd come. She is sure of it.

Almost.

She walks around the city revisiting some of the places where she has applied for work.

About noon, she returns to a hotel. As she approaches the desk, a man she spoke with two days ago, looks up from a computer and shakes his head. He is staring at her, but she looks behind to make sure he means her. No one else is there. From halfway across the room, she holds her hands out to him. Pleading.

"We don't have anything," he says and returns to his paperwork.

It's the same story she gets everywhere she goes. It seems there isn't a single position open anywhere. Or maybe it's just that there aren't any positions available to a girl who has to carry her baby around with her.

As sunset nears, Lizzie finds a bench where she can sit to feed her daughter and eat a supper made of items of pilfered food.

She sits, rocking Sarah Jane, with nothing except fear in her head. She has no idea where to go or what to do. She envisions a life on the street and wonders how they will manage to stay alive.

Dusk becomes dark and Lizzie is fearful to be outside on her own in this huge city. She walks to Union Station where she is at least in a well-lighted area and in the company of others. She finds a seat in a corner and dozes once more until someone nudges her foot.

"What?" Fear grips her. Has she done something wrong?

"Girl, you've been here for hours. What're you doing hanging around here all night with a kid?"

Lizzie looks up at the Amazon standing before her. She has never seen a woman this tall. She has never seen anyone this dark. She has never seen someone clothed in the way this woman is clothed, at least not in real life. A short dress clings to narrow hips and muscular thighs. A neckline plunges between insignificant breasts, yet it manages to reveal too much for Lizzie's comfort. Long coils of black hair reach very nearly to the woman's waist. Lizzie blushes when the woman catches her staring.

Lizzie's eyes dart around the room to locate where help might be if she needs it. The ticket agents work upstairs; the security guard is nowhere in sight. Sarah Jane frets, tired of her confinement.

"Now look what you've done." Lizzie fusses with her baby, relieved to have something to occupy her, to give her a chance to collect her thoughts. She glances at the woman from under lowered lids.

"Well?" The woman asks as if to say, I haven't got all day.

"I'm not bothering anyone. Leave us alone."

A grin spreads over the face of the giantess. "You can't live at the train station."

"I'm not liv—"

"Little girl. Do you see dawn breaking over the horizon? That means I'm ready to leave and that you've been here all night and nobody, I mean nobody, sleeps here when they have somewhere else to be."

"I'm waiting for a bus."

"Really? Going where?"

"That's none of your business. Why are you—?"

The giantess waves her hand in Lizzie's face. "Child, I am trying to offer you help."

Lizzie pinches her lips shut and stares at the woman. Could she help?

"My name's Samantha."

Lizzie remains silent.

"And yours is?"

Lizzie continues to stare, hoping the woman can't see her fear.

"Have it your way. I'll be back tonight. This is my turf." With that the woman sashays away, not even once glancing back at Lizzie.

Sarah Jane begins to cry in earnest, angry that she has had to wait for her breakfast. Lizzie nurses her while she sips from a stolen juice box. She's read that drinking something cold helps breast milk to flow. She doesn't know if this is true or not although she does get a terrible thirst during feedings.

After a quick wash up in the women's room, something at which Lizzie has become adept, she hits the streets, revisiting the restaurants and shops she was at yesterday. If a baby slung around one's neck is considered a shortcoming in a new hire, Lizzie will accept pity. She begs for work, explaining her dire situation. There are expressions of pity or indifference. They've heard it before. When the end of the day arrives, she trudges back to the hostel, still jobless, to gather her belongings from the locker.

As soon as the clerk leaves to fetch Lizzie's bags, Lizzie sneaks into the kitchen for the last time and fills the diaper bag with juice, bread, anything that's portable.

Mouthing an apology, she sticks her head through the kitchen's doorway to check for a clear passage. She hears footsteps approaching, zips the diaper bag closed and races on tiptoe to the front of the registration counter.

The woman drops Lizzie's bags onto the floor and wishes her well. She hands Lizzie two sandwiches. Lizzie accepts them and hurries outside where she bursts into tears.

The bags are heavier than Lizzie remembers as she drags her feet down the street. She thinks about Maria and wonders if the woman was serious about feeding her for free.

She sits on a bench and ponders her fate. Thinking about her next meal and where it will come from has become the most important part of her day. She's never been so focused on food before.

"What do we have to lose, right, Baby?" Lizzie walks the few blocks to the tiny Italian restaurant. Maria welcomes her at the door.

"Sit," she tells her as though Lizzie's an errant puppy.

Lizzie slips onto a chair and waits. Maria brings her a glass of milk. "Drink. You need it for the baby."

As soon as the glass is empty, Maria refills it. "I bring you food. You stay here."

It is too early for the evening crowd. There are only three other couples sitting at tables in front of a large window.

Within minutes, Maria returns with a romaine salad, warm bread and oil. Some time later, she brings a plate of lasagne.

Lizzie pats Sarah Jane's back and watches her benefactor. The food is the best she's ever tasted and as she eats she feels recharged. She can't figure why Maria wants to help her; certainly no one else gives a damn. The woman laughs with one of her customers and Lizzie takes in the fine lines that radiate from her large eyes and the corners of her sculpted mouth. The skin is softening under her chin and she has dark circles under her eyes, yet in spite of these signs of age, she is a very attractive woman.

Sarah Jane sleeps and Lizzie feels good to be seated in a nice restaurant, eating good food, not having to worry for a few minutes. When she looks up, Maria is on the phone and looking straight at her. The shock of comprehension hits Lizzie in the base of her spine. Maria is speaking to someone about her.

Lizzie drops her fork on the floor, and leaps out of her chair. With speed that surprises even her, she grabs her bags and clasps a hand around Sarah Jane's bonneted head then gallops out the door.

"Hey, you. Come back!"

Lizzie runs as fast as she is able, struggling against the yoke of her cargo. No one is going to take her baby away from her. Nobody.

Within minutes, she is panting and slows to a trot. She looks over her shoulder. No one has followed. Lizzie drops her bags to the sidewalk and pushes her fist into a stitch in her side, trying to drive it away. Sarah Jane screws up her face and lets out a squawk of indignation.

"Shush. Shhh. Please don't cry." Lizzie is near tears herself. She has a few dollars, a bag of food and three diapers. She can't see any options for herself other than to go home and face a life of fists and feet just like her mother. "There's no way out for us, is there?" She kisses her daughter and rubs her head. Slowly, Sarah Jane grows quiet and chews her fist. Lizzie hears the comforting sucking sounds. "We tried, right? That's got to be worth something. Maybe all that matters is that we're together. I can put up with Rue, if you're with me. What do you say, Baby? Should we go back?"

Lizzie hums a lullaby as she walks toward a park she passed earlier in the day. The beautiful green space beckons her. Trees make her feel at home even if they are different from the conifers she has known. She pulls a baby blanket from one of her large bags, spreads it out over the new grass, and lays her daughter on her back. She stretches out beside her and stares at the deep blue sky through the leafy branches.

She breathes deeply and tears flow down the sides of her head into her braided hair. She turns to Sarah Jane who is looking at her.

"At least we'll have a bed to sleep in. Rue'll buy you a crib. You'd like that, right? A pretty crib and a cuddly stuffed bear? Wouldn't that be nice? And I could give you a warm bath every day in a real tub. Rue'd never hurt you, baby girl. You'd be okay." She wonders if this is true. If this is the sort of justification Mama used when making her decisions. Lizzie strokes Sarah Jane's cheek. "You're so beautiful. You're the most beautiful thing I've ever seen. Who could ever hurt you?"

While the sun hangs in the lower quadrant of the sky, warming the ground, people pass by, laughing and rushing off to do whatever they have planned for the evening. Car horns honk and a red streetcar clatters past.

God, it's so noisy. Don't city people ever just rest?

Lizzie closes her eyes. She decides that, for one more night, she and her daughter will enjoy their freedom. They will ignore the traffic and the sound of crowds. They will breathe in the verdant smell of grass and leaves, the earthy smell of the soil, the perfume of the spring flowers in bloom all around them.

"One more night, okay, Sarah Jane? One more night just for us and then I'll call Rue and we'll go back to your daddy. Okay? One last night."

They lay in a lush green corner of the busy city and the sun sinks ever lower till it passes the horizon, taking its warmth away from them. Sarah Jane's skin becomes cool and then cold, and Lizzie knows she has to find somewhere warmer for them to spend the night. Summer isn't here yet.

She gathers their things, straps Sarah Jane into the baby carrier, and turns toward Union Station. When they arrive, Lizzie hesitates before going inside, peering through the glass, on the alert for the giantess.

The coast is clear, at least as far as she can tell. She enters and finds another corner to rest in. She reaches into the carrier and feels for a baby foot. It is warm and Lizzie relaxes.

Lizzie sits on the straps of her baggage, hoping to deter thieves. She wriggles into her spot and sings as Sarah Jane drifts off. The child rubs her nose and makes sucking sounds as she sleeps. Within no time and despite the lights and the foot traffic, Lizzie sleeps too, accustomed now to being in strange places.

"Well, look who's back!"

Lizzie lifts her eyes to the Amazon standing in front of her. She bites her lips together, unsure of what to say or do.

"So, I guess this is where you're staying now. Is that it?"

Lizzie shrugs. She does not trust her voice with this woman.

"It's Samantha. Sam." She holds out a shovel of a hand that Lizzie, raised to be polite, has no choice other than to shake.

"Cat got your tongue?" Sam looks down with mock concern. She sits next to Lizzie and crosses one long leg over the other. "You worry me, girl. Fresh out of the potato patch, aren't you?"

Lizzie shrugs again. "I'm going back home."

"Well, good for you. Good for you." Sam pats Lizzie's knee. Lizzie tenses, but fixes her attention on the people in front of her. It's a full minute before Sam speaks. "I've seen lots of girls like you here before. They come, they stay for a while, they vanish. I have a little game I play with myself, a game where I try to guess their stories, try to imagine why they're here."

Lizzie's foot begins to twitch.

"How old's that baby of yours? Still pink and mewly. Can't be more than a couple of weeks. Am I right?"

Lizzie doesn't answer.

"So, who you running from? Your daddy?"

Lizzie nods.

"What about the baby's daddy?"

Lizzie nods again.

"Well, well. A double-whammy. You got it tough kid." Sam leans over to adjust a strap on her high heels. "Tell you what. If you're still here in a couple of hours when I'm done my shift, I'll take you home for some breakfast. Get yourself and that baby cleaned up. See what your options are. Then you can decide if going back to what you left is really what you want." Sam checks her watch. "I'll be back sometime before six. You rest here till then." She pats Lizzie's leg again then notices her bags. "And you better get those into a locker. Why tempt those who might be tempted?"

Sam saunters across the room towards the exit and Lizzie loses sight of her.

She waits to see if she'll return. Once she realizes that Sam is truly gone, Lizzie nurses Sarah Jane once more before sleep comes for her.

She wakes to someone shaking her shoulder and jerks to her feet, jostling Sarah Jane awake. The startled infant wails in fear. Large tears spring forth.

"Just me, like I promised." Sam grins through red-rimmed eyes and flakes of dry mascara. "Come on. Let's go get something to eat. I'm starving."

Lizzie follows her strange companion from the station to a bus stop. She asks no questions. There is a preordination to her path, whether toward salvation or destruction, it matters not. She has run out of options.

They do not speak and after a short ride, Sam takes up Lizzie's bags and they walk what seems like miles to a derelict warehouse in the industrial area. A discreet sign has been painted over a mailbox: The Sisters of Sweet Charity.

Lizzie looks around nervously, wishing she had paid better attention to their route here. Suddenly, being a passive participant in her fate doesn't seem like a good idea.

Seeing the look of mistrust on her face, Sam laughs. "It's not me you have to worry about, it's the creeps at the station who'll get you. They rub their hands in glee, counting their money when they see someone like you arrive."

"Who are they?" Lizzie motions toward the sign over the door and Sam laughs anew.

"It's a private joke."

Lizzie surrenders, too tired for much else. *I'm in your hands, Granny Gee.*

Sam unlocks a deadbolt and enters a cavernous space that has been converted into a home. The floor of the foyer is made of grey stone. To the left is a stairway heading up. To the right is a living area with high ceilings and three large windows. Couches and chairs in patterns of red festoon the room. A large, flat screen television sits on a low table against an exterior wall. Beyond this is a dining area with a long table made of some heavily grained exotic wood and six high-backed chairs.

A woman with hair the shade of red Kool-Aid sits in one of them, smoking a cigarette. She says nothing, just squints at Lizzie through the smoke.

"ZoZo, take yourself and your filthy habit outside. You know better."

The woman shrugs and flicks an ash into the palm of her hand. When she stands her robe falls partway open revealing a bony ribcage. She saunters toward the back of the building, past a half wall whose opening offers a good view of a commercial-sized kitchen, and through a doorway that leads to a corridor.

"Do you live here?" Lizzie has never been inside a home as large as this one.

"With ZoZo. There have been others but they're gone now. I'll show you to a room where you can stow your things. You can shower if you want. I've got to get cleaned up myself and get breakfast started. First one home usually gets the glory. I guess she's not in the mood."

Sam lifts Lizzie's bags from the floor in one large hand as though they are filled with nothing heavier than feathers then leads her up the stairs to a hall lined with three doors, two to the side and one at the end. Sam dumps the bags in the middle bedroom and flicks on a light. "You can rest here. This room's got its own bathroom through that door there. And see here?" Sam turns the knob to a deadbolt. "The door locks. You'll be safe. I'll call when food's ready."

Lizzie sinks to the edge of the bed in disbelief. *What is this place?*

She retraces her steps to the door, closes and locks it. Feeling secure, she pulls Sarah Jane from the baby carrier and lays her in the middle of the bed. "I'll be right back."

She showers quickly and races back to check on her daughter, dripping water on the carpeted floor. She needn't have worried at leaving the child alone. Sarah Jane is alert and trying to fit her entire fist in her mouth, her attention caught by whatever comes into her view.

"Bet you're happy to get out of that carrier contraption for a bit, aren't you?" Lizzie bends to kiss the baby's round belly and breathes in the unmistakable odour of urine. "Pee-yew. Hang on and I'll get you smelling all pretty too."

She towels off, brushes her teeth, and pulls on her last pair of clean underwear. "Wonder if I can do laundry here?" Being clean and having a private room to stay in improves her mood, helping her believe her luck might be changing.

She rinses the tub and lets warm water fill it to a few inches while she undresses Sarah Jane and removes an overly soiled diaper. "Whew! We need to get you more of these, fast."

After bathing, Lizzie lines a hand towel with folds of toilet paper and wraps it around Sarah Jane's bottom. "Maybe there are other babies here we can borrow a diaper from." She dresses them both and lies with Sarah Jane to nurse her.

By the time they are finished, voices filter in through the space under the solid wood door. Lizzie cracks it open. The voices of women chattering below drift upwards. Sam calls her to the table.

"My turn for breakfast," Lizzie says. Anxiety swirls in her stomach as she retraces her steps downstairs.

"Well, here they are." A black woman with close-cropped hair and wire-framed glasses ushers Lizzie to the table. Her voice is soft and low. She wears jeans and a short-sleeved blouse. Her arms are muscled and lean. She has an air of restraint about her and it takes Lizzie several seconds to recognize Sam. In her home, she is a different woman altogether from the woman of an hour ago.

And then it strikes her. The recognition of Sam's identity, the incongruity of her size and physique coupled with her attire.

It is all Lizzie can do to hold in a gasp, to stop from gawking. She knows nothing of this. She isn't even sure what it's called. All she does know is what Rue called people like this: "fucking freaks."

But then Rue isn't exactly an ideal role model.

ZoZo is already seated and Sam makes formal introductions. A tray of pancakes is passed around followed by one of bacon and a bowl of fresh fruit.

Lizzie holds her daughter on her lap with one hand and fills her plate with the other as the dishes pass her way. The fork shakes in her hand and rests it on her plate with a clatter. She hopes no one has noticed.

"What's the kid's name?" ZoZo asks with a coarse Quebecois accent.

Lizzie answers despite her strong desire to ignore the woman. There is something foul about her. A hardness to her face, a brashness that Lizzie dislikes.

"Want me to hold her so you can eat?" Sam asks.

Lizzie shakes her head. She doesn't want any strange woman – or man – holding her child. She sits with one hand in her lap and one clutching her daughter and wonders why she's been led here.

"She staying?" ZoZo asks Sam while glaring at Lizzie. It seems she is no more a fan of Lizzie's than Lizzie is of hers.

"We haven't figured that out yet," Sam responds.

"What is it about you picking up strays?"

Lizzie's face burns at this rudeness, talking about her as though she isn't there, and knows no matter what else might happen, she and this woman will never be friends.

Sam tells the woman to hush. Her voice reverts to its earlier cheeky tone. "She's fresh off the farm. Be nice to her."

It's so condescending that anger rises inside Lizzie like a tornado. She wants to yell at them that she isn't from a farm, but it wouldn't matter. Farming, mining. What's the difference to these people?

"Eat your breakfast, Milk Maid. Don't let it go to waste," Sam says.

Lizzie switches Sarah Jane to her other arm and cuts her pancake with her fork. Pancakes dripping with butter and syrup. Just what she wanted. When she swallows the first bite, her appetite surges and she clears her plate quickly then asks for more. She eats until her stomach stretched and aching. When she tears her attention away from her spotless plate, she meets Sam's eyes and once more feels heat in her face.

Lizzie stands and moves Sarah Jane to her shoulder.

"Well, now. Someone's had an accident." Sam smiles. She is soft Sam now.

Lizzie looks down at her lap and, sure enough, a large wet mark is there. "I'm out of diapers," she confesses, embarrassed by this admission of destitution.

Sam asks ZoZo to go to the store to buy some while she and Lizzie clean up.

"I'm no dog. I don't fetch for nobody," the redhead states. She takes a cigarette from behind her ear. "I'm having my café and a smoke and I'm going to bed. You know. Fait do-do?"

Sam rolls her eyes in exasperation. "Come with me." She crooks a finger in Lizzie's direction and Lizzie follows her down the hall past the kitchen to a laundry room. "You can wash your things in here."

Curiosity and suspicion getting the best of her, Lizzie blurts out, "Who are you? What is this place?"

"You are right off the hay wagon, aren't you?" Sam says and then sighs. "I don't know that I can put this any more plainly. We're hookers, honey. At night, I'm glamorous, gorgeous Sam. During the day, I'm just plain old me."

"I see." Lizzie ponders what this information might mean to her. Has Sam brought her here as a new recruit? Her mind kicks in to high gear. Has she walked into a trap? Can she walk out of it and if so, where will she go? She chews on the inside of her mouth, searching for the right words to ask the next question that demands to be asked. "But you're a... you're a..."

Sam's face grows hard and Lizzie knows she is on her own to get through this.

"You're a man, right? I mean ... Are you?"

"I am a woman. You better get clear on that. I'm a woman who happens to suck dick for money." Sam glowers. "That is my job. This," she motions to the space beyond the door, "is my home and you are a guest here. Maybe you should act like one."

Lizzie doesn't know what to make of it all. She feels her breakfast rise in her throat. Her knees feel weak. Her chin quivers and she feels a cry coming on. She hadn't meant to offend the person who had shown her kindness.

"You better take care of that." Sam points to Lizzie's pants. She pours soap into the washer and bangs the lid shut as water fills the machine. "Get your things and I'll run to the store for diapers."

Sam marches away, leaving Lizzie to ponder this turn of events. She hears a door close and returns to the room she has on loan. She wraps a clean towel around her daughter's bottom before taking care of the dirty clothes.

Some minutes later, Sam enters the bedroom and leans against the wall with her arms crossed over her chest as Lizzie diapers Sarah Jane. "Listen," she says. "I'm only going to say this once and then you can make your choice about staying or leaving. It's a mean world out there for people like us."

"What do you mean, people like us? I'm not like you."

"People on the outside of things. People who don't have people."

Lizzie senses the truth in this. How much easier things would have been had she had someone to count on over the past days, months even.

"It's a dangerous world," Sam continues. "I set this up as a safe place. There have been others who have lived here before you. Till they got on their feet. We live here, nobody brings work home and we watch out for each other. If somebody's sick or hurt, they have somewhere that's theirs to stay. Everybody pays rent. Everybody does chores. Everybody gets along."

Lizzie isn't sure why, she only knows she is drawn to Sam. For as uneven as the morning has been, there is something elusively compelling about her, something in the way she acts so brashly and yet shows such compassion – if that's what it is. Lizzie straddles the line between wanting to stay and being fearful of trusting this man-woman.

"What does this have to do with me?" Lizzie asks.

"You need help, yes?"

Lizzie nods.

"I can help you."

"I'm not a …"

Sam clicks her tongue against her teeth, making a tsking sound. "Don't be silly. You are a child. I don't agree with children in this line of work. Tell me, what are you running from?"

Lizzie inhales, wishing she knew which way to go. Finally, she pulls her T-shirt away from her neck to bare her shoulder. A faded yellow ruffle blooms there, each furrow matching the space between Rue's fingers, each petal the size and shape of one of his knuckles. It had been presented to her as a joke. The punch his way of telling her not to be such a sissy over "some God-damned chick book."

Sam shakes her head. "Ahh. As I thought, you do know about cruelty."

Lizzie's eyes fill with tears. She is so tired, she cannot think clearly. Sleep threatens to drop her where she stands.

"Can you cook?"

"Nothing fancy."

"That's all we need. You cook, serve breakfast when we come in, get us some dinner before we go out, do some cleaning. You can stay in this room. I'll buy whatever you and the child need. Until you get on your feet."

"But— but, why?"

"Why not? You're not the first one. I don't think you'll be the last." Sam smiles and turns to leave, but Lizzie calls her back, embarrassed once more.

"I'm not sure this is right for me or my daughter." Her voice drops and she stares at her restless hands, twisting the ring on her finger. Standing up for herself isn't something she's accustomed to. "I don't know about you and … ZoZo and … Well, you know …"

Sam tilts her head to one side. Her face is filled with such sadness that Lizzie wishes she could retract her words.

"Guess you'll have to figure that out then." Sam walks out and closes the door.

Lizzie's head swirls with information and questions and when she sleeps, she dreams about tall, well-muscled women dancing around a fire.

Chapter Six

For the first time, she is alone in this strange house. Like vampires, the others have left their beds after sunset.

Sarah Jane sleeps in a new crib that was delivered that afternoon and set up in Lizzie's bedroom. Lizzie tries to watch television on the main floor, but is on edge, nervous of being in this place and afraid she may not hear Sarah Jane if she wakes.

Lizzie jumps up to check that the doors are locked and that Sarah Jane is safe and sleeping still. She paces the floor, flips through magazines and peers outside. Across the street and around the corner, a fish plant is in operation. Men and women unload cargo from trucks parked in front. They load boxes onto conveyer belts that carry the fish inside. Lizzie risks standing on the front steps. She listens to the sounds of people working – the hum of engines and periodic peals of laughter. She smells the unmistakeable odour of fish carried to her on the light spring breeze and marvels that anyone would choose to live this close to dead fish. Must have been cheaper.

At eleven, she turns off the lights and pads up the stairs to her room, her heart thumping at the thought of what bogeymen might do when her back is turned.

She reaches the hall at the top of the stairs and sprints to her room, slapping the door shut and throwing the deadbolt.

Forcing a laugh at what she tries to convince herself is utter foolishness, she tells herself she is perfectly safe.

"Safe as I've ever been, anyway," she says aloud.

The parenting book rests on the bedside table and Lizzie stretches her five-foot-seven inch frame on top of the comforter to read while she waits for her daughter to wake for the eleven o'clock feeding.

The bedroom window is open. The breeze billows the curtain and cools the room. Somewhere on the street, a loud crack cuts the darkness, jerking Lizzie from near sleep. Adrenaline surges in the seconds before she realizes what she's heard: a car backfiring.

Get a grip. Did you think it was gunfire?

She settles back on her pillow and opens the book. Her eyes skip off the page and wander around her new room, taking in the details. The walls are pale blue, the furniture is painted white and the linens are striped periwinkle and moss green and cream. It is feminine without being frilly and feels light and airy – like having her own beach house. Like everything could just float away. There is a deep blue side chair with a paisley cushion and an ottoman next to a pockmarked brass reading lamp. The door to the bathroom has a glass knob. It could have come from the pages of a magazine

As always, Lizzie is tired and wants to relax, wishes she could relax. Her body craves rest; her mind won't allow it as it flits from thought to thought. She is on edge. Just how safe is she here? Her room has a lock; still, Sam might have another key.

Her mind drifts to sounds from outside. The city is loud even at night and at a distance from theatres and restaurants. Large transports and other trucks rumble by on their way to who-knows-where, loaded with who-knows-what from ships at the dockyard and the warehouses that fill the district. Although most businesses are closed for the day, the fish plant remains open. The voices of men and women can be heard calling out to one another as the night shift begins. The work never stops.

If only she could rest peacefully.

Sarah Jane peeps and Lizzie leaps to her feet, happy to have something to do. She lifts her baby, nuzzles one soft cheek and lays the infant on the bed for a diaper change.

"Whew! You are a stinky girl tonight."

Sarah Jane waves a fist, punching the air. Her face scrunches readying a cry.

"Hey, now. I didn't mean to hurt your feelings. Let me get you cleaned up before I fill your tummy. You'll be too sleepy afterward."

Lizzie hums a nameless tune to distract Sarah Jane from her hunger. In minutes, the two are curled together on the bed. Lizzie tries reading over her daughter's head and fights her heavy eyelids.

The alarm clock wakes her hours later. She is disoriented, blinking into the daylight pouring into the room.

And then she remembers.

She has to make breakfast.

Lizzie rolls away from Sarah Jane, lifts her gingerly and places her in the crib. They have slept for six whole hours – a new record.

She tiptoes toward the door and is unlocking the deadbolt when Sarah Jane wakes with a whimper.

"Oh, no, no, no, honey. Not now. Mommy's got to cook breakfast." Lizzie vacillates, her eyes darting between the clock and her daughter.

Providing meals on time is her primary duty. "There's nothing uglier than hungry hookers at the end of their day. That food better be ready when we get home or we'll serve you for breakfast." Sam had laughed when she'd said it but Lizzie isn't so sure it was meant as a joke. She knows Sam has gone out on a limb with ZoZo, and now Lizzie has to prove herself.

Sarah Jane is fussing, her delicate fingers clenching a cotton sheet. When Lizzie lifts her, she discovers the blankets are wet. "Mommy doesn't have time for this right now." She strips the sopping clothes from Sarah Jane, too roughly in her haste, and the baby howls, her face crimson, her uvula vibrating in anger.

Lizzie wipes her clean and covers her wee bottom with a fresh diaper. "Shhh. Please don't cry. I'm sorry. Here, look. You're clean. Sort of." Lizzie takes a deep breath. Panicking isn't going to help. She carries Sarah Jane down the stairs to the kitchen. "Let's make a deal," she says, her voice forcing a cheerfulness she doesn't feel. "I'll get some eggs whipped up lickety-split and if you'll stop screaming, I'll feed you while I'm cooking. Deal?"

Of course, Sarah Jane continues to howl, waving a fistful of Lizzie's hair in one hand while she pinches the soft skin under Lizzie's arm with her razor-sharp nails.

"Ow! That hurts." Lizzie looks around the kitchen frantically, trying to find somewhere to set her child. "Five minutes, that's all I need. Just five minutes. Come on, Sarah Jane. Hang in there with me."

She grabs a handful of fresh dishtowels and makes yet another nest on yet another floor for the baby. "There you go. Good as anything."

Sarah Jane's mouth is turning blue, mucus is running from her nose and her fists rub it all over her scarlet face.

"Hush little baby, don't say a word, Mama's gonna buy you a mockingbird." Lizzie sings while she bangs frying pans onto the stove and grabs milk and eggs from the fridge. She breaks eggs into a large metal bowl as quickly as she is able. Eggshells fall into the mix and her fingers shake as she fishes them out. Her voice wavers then breaks and tears spurt onto her cheeks. This is not the way life is supposed to be.

A voice pulls her out of her misery.

"What in heaven's name is going on here this morning?" It's Sam. There are lines under her eyes, a tight smile on her face.

"I'm sorry. I'm sorry. I'll get this on in two minutes. Sarah Jane wants her feeding and I'm trying to figure this out and …"

Sam crosses the room in three long strides. She hip-checks Lizzie. "Go take care of your child. I'll handle this."

"But it's my job–"

"Get. And stop that child from wailing. Lord, what a noise she makes." Sam grabs a whisk for the eggs.

Lizzie scoops Sarah Jane from the floor and sits at the kitchen table. She lifts her T-shirt, but Sarah Jane is too incensed to take the comfort offered her. Her arms and legs flail as she chokes for breath. Lizzie forces a nipple into the angry mouth only to have it spit out. It takes repeated efforts to calm the infant enough for nursing. As the baby sucks, her body jerks. Tension washing from her.

Lizzie takes a wet cloth that Sam hands her and wipes Sarah Jane's snot-streaked face. "There, there, now. Mommy'll figure something out." Her stomach is in knots. Just how is she supposed to juggle mothering with house duties?

Girls do this everyday, remember?

Sam has sliced mushrooms and green peppers that she adds to the bowl. "You are lucky I'm in a good mood this morning, Milk Maid."

"I'm so sorry. I'll get this figured– "

"Take a joke, kid. I know it'll take a while for you to hit your stride. I'm not ready to turf you out yet." Sam's grin is broad and Lizzie feels relief wash over her. She smiles in return, but in the next second her mood swings, her lips contort and tears flow afresh.

"I was so scared you'd be mad."

Sam points at Lizzie with a spatula. "Never mind that. The one thing I don't tolerate well is tears. Don't fret so. This isn't a prison camp. It's not the Gulag." She turns back to the counter and drops bread into the toaster.

Lizzie gulps air and closes her eyes to force her tears back. She nods. "If it's okay, I'm going to wash her really quick and try to find somewhere to set her and then I'll help."

"That sounds like the first good idea you've had this morning. Scoot. I'm not going anywhere.”

As Lizzie enters her room, she hears the front door open and ZoZo call something to Sam.

“We don’t have a lot of time, sweet baby girl. Let’s get you cleaned up and looking pretty.”

Lizzie runs water in the tub. She washes her baby who startles herself when a wayward hand splashes water onto her face. Sarah Jane holds her breath and looks like she is about to cry. Lizzie swiftly rinses away soap bubbles and wraps the child in a towel. “Don’t fuss. You’re okay, little one.”

The air from the open window is already feeling warm this early in the day. Lizzie dresses her daughter in a cotton undershirt and diaper.

By the time Lizzie settles Sarah Jane on a blanket on the living room floor, breakfast is ready.

The first day of her new life has begun.

Chapter Seven

Every day, a new gift arrives. Samantha buys a rocking chair for Lizzie's bedroom and a playpen for the main floor. She brings home stuffed animals, a mobile that plays sounds of the rainforest and an infant gym with buttons to push, springs to bounce, brightly coloured shapes that swing when touched. A change table and dresser arrive, ready for the wee clothes and other necessities that she drags Lizzie out to select. She even purchases a few essentials for Lizzie: nursing bras and toiletries. When she hands Lizzie a bus pass, she says: "Don't stay stuck inside especially during the day. You've got to get out, find where things are."

Lizzie doesn't know how to act in the face of Sam's joy. It's like Christmas has arrived early, a very opulent and alien Christmas. Lizzie is bedazzled as she watches her new benefactor lavish gifts on her daughter, waiting with growing anxiety, waiting for some demand to come of this generosity.

As the days go by, however, it seems that Sam's delight in buying these things is genuine. She presents each gift with a grand flourish. Her eyes dance. She holds her breath until Lizzie tells her it is just exactly the right thing. This woman, who has hardened herself to do what most women consider to be the worst job possible, seems so vulnerable in the presence of one helpless baby.

This morning, Sam has two storybooks and two CDs. She snuggles Sarah Jane onto her lap. "Look, sweetie. It's The Elephant Show and Sesame Street. The stuff I watched when I was little and it's for you. Here. I'll show you." She slips a CD into the stereo and the sound of children laughing fills the room. The first song begins and Sam dances Sarah Jane around the room, cradling her head with a large hand and kissing her fat baby cheeks.

Sarah Jane blinks owl-like and blows a bubble.

"You are the most precious thing ever," Sam tells her so softly Lizzie only just catches the words.

Lizzie watches from the sidelines, studying Sam's interactions with Sarah

Jane and wondering about her – who she is and what it has been like for her to live as she is. Lizzie feels sadness emanating from the woman belying her outward happiness. It is this perception that tells her to let Sam play with Sarah Jane, to allow Sam this opportunity to give and receive affection innocently, tenderly.

Over days, a seed of admiration for Sam starts to grow in Lizzie. Sam's height may contribute to that – she is not only the tallest person Lizzie has ever seen, but when she puts on her heels and her hooker persona emerges, she fills a room. She's magnetic. Yet it is Sam's other self that Lizzie admires most. The person who emerges during the day is the real Samantha, Lizzie believes. The woman with the well-modulated voice and understated dress. There is an elegance and self-assuredness to her that Lizzie envies.

Despite Sam's infatuation with the baby however, Lizzie is unable to form a connection with her. One wrong word and Sam's alter-ego shows up. It makes conversation between them difficult.

And then there is ZoZo – as vulgar as a Vegas wedding.

Contrary to Sam's contention that everyone is to help keep house, ZoZo never lifts a hand.

"You're here now. That's your job," she tells Lizzie. "Me, I work and I pay rent."

And that apparently gives her license to do exactly as she pleases. She leaves dirty dishes everywhere, smokes indoors whenever Sam is out and drinks. Frequently. One shelf in the fridge is taken over by beer and white wine and fizzy coolers. All for ZoZo.

Lizzie can only imagine the filth of her quarters, but will not clean it. That is simply too much. She isn't the woman's servant. It's bad enough that she has to pick up after her throughout the rest of the place. Cups and saucers, plates and glasses, cigarette butts strewn like a trail of breadcrumbs behind her.

"You'll never get lost," Lizzie teases, in an attempt to build a rapport, but ZoZo doesn't know the story behind the joke and scowls as she nearly always does when Lizzie speaks to her.

No matter how she tries to figure it out, Lizzie is perplexed by Sam and ZoZo's relationship. She cannot fathom why Sam would choose such a person to live with. ZoZo seems much older than Sam and, Lizzie suspects, has had a tougher life. She has that look about her. Coarse, jaundiced skin and a permanently suspicious expression. She cannot be cajoled to do anything that isn't in her immediate self-interest. Even long-term planning is beyond her. If her spending habits are any indication, she has no dreams or goals beyond what she earns and can buy today. How she will manage in her old age when demand for her services declines, Lizzie can't conceive.

Another thought begins to nag as well. Given Sam's largesse, what can Lizzie do to repay her? Something that will demonstrate Lizzie's appreciation and gratitude – and at a cost of... well... nothing.

It's a challenge that plagues Lizzie until one morning when early summer warmth is upon them, encouraging Lizzie to take Sarah Jane for a walk in a nearby park. It is after breakfast, a time that would normally find Sam already in bed for her day's rest. Lizzie notices Sam watching her as she pulls the old stroller left behind by one of Sam's former reclamation projects, out of the laundry room.

"Would you like to come with us?"

"I should get to bed." Sam's tone is impassive yet Lizzie observes a flicker of longing ripple across her face.

"It's just a short walk to the park. It's nice there under the trees. You might even be able to sleep. I have a blanket to stretch out on."

Sam takes a moment to answer. "No. That's fine."

Lizzie realizes it could be possible that she has misinterpreted Sam's expression but she doesn't think so. "I'd like you to come." It seems, for whatever reason, Sam doesn't feel that her company is wanted. The insecurity of this powerhouse baffles Lizzie. "Please come. Sarah Jane loves having you around."

A grin lights Sam's sombre expression. "You know I can't say no to her."

The three of them stroll down the two blocks to the park.

To the uninformed, it seems an odd choice for city planners to have created a patch of green in this lonely area between the warehouse district and the dockyards of Lake Ontario, yet when it was conceived many years ago, families lived here, Sam tells Lizzie. Families of the small business owners who used to live where they worked – importers, fish merchants, garment makers. When that way of life died, larger enterprises moved in and built warehouses for storage.

The few residents of the dilapidated neighbourhood next to this district are, at this time of day, either heading to bed or rushing to their menial jobs. None are interested in early morning strolls with the exception of a few dog owners who use the park as an easy-to-access canine toilet. The wise pedestrian watches where she steps.

The park isn't completely abandoned. It is true the walkways are cracked and wild flowers and weeds have taken over tired perennial beds. Still, the city mows the grass every few weeks in an attempt to keep vermin under control and garbage — made up mostly of dog feces and pop or beer bottles — is collected from the plastic-lined cans every now and then.

Despite its shortcomings, there is something Lizzie loves about this place. It's a still-fertile relict, refusing to accept its diminished status. It lives on, breathing and growing, and providing homes for birds and small animals. The air is special too. Away from the exhaust of the large trucks that circulate the surrounding streets, Lizzie smells earth and trees, different from her northern home, yet recognizable enough to give her respite from the grime and rush of the city.

They find a spot in the shade under a rambling maple. Sarah Jane dozes in the carriage while Lizzie parks herself next to a prostrate Sam and picks at pieces of grass that trim the periphery of the plaid blanket. Questions burble about in Lizzie's head and she can think of nothing other than trying to satisfy her curiosity about her companion. She silently words and re-words questions, knowing there may be no right way for her to ask Sam anything.

In the past week, her thinking has progressed from viewing Sam as shocking — sickening even — to wanting to understand. How can she do this if she can't ask questions?

Lizzie looks up from the grass to meet Sam's stare. She blushes at being observed and wonders if Sam can read her mind. She clears her throat. "I was wondering, thinking that— Actually, I don't know what I was thinking… It's just that I… don't really get you."

Sam continues to stare and Lizzie squirms.

"I mean… I've never met anyone like you before."

Sam snorts. She rises to a sitting position them waits as seconds tick by. When she speaks, it is the other Sam's voice that comes out. "That may be so, Milk Maid or it may not. What do you think the chances are that anyone like me would reveal herself in that burg you're from?" Sam adjusts the crease in her shorts and Lizzie wants to crawl into a hole. "I had to leave home, give up everything I'd ever known so I could be myself. How different is that from you, do you think?"

"I'm sorry. I shouldn't have asked."

Sam seems to contemplate how to respond. "Never mind," she says eventually. "I suppose it's better you ask."

"I just never knew anyone like you existed. Papa said gay was against God and –"

"First of all, I'm not gay and second, well, your daddy's wrong about a lot of things, isn't he?"

Lizzie wants to cry. Why can't she ever have a reasonable conversation with this woman? Why can't it ever go as she intends?

Sam glances at her and takes a deep breath. "I tell you what. You don't ever, ever quote your daddy to me again and I'll cut you a break on this conversation we're going to have. Deal?"

Lizzie nods.

"First of all, not every tranny is gay. Got that? We come in all shapes and sizes and desires. You're best not to generalize."

"So if you're not gay …" Lizzie's question trails off. She isn't even entirely sure what "tranny" really means. Her only point of reference is The Rocky Horror Picture Show. It seems the more she knows, the less she knows.

"I'm a woman. In here and here." Sam touches her head and her the spot where her heart beats below.

Lizzie tries to absorb this. Leave home? That suggested Sam had felt this way for a long time.

Pictures from her advanced biology class swirl in her head. Images of cells and chromosomes. Charts of testosterone and oestrogen levels. Ultrasound images of unborn fetuses, moving and growing in the complicated soup of human chemicals. She thinks of a tiny penis that grows from the same cells as a clitoris, marvelling that genetics and whatever else goes in to building us manages to align our parts as well and as often as it does.

But what about when development is out of sync? Because it happens, doesn't it? Sometimes.

If babies can be born with two different colours of eyes; if fraternal male twins can have different sexual orientations from each other; if brains can be manic or depressed, high IQ or low; if brains can be short-circuited from bodies, causing any number of quirks and tics and, in some cases serious ailments or diseases; if babies are born with ambiguous sex organs or sex organs of both genders; if all of this is true – as it is – then why is it so hard to believe that sometimes a person's body and brain might not be in perfect harmony?

It would have to possible, wouldn't it? Sometimes.

Would it be?

How could it not?

Lizzie sucks her lips between her teeth. She should be out of breath. Her brain has run a marathon. She looks at Sam, letting air escape slowly from her nostrils.

There is a look of consternation on Sam's face. "Where did you go?"

Lizzie grimaces and shakes her head. "I think I just figured something out."

Sam's expression asks for an explanation, but Lizzie isn't ready to share. She doesn't want to risk Sam scoffing at her or making fun. Not right now. Lizzie doesn't want her revelation to be mocked. She moves items around in the diaper bag as though organizing it. She purposely knocks a bottle of water to the ground and grabs at it to give her something to avoid conversations. Sam returns to pondering the horizon.

After a few minutes of silence Lizzie asks, "Where're you from?"

"Well now, how about if I was to ask you that? Seems to me, you've been really quiet about that so far."

"I'm from up north," Lizzie says. "A mining town."

"And how did a young thing like you get to the big city?"

"I used to love suspense books, you know? And whenever someone needed to get lost, they'd find different ways to travel. I thought if I broke the trip into segments and switched up how I was travelling, I'd be harder to find – that is, if anyone was looking." Lizzie smiles, her self-assurance growing. "I hitched a ride out of town. Waited for one of those big rigs down the road from one of the truck stops. I thought if I was reported missing, somebody driving a long haul might not see the local news.

The look of wonderment on Sam's face was worth telling the secret. Lizzie warmed to the topic. "I got off in a town where I knew there was an airstrip. I scoped it out as soon as I got there."

"What about the baby? The birth?"

"That scared me, I won't lie." The words were poring out now. "She came early – at least according to my calculations. I didn't think I'd still be in on the road." Lizzie bends over her daughter who is now awake and watching the millions of leaves overhead waving in the summer breeze. "I put off leaving as long as I could to save as much money as possible."

Lizzie leans over the stroller and Sarah Jane grabs a handful of her mother's hair. Lizzie yelps then pries the tiny fingers one-by-one from her long strands.

"She's a strong one," Sam says.

"That's good. We girls have to be."

"Ain't that the truth?" Sam's good humour fades and her dark brown eyes fill with hurt.

Lizzie thinks of the last time someone yanked her hair and her hand travels to the crown of her head to feel for the bare spot. She brushes her fingertips over patch of hair only a few inches long, pleased that her hair is growing back.

"For a hayseed, you are full of surprises. How old did you say you are?"

"I didn't. I guess I must look pretty young and dumb to you. Well, you know what? Maybe I'm smarter than I look."

Sam throws her head back and a deep chuckle rises within her. "Aren't we a pair? You and me. Neither one of us are what we look like, are we? And here I am feeling so misjudged. You got me back. Yes, you did."

Lizzie rocks the stroller with her right foot. She cocks her head to the side, feeling confused. "So, you're not mad at me anymore?"

"No, Milk Maid, I'm not mad at you." Sam pats Lizzie's arm.

"I'm seventeen," Lizzie offers. "I have a scholarship for the University of Toronto. Or I would have if I'd been able to finish my last term. Someday I'm going to go there."

"That's the spirit." Sam's eyes lose their sparkle and she looks thoughtfully at a scraggly cluster of geraniums. "I left home when I was seventeen too."

"Did you ever go back?"

Sam shakes her head and leans back on her hands, drawing her knees toward her. "That wouldn't be possible."

"Are they dead?"

"My father is. And I am. To them both when he was living; to my mother now."

Lizzie wants so much to reach out and touch Sam, to let her know that she's sorry for thinking her strange. But she doesn't. In her world, touching has often been a terrible, hurtful thing. She isn't sure how to do it except with Sarah Jane. She swallows, hoping something will come to her. Something to save the moment. Instead, she asks Sam how long it's been since she left home.

"Six years. I'm twenty-three."

"You haven't seen your parents in six years?" The time is almost a third of her life, and as she repeats it, she realizes this will be her fate as well.

"My mother came to see me once." Sam's face is tight and angry. "She wanted me to 'give this nonsense up' and come home. Said my father was dying and wanted to see his son. I almost did it too. Just before I got in her car, I changed my mind. I wasn't the son he wanted to see."

Lizzie's attempt at an encouraging smile goes unnoticed. Sam doesn't look her way. Instead, she stands, dusts off her shorts and says, "Well, isn't that the saddest thing ever? Come on Milk Maid. I need my beauty rest. We should head back."

Without waiting for Lizzie, Sam starts down the path leaving Lizzie scrambling to tuck padding around Sarah Jane so the child doesn't slump in the too-large seat.

"Hey," she bawls at Sam's retreating form. "Do you think you could quit calling me that?"

Chapter Eight

The image of her father's hands keep Lizzie from falling asleep some nights. Broad and meaty with thick nails that curved like talons over the ends of calloused, sausage-shaped fingers. Large hands. Bigger even than Sam's. Competent hands. Hands that were once gentle.

They are the hands that rubbed the rust off her first bicycle after a long winter and a cold, damp spring. The hands that used to slide down Mama's spine and rest in the small of her back. The hands that brushed Lizzie's long hair till it shone in the lamplight while they watched television on Sunday night. The rough, working hands that became cruel when they worked no more.

She can't remember how old she was the first time she'd seen him hit her mama – grade four or five – although she remembers every other detail. Papa had been out of work for some time and dinner was late, then burned and then fell to the floor in the rush to get it onto the table. Papa was furious. "I'm still the head of this house and I will be served dinner on time." It was a backhand swing, delivered as though it had no consequence, that caught Mama under her jaw and was powerful enough to lift her right out of her slippers. At least that's how Lizzie remembers it.

It had been like a Saturday-morning cartoon except it hadn't been funny. There were no stars swirling around Mama's head or bulging eyes that snapped back into place when the pain stopped. There was just that awful thick sound of flesh hitting flesh and the resigned look on Mama's face as she gathered the pieces of broken dish and spilled food. It was the lack of surprise on her face that told Lizzie this wasn't the first time and the look of resignation that told her it wouldn't be the last.

Lizzie doesn't recall what was eventually served for dinner. The picture of Mama on her hands and knees, gathering the mess is the last recollection of that night that Lizzie has.

The events of the next day were less dramatic but proved to be equally devastating.

Lizzie had woken with grey-smudged and bloodshot eyes and a sick stomach. The reflection that stared back from the bathroom mirror that morning was haunting. She barely recognized herself, recalling a picture she'd once seen in an art book at school – The Scream by Munsch. It made her uneasy then and seeing it looking out at her, frightened her again. In the years since that morning, she'd avoided all reproductions of the famous image.

Over a silent breakfast, she stared at the bruise on her mother's jaw while she played with the eggs on her plate. Mama didn't meet her eyes, not even once, and Lizzie knew she was ashamed. Lizzie was, too. And terrified of what was to be. But it had been the shame that made her feel worse. To feel that way about Mama – the person who suffered so much – was reprehensible. Lizzie couldn't articulate that at the time. She only knew that her feelings were somehow wrong and that she herself was somehow bad for feeling the way she did.

When it was time to leave for school, she said goodbye and took a different route to avoid her friends.

That one slap broke a barrier of self-restraint with Papa. It seemed like if Lizzie had seen it once, it didn't matter if she witnessed it again and again and again.

Yes, the image of those hands keep her awake some nights. The nights when the converted warehouse she now calls home creaks from a new direction or a wind off the lake rattles grit against the windows. Sometimes the memory of those big hands snaps her from a deep sleep and pummels her full of fear till she lies shaking under the covers.

Thinking of his hands shakes loose other memories. A time when Papa stopped thinking of her as a child and started to blame her, along with Mama, as the cause of his failures.

First Mama had trapped him – a Jezebel with swaying hips – and then Lizzie locked the door of his prison by virtue of being born.

She might speak too loudly or maybe too softly. Her clothes might be the wrong ones. The house might be too messy; then again it might be too neat. Of course, her worse crime was no crime at all – that of being. Just being. Growing and learning. Maybe succeeding at things Papa had long given up for himself.

By the time the mine and the sintering plant reopened, his bitterness had set too far into his mind to shed. His need to strike out had grown too strong. Like a junkie on heroin, he couldn't kick the habit of blaming everyone except himself for his addiction.

The brutality began when he lost his work; debt, meanness and ignorance kept it going after work returned. It was like stopping might imply he'd been wrong to have done so in the first place. Wrong was something he could never be – not even in the time before when life was good.

If it weren't for old memories, Lizzie might relax into her new life. Maybe discover what contentment was. She is safe. Sarah Jane is safe. Whatever reservations she had held against Sam have drifted away. Life isn't bad at all. Different, but not bad. In a million years, she'd never have thought she'd end up where she is right now yet, for all that surrounds her, she is the most secure she has been in years.

Lizzie lies in her new bed, staring through the dark at the ceiling, picturing the items in the room and trying to feel like they belong to her. She imagines what it might be like to be able to waltz through a furniture store and pick whatever pleased her. She sighs. It's a long way from being a teenaged mother working as a maid for a couple of sex workers.

A car drives by; its headlights flare in her window. When it passes, she realizes she's been holding her breath. There is nowhere she can let everything go.

She is restless and turns from one side to another before rising to look out the window. Night time is never more than grey in this new place. There is no black sky decorated with millions of brilliant stars, their lights so bright a person might go blind if the sky wasn't so black it swallowed their aureoles. She wishes she'd learned the names of constellations before they were lost to her in this false night.

She misses the dark. Although she is nervous in this unknown place, in the past, darkness gave her peace. When the house settled for the night and she and Mama had retired for the day, Lizzie knew they were out of harm's way. Nothing bad happened after bedtime. There were minutes of calm before sleep.

Lizzie likes the moments of total blackness that envelop her the instant she flicks off the bedroom lights. She can feel the peacefulness of invisibility for a moment or two – those moments before her pupils adjust are wonderful. She stands motionless and breathes. Just breathes until the outline of her room appears before her and the lights of the city return.

Lizzie returns to bed, rolls onto her side and stretches her arm through the bars of the crib for the round outline of her sleeping daughter.

The image of her father's hands fly to her and Lizzie whimpers, wanting so much to be ready to ward off harm coming to her daughter.

Stop! She cries silently and begins to pray. Not to God, who has done nothing for her as far as she can see, but to her guardian angel.

"Granny Gee, tell me I did the right thing. I was so scared. I had to get away. Get my baby away." She pauses. "I wish I could see Mama. Maybe someday I can send for her." Hope springs in her chest then the imaginary fist smashes the hope gone.

Lizzie curls into a ball and cries.

Chapter Nine

The hole in her sneaker has grown. It's larger than a quarter, about the size of the old fifty-cent piece Mama keeps in her top drawer "for luck." Like it ever did her any good, Lizzie thinks with a sneer.

The hole began as a sliver; a small split where she'd stepped on a piece of metal lying on the street. It's large enough now that she has to clench the muscles of her foot to keep her big toe from scraping along the ground. At the end of the day, she scrubs her foot to clean off the dirt that filters into her shoe through the hole. She refuses to tell Sam who will insist on buying her new ones and she is indebted to the woman enough already.

Lizzie has tried lining the sole with layers cut from grocery bags that wore too quickly and cardboard inserts that dissolved from a combination of her sweat and scuffing.

Today, she has cut the shape of the ball of her foot from the plastic lid of an empty margarine container. She peels the liner from her sneaker and inserts the plastic form then lays the lining on top.

She pulls on her shoe and rubs the hard plastic with her big toe. It feels better than pavement. She hopes it will get her through the day.

With that task finished, she scans the Yellow Pages for pediatricians. The book is massive, never mind that there are two of them. Two fat books – one white, one yellow. She's in a quandary. There are pages and pages of physicians, column after column of baby doctors and she doesn't know how to choose. The baby book advises regular check-ups starting at two weeks and Sarah Jane is a month old already.

Lizzie is worried about approaching a doctor who will ask all kinds of questions. What can she say? How will she answer them without looking like a liar? She won't be eighteen for months yet. Could they take Sarah Jane away from her? Could they send her back to Rue? Authorities. Those faceless, nameless people with their untold power.

She's still wearing the engagement ring Rue bought her. It's not much of a ring. Nothing more than a microchip of a diamond on a band of white gold. Maybe silver. Maybe it's not a diamond. She doesn't know and doesn't care. She doesn't like wearing it, the constant reminder of him. She hopes appearing as an engaged woman rather than the stray she is gives her some standing in public.

She twists her ring round and round while she scans the pages.

ZoZo enters the kitchen sniffing into a tissue. Her scarlet hair is on end like a halo of flames encircling her head. An unlit cigarette is, as usual, tucked behind one ear. She has the summer flu, "the worse kind" according to her, and won't be working tonight. She claims she picked it up from a customer last night. "He was gross, sneezing all over me."

The worst kind of flu can kill you, Lizzie wants to tell her. Not to mention that thing called an incubation period. It takes more than a few hours for germs to develop. Maybe it's a message from your lungs. But Lizzie stays quiet. She knows better than to taunt a sewer rat.

Lizzie regards ZoZo with equal parts fascination and fear. Whatever has happened in ZoZo's life has made her uncaring to the point of callousness. It shows in the way she laughs at the misfortune of others when she shares stories about other women or the johns she meets. It shows in her house attire: a short robe held together only at the waist. Her scrawny chest and pubic area are continually on view. ZoZo doesn't care if she flashes some skin. Lizzie wonders why she bothers to wear anything at all and is sure the woman parades herself on purpose to see if it bothers Lizzie. Lizzie keeps her thoughts to herself concentrates on ZoZo's face, wishing she could avoid her entirely.

"What are you looking for?" ZoZo asks in reference to the phone book.

"A doctor for Sarah Jane. She needs a check-up."

"Bah. My mother never worried about doctors for me and I turned out okay, eh? You gonna spoil that kid and she'll end up being weak." She fills a mug with coffee, grabs a muffin from the plateful Lizzie baked that morning and plants her derrière against the granite countertop. She points a bony finger. "How you hook up with Sam?"

Lizzie clenches her jaw muscles. She'd rather not discuss anything about her life with this horrible woman. She attempts nonchalance. "She offered me a place to stay till I get settled. Seemed like a good idea. How about you?"

"Pfft. You want to know about me."

"Why leave Quebec? Why not pick Montreal instead of here?" To Lizzie,

Montreal sounds all too glamorous. She can't imagine why someone would prefer smoky, grey Toronto.

ZoZo yawns. "Montreal? I been there. I was a dancer, you know? Exotique? Did the circuit. Sydney, Montreal, Quebec, Sudbury, Winnipeg, Yellowknife, Fort McMurray."

The names of the towns are tattooed in tiny black script that runs up one arm and down the other, like two long indecipherable scribbles. Words written like a foreign language running together like the seam on pantyhose.

It's an intimidating list. Travelling to strange places week after week or month after month, to take her clothes off on a stage in front of a room full of hard-drinking men. Lizzie shudders and despite her dislike of ZoZo, feels a twinge of sympathy for her.

"You name somewhere, I been there," ZoZo continues. "But then, you know, there was too much coke. I got strung out, then I got clean and now I'm here. And why not?" She gives a Gallic shrug that belies the hard glint in her eyes. "Don't much matter where you are. The men are all the same, eh? Pigs." She peels the paper from the bottom of the muffin, dropping crumbs on the floor. "Did you see Sam this morning?"

Lizzie shakes her head. Sam had come home unusually early, waking Lizzie when she dropped her keys unlocking her bedroom door.

"She got a rough customer. Gave her a poke in the eye. Quit early just for that." She snaps her fingers and laughs as if to prove Lizzie's earlier judgement of her.

"Is she all right?"

"You and her, such babies. Like a jab in the eye's so bad. It's not hardly even black. Barely shows. That Sam, she thinks she's so smart but sometimes she don't know what end's up."

ZoZo pushes her hips away from the counter. "Ah, well. Who cares, eh? Me, I feel like shit. If Sam ask for me, you tell her I don't do nothing today." She clomps outside to sit on the front stoop, smoke her cigarette and yell at the guys unloading a truck across the street. They yell something back and ZoZo cackles so hard she has a coughing fit. A few minutes later, she retreats upstairs and Lizzie listens to her feet stomp down the hallway to the end bedroom.

She shakes her head. That woman is a funny one. Maybe a dangerous one as well. Lizzie is aware that ZoZo regards her with disdain, that she sneers when she sees her doing housework. Work ZoZo considers beneath her. Money for sex, that's okay. Money for cleaning a floor, that's for grunts. "Nobody get rich that way," she's told Lizzie more than once. Of course, Lizzie hasn't noticed any riches falling from ZoZo's fingers either, but she is smart enough not to say so.

She pulls her attention back to the phonebook, trying to recognize street names to select a doctor nearby. She is still struggling when Sam enters in a beautifully embroidered kimono and places a plastic bag on the table in front of her.

"What's this?"

"Open it and find out."

"ZoZo said you were hit. Are you all right? Are you hurt?" Lizzie studies Sam's face, able to detect nothing more than a blood-shot eye. Perhaps it was the insignificant incident ZoZo portrayed.

Sam pours herself a glass of orange juice. As she sips her drink, Lizzie notes a small blue bruise over the bridge of Sam's nose and reaches to feel for her own scar in the same place. She runs a finger over the tiny, pink indent. Sam's injury will heal so much faster.

"I'll be fine. Hazards of the trade. Put ice on it when I got home and the swelling's already gone. Now go ahead. Open your surprise."

Lizzie reaches for the bag and peaks inside. "A baby monitor!"

"So you can hear her wherever you are."

"Thanks, Sam. That's really sweet of you. You even remembered batteries. You're too much sometimes."

Sam smiles then catches sight of the still-warm muffins. She grabs one and bites into it. "These are good. Carrot and what else?"

"Applesauce. Cuts down on the fat."

"I could use a little." Sam pats her curveless hips.

Lizzie gets a glass of milk and places two muffins onto a plate for herself. She glances over the directions for the monitor. It is a thoughtful gift. She often worries that she won't hear Sarah Jane wake when she is doing something in another part of the house.

Sam reaches for another muffin.

"There's fruit salad to go with that," Lizzie tells her.

Sam gets a bowl to fill with fruit and helps herself to a third muffin. "What's with the phonebook?"

Lizzie explains her doctor dilemma – how to get health care without having to answer too many questions and how to select someone from the multitude of choices.

"There's a walk-in clinic a few blocks from here. I can take you later if you want. They don't need to know your business, but I think you're worrying for nothing."

"I can just show up anytime?" Where she is from, there is no such thing as a walk-in clinic. There are two doctors who have delivered and buried everyone in town and know more secrets than the priest, the lawyer and all the bartenders combined.

"God, Milk Maid, you are so naïve. You're lucky I found you before someone else did."

Lizzie disregards the nickname it seems she is to be stuck with. "You'll take me later? Before you go to work?"

"Promise."

Lizzie follows Sam upstairs, each to their separate rooms. Sarah Jane has slept longer than usual today and Sam will miss the morning stroll. Lizzie enters her bedroom to find her daughter stirring and ready for breakfast. Her fists are waving in the air; her mouth is puckered, gearing up for a yell.

"Hush, my sweet one. Mommy's here." Lizzie lifts the infant and cozies up with her on the bed. This is Lizzie's favourite time of day. After the others are sleeping, when she is alone with her daughter.

Lizzie handles Sarah Jane's morning routine with practiced efficiency and loads the diaper bag with items to carry necessities to the main floor. "We're running out of diapers. It's hard to believe how quickly you go through these."

Sarah burbles in response.

"It's so nice not to have a care in the world, isn't it?" Lizzie kisses her cheek, the baby skin impossibly soft against her own. This simple gesture makes her think about her own mother and how she used to cuddle against her, listening to a story before bedtime or in the morning before school.

A catch in her throat takes her by surprise as it has hundreds of times since she left home. It must be true that for every good feeling, there is a bad one to accompany it and she fights to hold her tears from falling.

Chapter Ten

Sam is unreadable to Lizzie this morning. Her face is blank and as they clear the breakfast dishes, she moves without her usual fluidity, wincing when she bends. She even asks to forego their morning walk.

"What's wrong?" Lizzie asks.

"Last night. On the job. It's nothing."

Lizzie tries to hide her disappointment, but when their eyes meet, Lizzie knows she has failed. Sam insists she is fine and off they go.

Lizzie hesitates to ask for more details. Sam draws a rigid line between home and work. It is how she maintains her sanity, she says, keeping the two distinct.

On their way out the door, Sam grabs a map of the city from the front hall table.

Pushing the stroller, Lizzie sets a sedate pace, hoping this will be better for Sam. They make their way to the park that is, as usual, almost empty.

Sam spreads a blanket, grimacing as she fixes the corners then settles onto her back, covering her eyes with her forearm.

"What happened?" Lizzie can't hold back.

"Never mind. It's fine. I'll be fine."

"You're hurt."

"Shush. I don't want to discuss that world when I'm in this one."

Lizzie lays Sarah Jane on the blanket in the narrow space between herself and Sam. The baby coos to the leaves overhead.

The sound of contentment brings a smile to Sam's face and she turns to Lizzie. "Hard to be miserable around this one."

Lizzie observes Sam as she marvels at Sarah Jane. Along with what Lizzie interprets as Sam's enduring sadness, there is tenderness on the woman's face and something Lizzie can only describe as hope. Yes, that's it. Sam looks hopeful. Though Lizzie isn't sure why, she thinks it has something to do with these morning walks and the idea that she has done something to make Sam happy makes her happy.

Sam pulls the map from the stroller and sits to spread it on the blanket. "You have to learn your way around," she says.

Lizzie looks at the mess of ribbons and knots that represent streets and highways and intersections. "This is impossible."

"Look. Here we are and here's the closest library. See here? That's that university of yours." Sam stabs at the map with her finger. "Maybe you could go there and talk to them in person."

Lizzie's stomach flips. Could they help her?

"You have to get out. People are going to think you're a prisoner. Some kind of sex slave or illegal immigrant."

"Who? Nobody knows I'm here."

"Potentially."

"I'm not stupid; I'm just used to a place where all the main roads meet in the middle of a downtown area. A place where four roads connect to the outside. One that runs to the mine, one to the box stores, one to Sudbury and one that meanders south. That's it. I don't know how anyone finds their way to anywhere here."

Sam laughs, throws her arms wide and as she falls onto her back, she yelps and tenses, her shoulders remain off the ground

"That is my fault." Lizzie feels miserable. "You're hurt and I made you come out. We should go back."

"Never mind that now. Let's just enjoy this." Sam is silent for a moment then exhales slowly, sinking onto the blanket. In another moment, she returns to their earlier conversation as if nothing is wrong. "Milk Maid, how did you ever find your way from nowhere to here if you can't even figure out where south is?"

Lizzie's cheeks turn pink. Sam has a way of making her feel goofy and special at the same time. "I had time to work it out."

"If you can find your way from the wilds to the city, you can most certainly learn your way to a few key spots."

Lizzie rolls her eyes.

Sam moves onto her side, rests on her arm and points to the map. "We're here. See? Right by the lake and the train tracks. Over here is the CN Tower. Follow this north." Sam's blood-red nail traces a line representing Yonge Street on the map. "Here's the Eaton Centre. You've heard of that, right?"

Lizzie nods though she has never heard of much of anything to do with fancy city life – the right places to eat or the best places to shop or the latest fashions to wear. That information never permeated remote regions and even if it had, what would it matter to those with little access and less use for such things?

"South is water. North is city and beyond that, suburbia, and beyond that farmland. See this?" Sam draws her finger north and south and it dawns on Lizzie that there is sense to be made of this. There is a recognizable grid to the layout of the streets. Sam shows where to find the nearest convenience store and which areas of the city to avoid.

Sarah Jane blows a raspberry and laughs at her new sound. Drool coats everything south of her dainty mouth.

"Isn't she too young for teething?" Sam arches a finely shaped brow.

"No such thing. Mama says I started the day I was born."

Sam's lies down and thrusts her hands under her head and closes her eyes. Lizzie examines her. Her natural hair is cropped close to her head, her complexion flawless and smooth. Her lips are perfectly formed, her ears small for such a large person. Her neck is long and missing the bump of an Adam's apple. She wears a canary yellow camisole that contrasts brilliantly against her dark skin. She's beautiful, Lizzie decides, especially with her work makeup washed off.

Lizzie had never studied Rue as closely, nor reflected on him as deeply. Comparing her first love with Sam is odd and yet, with the exception of family, these have been the two most important people in her life. Though Rue had been a magnet for her, she hadn't pondered his soul in the way she does Sam's. Something niggles at her as she thinks this. A warning? A piece of sudden knowledge. She bats it away. It's too nice a morning for deep thoughts or worry. She lies back and her lets her mind drift.

When she'd first seen Rue in grade school, she hadn't paid him any mind. She knew of him in the same way that everyone in a small town has at least a passing acquaintance with everyone else. As they grew, she watched him as those younger tend to watch those older. Three years her senior, Rue started high school and exited Lizzie's orbit. When she started the ninth grade, she saw that he had developed the sort of dark and dangerous looks that attracted her and every other pubescent girl. She would have risked anything to be with him. He was the first and only boy to make her feel any excitement by doing nothing more than entering a room or walking past her. From his behaviour, she knew he was no more interested in her than he was in his studies.

When she turned sixteen, that changed. His band had played at a school dance, while Lizzie stood at the edge of the stage, watching him and dreaming about his full lips on hers and what they might feel like.

He saw her – really saw her – at the start of the band's first break. Noticing, like the other boys had that year, that she had left childhood behind.

Oh, she could tell they noticed her by the way they spoke to her, staring at the rise and fall of her chest. The way they found excuses to bump against her and lean over her shoulder in class as if they were checking her answer to a homework question. They knew that she knew they were only trying to get a glimpse of what lay beneath the buttons of her blouse, but the game was too exciting not to be played. A transparent ruse. Once in a while, she would lean her head to the side and squeeze her arms together to give them a brief peak for the visceral thrill of it. The power of it.

Even as she enjoyed this newfound popularity, she knew it for what it was. Developing later than other girls, she'd seen the trials of the early-bloomers. The unending drama, the alienation, the accusations, the heartache. It was sickening when she thought about it and it was this revulsion that kept her chaste and, eventually, stopped the boys from pursuing her any further.

Still, her time at the centre of all that buzzing gave her a sense of herself and some of the confidence she'd been missing. She stood in front of her bedroom mirror, angling her face this way and that and determined that her sculpted cheekbones and strong jaw line would do. She saw that she'd become attractive. Not cheerleader-pretty in the way of the most popular, but strong and womanly in the way of her ancestors. Her father's battle maiden at last.

That night, as Rue strummed his final chord of the set, he looked her way and their eyes locked. He set his guitar aside and strode toward her, licking his lips. She was riveted and continued to be. For long enough anyway.

The next day he walked six miles just to see her. His car had broken down and he acted as though his trek was nothing more than a casual stroll. Lizzie had been doing homework at the kitchen table, her parents in the living room, a ball game on the television. Mama was darning Papa's work socks. They were thick and warm and too expensive to throw away because of something as minor as a hole.

When Rue arrived, he sat at the table. Lizzie's books were spread out between them as if there were a chance she might return to studying at any moment.

She served him tea. Cup after cup. Coffee seemed too complicated – all that measuring.

Rue sat there with his lazy, sexy smile, his thumb circling the lip of his mug and Lizzie couldn't believe her good fortune. Six miles he walked for her. And six miles back. It was a knight's errand.

It presented her with a fork within a fork within a fork in her road. Pick this or that or some other thing. On one side chastity, on another lust and Rue. On yet another path was the way to something else. Something big.

It was the year she found a job at the airstrip after school and on weekends, earning a regular paycheque and with it a taste of independence. She had money to buy things for herself and she began saving – for what she didn't know; yet save she did. As the money in her bank account grew, she thought about what she might do with her riches. Once she started thinking about that, her mind expanded beyond Black River and Rue to the possibilities of life.

That was when she got it in her head to go on to university. It was an idea that grew on her slowly. Or rather, it was an idea that just was, waiting to be recognized, to come into focus. It came to her as a matter-of-fact one warm September day as she was bent over her desk, examining a bit of feldspar under a banged-up microscope in the science lab, when there it was, a desire to go on doing what she was doing forever.

She told Rue and he'd laughed at her, but she didn't mind at the time. She was used to keeping her thoughts and feelings to herself. She hadn't known that this was something he'd never agree to, that he'd go so far as to fight to stop her. She talked to her guidance councillor and studied under a school-supplied tutor for the remainder of the year. By end of first term, she'd made it onto the honour role and Rue stopped laughing. By the end of first semester, her teacher said she had a good shot at a scholarship. That was when Rue got mad and told her there was no way she was leaving him for a "fuckin' degree."

She kept at it, oblivious of just how serious he was until he reached the narrow limits of his patience and tried to "knock some sense into her."

From then on, Lizzie kept her studying to herself.

She hid her books and sneaked out to the library or found excuses to stay after school, and eventually she too began to boil. She simmered over Rue trying to hold her back, over Papa for what he did, and over Mama for never standing up to him.

All of this subterfuge taught Lizzie something. She was a wily girl.

And then buxom Mona and her family moved to town and Rue's eye followed her sashay whenever she drew near. Jealous, Lizzie chose the wrong fork in that particular road and ended up pregnant. It must have happened at the start of grade twelve although she hadn't figured it out until almost Christmas. She'd never had regular cycles and it wasn't till she started to feel nauseated when she got up in the morning that she'd taken a home test.

When she read the positive result, she threw up. What was she to do?

She chose to keep quiet till she could figure that out for herself. Holding her own counsel was something that came easily to her. Who had she ever had to talk to?

Getting pregnant was something that might have stopped some girls. Not Lizzie. She became ever more determined to do what she wanted to do. She applied for a scholarship for the fall semester without telling anyone. By the time she received her acceptance letter, she'd had her escape planned and the money — she thought — to make it happen.

The money had proven not enough and then Samantha appeared, like a garishly made-up angel.

Lizzie glances at her and rubs her hands as though washing them. She is torn – wanting to ask so many whys and whats, and not wanting Sam to be angry with her.

As if reading the furrows on her brow, Sam says, "Go ahead. Ask. I can feel you ready to burst."

Lizzie reaches for her bag and grabs a diaper. She concentrates on changing her daughter, even though, strictly speaking, a change isn't required.

"Why…?" She is unsure how to continue. Embarrassment flushes her cheeks.

"Why what? Why am I the way I am? Why do I sell sex? Why am I allowed to live, to take up oxygen? Which why do you want answered?" Sam's voice stings like nettles in an otherwise lovely garden. Their eyes meet and Lizzie looks away in shame.

"I am who I am. There is no one else for me to be. As for the other – what else is someone like me going to do? I'm a freak to people like you and yours, right? Normal people. People who operate in the regular world just fine. Everyday, run-of-the-mill people who can destroy each other and cause their children to run away."

"Sam, please. I don't mean to offend you. I just don't get it, you know? If I can't ask you, how am I going to figure it out?" She can tell Sam is listening even though her eyes are closed. This gives her courage to ask the next question. "How come you became a prostitute?"

"Isn't that the sixty-four thousand dollar question? Have you had a good look at me? Take one look and every thought you have about me has to do with sex. You don't wonder what I'm studying or whether I landed some big deal. You think, does she have a dick? Or who does she fuck? What else is someone like me going to do?" Her voice carries the hurt of years of rejection and disappointment, and Lizzie is sick, not with herself finally, but for anyone who would shun Sam.

"Now, can we not talk about this anymore?" Sam asks.

Lizzie shrugs. "I've never met anyone like you before."

"Yeah, so you've said. I'm not your science project, Milk Maid. You don't get to inspect me."

"That's not what I mean. I—"

Sam rolls gently onto her back, distancing herself from her inquisitor.

"I just want to know you better."

"Why?" Sam snaps her head to the side and pins her gaze onto Lizzie's.

Lizzie feels the heat flush her cheeks, but soldiers on. "I think you're amazing."

Sam's mouth opens then closes. She blinks. "You think I'm amazing?" Her voice is incredulous and Lizzie nods.

"Look at everything you do."

"I'm just a hooker, Milk Maid. Don't get all sentimental over that." Sam's sardonic tone is back, establishing distance between them.

"No, Sam. Look." Lizzie grabs Sam's arm then releases it like she's been burned, still unsure about safe touching. She leans forward in earnest. "You created this home and you've saved Sarah Jane and me. You do an awful job then you come home every morning and shuck it off like it doesn't touch you. Or you try not to let it. You do so much for everybody and you take so little for yourself. Maybe you think nobody sees it but I do. I see you."

Silence reigns, allowing the sounds of their surroundings in. A bird sings in the tree overhead. A squirrel can be heard chattering at something or someone. A dog barks and his owner whistles for him. In the distance, the clanking of chains loading and off-loading freight can be heard from the harbour.

A Rottweiler rushes toward them, his owner trundling along behind. "Come on, Brandy. Leave those people alone." Lizzie snatches Sarah Jane from the blanket.

The Rotty stops at the edge of the blanket. Sam is on her knees, ready to lunge if need be, ignoring the doggy smile that inches its way across the dog's muzzle. His lips are pulled back over sharp teeth, wrinkling his snout, his large pink tongue lolls out the side of his mouth.

The winded owner arrives. "I'm sorry if he scared you. Brandy is harmless. Honestly." He snaps a leather leash to the dog's collar.

Sam remains silent. Her jaw tightens – in displeasure or fear, it is hard to tell.

"That's okay," Lizzie says to the dog owner. "We didn't know and the baby… well, you know."

"Yeah. Coulda been like that dingo." The dog owner chuckles then takes a long look at Sam, his face filling with confusion. Sam comes to her feet as the dog owner's eyes travel the length of her imposing figure. He bobs his head and gulps. "Sorry again. Didn't mean to scare you." The owner pulls his pet away at a jog.

"See. Like that. You looked like you were going to do battle with that dog. To protect us," Lizzie says.

Sam lowers herself to the ground stiffly. She returns to her original pose, on her back with her arm over her eyes.

Her voice is quiet, yet there is something else in it too. Something hard. Unfeeling. Final. "It's nice you notice, but I can't get all chummy. That's not the way my life is right now."

The weeks of building camaraderie between them has evaporated so quickly, Lizzie wants to cry; she is so alone in this large, strange place and maybe her only friend is not a friend after all.

Chapter Eleven

The centre of the massive library soars to a glass dome above five floors of books, computers, study carrels and reference materials. It is old and formidable, a larger version of the stately library in Black River. Both were built at the end of the nineteenth century when such edifices, along with town halls and post offices, were considered worthy of fine architecture. Archways and Greco-Roman columns. Pediments over doorways and leaded, arched windows with horizontal headers. Dentil work under substantial cornices. Marble stairwells and statues of founding fathers – never mothers – let the public riffraff understand the reverence expected in these spaces.

A computer screen comes to life before her. The Internet icon flashes in the corner. Lizzie clicks on it and opens her email account. There are more than six hundred messages waiting for her. She scans through page after page of junk.

Penis enlargers, hardeners and shavers. Cheap prescription drugs. Men and women from around the globe who care about her sexual satisfaction and want her to enjoy mind-blowing orgasms. Requests to help lawyers in Africa liquidate their late clients' funds. She has even won contests without having entered any. It's a miracle. There are hundreds of updates from her friends' social sites, photo tags, invitations to join groups, messages. She deletes page after page without reading, winding her way back to May and the last date she'd logged on.

Midway through that month's messages, she sees it. An email from Mama. Lizzie's heart races, she sucks air sharply and double-clicks the link.

> Dear Lizzie:
> I hope you are safe and well and the baby is too. I am so worried. Please contact me though this address. Your father doesn't know about it. I'll check at the library everyday. Please let me know where you are. I love you so much. I miss you.

Please write soon.

Mama

P.S. Mr. Patel helped me with this.

Mr. Patel, Lizzie's tutor. Lizzie exhales slowly, wondering who contacted whom. Mama had never used a computer. An email address gives Lizzie a safe way to contact her.

Or does it?

What if this isn't really Mama? What if it's Rue being exceedingly clever? Or the police?

What if it's someone helping Papa? Her heart sinks and she pulls her hands away from the keyboard as if he can see her through miles of cyberspace.

She imagines the inflection of his voice, sounding forever angry because of his heavy German accent.

Papa was a Protestant, from one of the stern sects that allow little laughter and no frivolity. Although he had walked away from his church when he arrived in Canada, he remained a solemn man, one who rarely smiled, one who expected to work hard and be rewarded for this and only this. It contributed to his hardness. Life had not gone as he had assumed it would, hadn't lived up to his expectations. Erik von Valör – a proud though impoverished descendant of princess-abbess Maria Clara von Spaur, Pflaum und Valör of Essen – had emigrated from Germany believing he would find farmland in western Canada at bargain-basement prices. Lizzie wondered how he had ever formed such an idea – that fertile land would be cheap. An out-of-date immigration book or an ancient rumour mill? Who knew how ideas about Canada arrived in foreign places?

How he ended up in Northern Ontario working in a mine was another question open to debate. Some days he said that his birth in a large steel centre fabricated his destiny, that there was a special magnetism in the blood that ran in his veins, calling him to the iron ore that lined the rock of the Canadian Shield.

Other days, he told the story of his voyage to Canada, shovelling coal into the ship's engine across the Atlantic to pay for his passage. On the ship, he'd met a man who told of the mountains of money that could be made in the nickel, silver and copper mines of the North.

Better to have money to bankroll a farm than to arrive on the vast prairie empty-handed, Papa had decided.

So, north he travelled to Black River, directly to the mine office where he was hired as soon as the words asking for a job were out of his mouth. Weeks later, on a sunny day in July, he sat in a diner celebrating his good fortune and his first full paycheque with a steaming cup of coffee and two large pieces of chocolate pie. As he looked out the window, Erik Valor – having dropped the von and umlaut from his last name to sound both brave and Canadian – watched Doris Butler cross the street.

Fresh out of high school with curvy hips just right for farm work and breeding, and a ponytail that swayed in time with those hips, Doris caught Erik's imagination. He wooed her and wed her before the summer was over with promises of leaving the stifling northern forest for the open horizons and blue sky of Saskatchewan.

To the mines he went, scrimping and saving yet never accumulating enough for his land – the land he discovered had to be bought at great cost along with massive machinery that drove many into bankruptcy. In the mines he stayed, long enough for the slowdowns and layoffs, and eventually, the closures that ate away his savings. He never did build his mountain of cash.

He became a bitter and angry man, blaming his wife and child for the loss of his dream of becoming a person of note with large tracts of land to his name.

Never his fault, Lizzie thinks with anger. Never. And what was so damn bad about their lives anyway? Things got bad for them as it had for most of their neighbours. The Valor family wasn't singled out or specially disadvantaged.

They had been happy once! He was the one who took that away from them.

Lizzie makes a fist and hits her open palm. She bites her lips together, thinking. What is she going to do about the email?

She pictures Mama pecking at a keyboard to create her note, Mr. Patel at her side showing her how to send her first electronic message. Or maybe Mr. Patel did the typing while Mama dictated. Both are comforting notions, but Lizzie forces herself to be practical.

The police can tell where emails come from. Which computer is used. At least they can on police dramas. If she were to reply, she'd have to travel to another computer at a library at the other end of the city. Maybe as far as one of the suburbs.

Is there some way for her to verify it was Mama who sent the mail?

Lizzie leans forward, resting her chin in her cupped hands. She has to think this through. She can't make a mistake.

Quit being a wimp.

She will do this. Figure it out. She's been in predicaments before, situations where she has had to rely on her own smarts to get by. How else did she find her way here? She has found answers before and she will again. The trick is to take her time. To not jump in. That is the key.

Today, she has another issue to tackle: school.

She logs into to her account with the university. Maybe Sam is right and she should make an appointment to see them. Maybe they have resources to help her out.

There is a message waiting for her. Admissions would like to know her decision about attending. They need her final transcript. Will she attend or not? Others are waiting if she would like to decline the school's offer.

Lizzie hits the reply key. She wonders if staff at the admissions department is aware of her situation. Not possible, she realizes. Her parents don't know about the scholarship. They wouldn't know to contact the university.

Unless more mail has been sent to her at home. Unless Mr. Patel told her mother. Or her father. A dull ache grows between her eyes as her mood dips once more.

Every step is filled with possible danger and her nerve falters.

I'm only seventeen. I can't do it all on my own.

In spite of her earlier resolve, she is filled with despair and self-pity. She sees the arc of time racing past her with opportunities lying beyond her reach as she raises a baby and sinks into the life of a domestic.

She cannot let that happen. She cannot raise Sarah Jane into a life of poverty and limited potential. She has to find a way to go to school and create a new life for them both.

Lizzie bangs the mouse against the desk louder than she intends and a person at the reference desk frowns at her.

"Sorry," Lizzie mouths at her.

She stares at the empty box where her response is supposed to go. Maybe she should ask for a deferral. "Definitely plan B," she mutters.

She can't get ahead if she lets fear rule every decision. At some point, she has to jump in and do something. She's frightened of responding to her mother and to the school. She has to thaw. Make a move.

Replying to admissions holds limited risk, she decides. Even if they contact the cops, Toronto Police won't have the time to follow-up. Her disappearance is of little importance in the scheme of things. How long do they even look for missing teens? The police must be overwhelmed with similar cases. Not to mention the real crime they have to solve. Murder and organized crime. It's not the same pace as in a small town.

She takes a deep breath and writes that she most definitely wants to attend this fall but has run into an obstacle and would like to meet with someone to discuss what options there might be for her. Before she can chicken out, she hits the send key then logs out.

She has one last thing to do before she leaves. She keys in the search term "transsexual" and begins to read.

Hours later, with her new library card securely away in her wallet and new information swirling in her head, she arrives home with Sarah Jane to find ZoZo up and watching television.

"You're awake early," Lizzie says as she lifts Sarah Jane from the stroller. "Couldn't sleep?" Lizzie tries to ignore the feeling that ZoZo can't stand her.

In response, ZoZo turns up the volume. She crosses her thin legs, one bouncing up and down like it is one end of a seesaw.

"Hey," Lizzie raises her voice. "Can you turn that down? I won't talk to you, if that's what you want."

ZoZo presses the remote until the sound is again at a reasonable level. She glares at Lizzie and turns her hand palm up as if to ask if she is satisfied. Her face is flushed.

"Are you all right?" Lizzie asks in.

The volume increases once more.

"Okay, okay. I surrender." Lizzie rolls her eyes and wonders what has happened. ZoZo is never up before five or six in the evening.

Lizzie nurses Sarah Jane and lays her down for a nap in her crib, then looks through a cookbook for something new to make with leftover roast beef. She settles on a beef and blue cheese salad with garlic bread on the side.

Sam is up. She greets ZoZo who leaps off the couch and bounds into the kitchen ahead of her. They pour themselves large mugs of coffee.

Sam looks at ZoZo in amusement. "You're energetic today."

ZoZo lifts her mug in salute and sloshes coffee onto the floor. She plonks her drink onto the counter, spilling more and feels behind her ear. "Tabernac!" she exclaims and springs to the coffee table in the living room to fetch her cigarettes. Forgetting or ignoring her coffee and doing nothing to clean her spills, she grabs a beer from the fridge and walks outside.

Sam's eyes narrow as they follow ZoZo in and out of the room. She purses her lips.

"What's up with her?" Lizzie asks.

Sam runs her hands over her hair and looks into the distance. "If I didn't know better I'd say she's using again."

"Using?" Lizzie is shocked and knows she shouldn't be. Someone who has been an addict once can easily be one again. Someone in the sex trade using drugs could hardly be unusual. Despite the relative comfort in which Sam and ZoZo live, theirs is a brutal life. Hadn't Lizzie watched after-school specials? Coming face-to-face with the realities of the life however, is a far cry from a video in health class or a documentary on You Tube.

"That's how we met. You wonder why I have her live here? We met at a twelve-step program after I'd detoxed in rehab. We both fell off the wagon more than once, but eventually we helped each other stay clean."

"I never would have imagined you …" Lizzie's speech trails off. What's she going to say? That she can't imagine someone like Sam, a transsexual sex-trade worker, seeking solace in her drug of choice?

"I've been worried about her for a while. She's been agitated and moodier than usual. Not that she's ever easy to deal with. She's tougher than old leather, but she's been even more difficult lately. She says it's nothing – I should have called her on it."

"You mean she's worse since I got here."

"No. Before that." Sam hesitates. "Maybe. I don't know. We used to talk. Sometimes we'd meet for a coffee if we weren't busy. That stopped somewhere along the line and I'm afraid that she's slipped back." Sam smacks the counter-top. "I knew it and I let it slide."

"Maybe that's not it," Lizzie offers. "You don't know for sure."

Sam looks at Lizzie like she's an imbecile. "That's what lets addicts get away with their addictions. People who want to pretend they don't know what's happening. I know and I have to do something." Her face softens. "Even if she isn't using yet …" She shakes her head. "No. I've seen her; I can't pretend otherwise."

As much as Lizzie wants to feel concern for ZoZo, she doesn't. She thinks of Sarah Jane. She can't raise her daughter in a house with an addict. How much longer will she be able to stay here if ZoZo continues to use?

Chapter Twelve

Lizzie holds a nasal syringe, about to insert it into one of Sarah Jane's nostrils. She's nervous about this procedure, but can't bear to see her daughter suffering without trying something.

Sarah Jane is sick and listless, likely from ZoZo's cold or flu or whatever it was. It's horrible to see her baby so stuffed she can't nurse or breathe, so Lizzie is attempting her last resort. She has tried numerous remedies though none have helped. Sarah Jane might as well be filled with glue.

Lizzie re-reads the instructions on the box. Depress bulb. Place in nostril. Release. Sounds easy enough.

She places the tip of the syringe into a small nostril. Her hands shake. She takes a breath and her hand slips. Instead of suctioning out mucus, she injects a stream of air into Sarah Jane's nose.

The child throws her arms back in surprise. She tries to inhale and can't. In an instant, her eyes are wide with terror, her face turns red, then her lips turn blue. Lizzie yanks her daughter into a sitting position. In another second, Sarah Jane catches her breath and begins to wail.

"Oh my god!" Lizzie cuddles Sarah Jane. "I almost killed you."

Sarah Jane's eyes are glazed. Her crying fades and then stops. Her body is limp and hot. Her down-covered head droops to the side.

"Okay. Bear with me. We're going to try this again. I don't know what else to do for you."

She rests Sarah Jane onto the diaper table and grabs the syringe. With great care, she presses the sides of the bulb together, inserts the tip into Sarah Jane's nose and loosens her grip. Sarah Jane's eyes fly open, but this time there is success and the syringe sucks mucus from her nose. Lizzie repeats the process three times to each side. Her stomach turns as she washes the syringe in her bathroom sink. Being sick is gross.

Mama hated sickness. She tackled it like she was the lone crusader battling evil itself. She'd slather ointment onto Lizzie's chest and cover it with heated cloths that felt like they might burn through her skin. She'd brew old-timey concoctions for Lizzie to sip. Mixtures that tasted every bit as vile as they smelled. Mama would scrub the bathroom and kitchen with bleach to stop the spread of germs and change Lizzie's bed linens with the fervour of the newly evangelized.

Granny Gee thought Mama was nuts. "Don't know where she got that. Not from me, I can tell you."

To Granny Gee, germs were a natural part of life. Not that she didn't keep a clean house. She did. She simply felt that people got carried away with all the hand sanitizers and antibacterials and obsessions with wiping out every germ. "We'll end up killing our own immune systems," she said. "That girl of mine's a throwback. All that fussing. All those old-fashioned remedies. Tsk. It's non-sense, you ask me."

Mama however, didn't ask for her opinion and acted like she didn't hear the critical comments while she carried out her private war.

She was equally fanatical about public washrooms. "Don't touch anything," she'd warn.

Like that was possible.

Still, it had bred a distaste of these public places in Lizzie. She handles re-stroom taps and door handles with paper towels or the fabric of her own clothes, placing her hands under her the bottom opening of her tops or pulling her sleeves over her fingers.

Having had to bathe her daughter in germ-ridden sinks had been disgust-ing. She'd never have done it if she'd had a choice.

As for colds, Lizzie has been following the suggestions in her motherhood book, trying infant medicines and using a vaporizer. Nothing helps until she buys the four-dollar syringe. With alleviated airways, Sarah Jane is able to nurse and immediately falls into a deep sleep.

Lizzie is able to rest too. They sleep past supper and when Lizzie wakes, it is dark outside and the house is empty. It's disconcerting to awake to a vacant house. She checks on Sarah Jane then turns on the baby monitor and goes downstairs to get something to eat.

She can imagine how annoyed ZoZo must have been that Sam allowed Lizzie to sleep in, forcing ZoZo to make her own dinner. ZoZo has made it clear that she regards Lizzie as a drain on resources rather than a contributor to the household. This latest incident will only give her more ammunition against

Lizzie the Interloper.

On the other hand, ZoZo has been quiet, circumspect even, over the past few days. Sam and she must have had words. Now that she thinks of it, Lizzie recollects that the two women have barely spoken to each other and wonders if this avoidance has been on purpose or coincidental.

Lizzie makes toast and spreads blueberry jam over it, pours a large glass of milk and heads to the television. She munches and sips while she surfs up and down the range of channels. Nothing.

It's ten-thirty on Saturday night. She's seventeen, wide-awake and house-bound. She turns the television back on and watches a reality show without interest.

Her mind drifts to the email in her inbox ostensibly from her mother. She hasn't come to any conclusion about what to do about it. Her mood swings from elation over the fantasy of convincing Mama to come to Toronto to hope-lessness at the risk inherent in contacting her. For all Lizzie knows, Papa co-erced Mama to write. If so, he would accompany her to the library to check for Lizzie's reply. Could Mama have found the gumption to take such a rebellious step as sending an email by herself?

Lizzie hates feeling immobilized.

She will take action.

If only she can sort out which path in this new fork in her road is the right one to take…

The next thing she knows, Sam is rousing her from sleep. "What are you doing down here?"

Lizzie's head is heavy. Her brain is wrapped in cotton. She wants Sam to be quiet so she can fall back a sleep. "What time is it?"

Sam tells her then asks about Sarah Jane.

"She's been sleeping forever." Alarm bells ring inside Lizzie's fuzzy head.

She trots to her room and finds Sarah Jane awake with streaks of snot across her cheeks and on her hands, but her eyes are bright and her fever has broken. "Look at you!" Lizzie says. "You're getting better."

She bathes and nurses the child and when she returns to the main floor, Sam has showered and changed into jeans and a brightly coloured camisole. She whisks eggs in a blue and yellow ceramic bowl.

"I'll do that," Lizzie offers.

"I don't mind. You've got your hands full." Sam pours the eggs into a heat-ed pan and lowers bread into the toaster. "I don't suppose you've seen ZoZo this morning? She should be home by now."

Lizzie shakes her head. Not seeing ZoZo is a good thing.

"Maybe you should take over. I'm going to call her."

Lizzie moves the rubber spatula through the egg mixture while Sam hits a speed-dial button. She leans against the counter with her cell phone pressed to her ear. She purses her lips and ends the call. "She's not answering. If she's not home after we eat, I'm going looking for her. We're supposed to call if we're going to be late."

Lizzie puts Sarah Jane on a blanket with her baby gym and serves the eggs and toast. They eat in silence; Sam checks her phone open at regular intervals.

"She's fine," Lizzie says. "She knows how to take care of herself. Out of anyone I know, she's the last one I'd worry about." She hears the callousness in her voice and bites her tongue, not wanting Sam to notice.

"You're probably right, but it's not a chance I can take. I'm heading out. Call me if she shows up."

Sam leaves and returns three hours later without ZoZo. "No one I've checked with has seen her for hours. Where the fuck is she?"

As she lifts the handle from the house phone, ZoZo strolls through the door.

"Where have you been?" Sam pounces on her. "Did something happen? Are you all right?"

ZoZo rolls her eyes. "Relax why don't you?"

Sam's eyes shoot daggers and Lizzie's gaze darts from her angry face to Zo-Zo's expression of disdain. "Lizzie, you better leave. With the baby."

Lizzie wastes no time. She flees to her room, closes the door with her foot and parks Sarah Jane on the bed.

Within minutes, she hears voices rising from downstairs.

"You know why we're supposed to call, ZoZo! What the fuck are you doing with yourself?"

Lizzie can't hear the response. She slips to her door and cracks it open.

"You're stoned right now."

"Don't be so dramatic, Sam. I'm not the one that's fucked up."

"You're not seriously trying to tell me that, are you? Like I'm not going to know? Me?"

"Seigneur! Calm down. It's just a bit of coke. Not crystal. Just coke."

"Just coke! Oh well then, okay." Sarcasm drips from her words. "Coke doesn't count. I forgot. How stupid are you? You can't start using again and stop whenever you feel like it. And you know you. You won't want to."

"Jesu. I'm too tired for this. I'm going to bed. To sleep."

"Don't think we're done. You know the deal we made. You use, you're gone. You won't be able to stay here."

"Like you're going to throw me out."

"Don't push me. You know what I went through getting clean." Sam's voice shakes and Lizzie realizes how frightened she is of falling down the rabbit hole again.

"Sure. You're going to throw me out now she's here. You got a new friend; you don't need ZoZo no more."

"That's not why …"

Sam's words grow faint and Lizzie can no long hear what she's saying. She closes her bedroom door in time to hear footsteps come up the stairs and stomp down the hall.

Chapter Thirteen

Someone knocking at the front door wrenches Lizzie from sleep in an instant. The sound stops and with her heart racing, she waits, hoping whomever is there has gone away.

Rapid-fire banging begins afresh. The urgency of it frightens her and she locks her bedroom door behind her, slips the key into the Spanish moss that surrounds the trunk of a potted and sickly ficus next to her door and pads down the stairs.

She slides the chain into the lock and cracks open the door. Before she can see who is there, the chain snaps from the wall and the door crashes into her head.

Lizzie screams as she drops to the floor, blinded by pain and an explosion of blood that shoots from a gash above her brow. She paws at her eyes in panic, attempting to clear her vision. She gropes for the stair railing to help herself to her feet. Through her one clear eye, the leering face of the intruder is hazy. Looking through the other, the world appears in red.

"Well, hello. Look who's here."

Lizzie's stomach lurches. It's a voice she knows so well.

She wipes her face with the bottom of her nightgown and, stepping away from the man. "Rue."

Emotions race through her. Disbelief, horror, shock.

Acceptance.

He grins, his eyes cold and sure. "Happy to see me?"

Lizzie is struck dumb. Her knees shake and she clings to the railing to steady herself.

"Talk to me, Baby. Tell me how much you missed me."

Lizzie swallows. Her throat sticks, the inside of her mouth turns to paste.

Rue backhands her and her head snaps to the side. "Who the fuck did you think you were dealing with, you little piece of shit?"

Tears run down Lizzie's cheeks, mingling with blood. Her vision is still blurry around the periphery and she blinks, trying to see a way out of this.

Can she get away from him? How long till Sam gets home? Her mind whirs. How can she keep him from Sarah Jane? The bedroom door is locked she remembers, relieved for this one thing. Don't wake, baby girl.

"What do you want?" she asks, frightened of what the answer might be.

"What the fuck do you think I want?" he roars. "My piece of shit fiancée and baby back home where they should be." His eyes flash. "Where's my kid?"

Lizzie's eyes dart up the stairs and she stumbles forward as if she might be able to block his way.

"Well, cock-a-doodle-doo!" Rue pushes past her as though she were no more than a gnat in his path. He races up the stairs two at a time.

Lizzie hesitates, her eyes moving from the phone in the living room to the direction of her daughter.

She lunges to the phone as she hears Rue fight with the first locked door.

"What the fuck?" he shouts. The sound of stomping boots echo overhead.

Lizzie dials Sam's cell phone number. It rings once and then twice. There is a click and the phone disconnects.

Lizzie dials again. "Come on, Sam. Pick up." Sweat breaks out on her face and back. She wants to be sick. Rue is at the end of the hall, ramming his body against what Lizzie hopes is ZoZo's bedroom door.

The baby monitor sighs to life as Sarah Jane's sleep is disturbed.

Rue runs the length of the hall and throws himself at a door. "God damn it! You goddamned bitch, where the fuck is my kid?"

Lizzie hears the phone ring once, twice, three times, then Sam's voice. "What's up?"

"It's Rue—"

The phone is ripped from her hand and Lizzie screams for help as it crashes to the floor.

"What do you think you're doing?" Rue has a handful of her hair and pulls her head backward. "Who the fuck was that? Your new boyfriend?"

Lizzie shakes her head.

A baby's wail fills the room and Rue's attention is gripped by the monitor.

"Is it a boy or a girl?" He yanks her hair.

She whimpers, but says nothing.

"A boy or a girl?" He pulls again, harder.

"A girl," she squeaks.

"Where's the key?"

Lizzie stares at him. She cannot tell him this thing. She closes her eyes. Be strong. Be brave. Don't tell.

"Where's the fucking key?" His fist connects with her ribcage and she can feel her damaged bone creak like a tree battling a great wind.

"No." She spits at him and he loosens his grip in shock at her resistance. She pushes away and races to the front door that remains ajar. Her fingers reach for the knob to propel her outside as a slingshot might. Rue grabs her nightgown from behind and twirls her into the room.

"You bitch," he snarls. "You are going to pay for that. And I know just how you can make it up to me."

He advances, unbuckling his belt as Sarah Jane's cries reach a crescendo.

"No, Rue. Please. Not this."

"Come on, Baby. Tell me you love me." His dark eyes glint with the cold reflection of obsidian and Lizzie's fear turns to panic.

"I l-l-love you, Rue."

"Love me? Baby, you can't do anything right without me. Look where you're at. Living with a bunch of whores. Well, Baby, you want to live with whores, you might as well be one."

Lizzie closes her eyes. She hears the sound of his zipper and tells herself it doesn't matter. She's been with him before. It won't be so bad. Maybe he'll go away afterward.

She floats to the ceiling. Away, away. Numb.

When it is over, she stumbles to a chair where she sits, feeling as worthless as he says she is. She cries into her chest without feeling the tears track down her face.

Rue zips his pants and smiles. "Now you go get your things and stop that kid from caterwauling. Jesus, if she's that much of a handful maybe I don't want you back." He gives Lizzie a playful pat on the shoulder. "Naw. Just kidding. Now go. Get your things. We're going home."

Lizzie can't move. She hurts everywhere. Her vision has cleared, but her head is pounding. Her insides feel raw with his contamination.

She is afraid that as soon as she opens the bedroom door, Rue will grab Sarah Jane and take off. Not that he would truly want her. He just can't stand someone else to have anything he thinks of as his. That and knowing it would hurt her. Hurting her seems important to him tonight.

"I told you to get moving. Fuck. Like I want to stay here longer than I have to."

Lizzie stands. A trail of semen leaks down her leg. This evidence humiliates her, enforcing how he has debased her. She needs to shower. Must shower. Scrub it off. Now. Her legs tremble and she sinks to her knees before him.

Rue grabs her arm and lifts her to her feet, laughing. It appears that things are really going his way. "Maybe later. I don't have time for that now. Go get your shit and the kid. I won't say it again." He flops on the couch and reaches for the remote.

"How did you find me?" Lizzie has to know where she failed.

Rue starts to laugh. "Checked the bus and train stations. That big slut you've taken up with stands out. She's fucking huge."

Of course he'd check there. She thinks back to the ticket agent that had given her the once over. He would have remembered her and that would have led Rue to Toronto. Checking Union Station would only make sense, but how would anyone even have noticed her? She should have found somewhere farther from Black River before hopping a bus here.

"I had her description. All I had to do was wait for her to show up. I followed her here this morning."

This morning. While they ate breakfast, Rue had been outside biding his time, planning his attack. Where had Lizzie's intuition been? Why hadn't she sensed something? Smelled something foul?

She drags her feet across the floor. She'd known it would turn out this way. She had, hadn't she? She reaches the stairwell and looks at the man-child she once loved. King of his domain.

Life is like this. Her life is like this and will be like this and who did she think she was to escape it?

The sound of a car's engine reaches Lizzie who looks beyond the open door to the red dash light of an unmarked police car. A door slams and Sam flies up the walk then bursts into the room. A man wearing a windbreaker saunters behind her. Lizzie sees the anger on Sam's face a split second before Rue jumps to his feet.

Sam barrels across the floor, dropping the stilettos she has been carrying, and tackles Rue to the ground. She smashes her fist into her adversary's face. One hit is all it takes to knock Rue out cold; still, Sam keeps hitting. Four punches are needed before she is able to stop herself, before Lizzie can let herself breathe.

Sam stands, shaking her sore knuckles and the stranger, who has been standing in the doorway, enters to stand guard over the prostrate Rue.

"Your face," Sam says. "What did he do to you? Where's Sarah Jane?"

The monitor has gone silent. Lizzie races up the stairs, unlocks her bedroom door and rushes to the crib. Sarah Jane's little face is sweaty and red. She is sleeping fitfully, her fist shoved between sucking lips.

Lizzie decides to let her be for a moment and checks her own reflection in the bathroom mirror. "What a mess." She turns on the taps and lowers her head, scooping warm water onto her face. She touches the back of her head and a few stray hairs pull away in her hand, too reminiscent of the last beating given her. She blows her nose then rinses between her legs. It's the best she can do for now. She turns to the stairs. Voices meet her on the landing and she runs to the front room.

"Jesus Christ. You're a fucking—"

"Don't finish that." Sam's voice is low and menacing. "If I ever see you around here again, you won't have the opportunity to go back to the rock you crawled out from under. You've used up your one chance. Are we clear?"

Sam's companion grins like a wolf, his skin pulled too tightly across his teeth, and pulls out a police badge. "This town is off limits to you, dumb fuck. If I so much as smell your wind, you're dead. If I get another call that pulls me away from the loving arms of my wife because you're causing havoc, you're dead. If my friend here even thinks you might be an ongoing problem, you're dead. Hey, if I am feeling bored some day, I might make a call to the police chief in, what is it?"

"Black River," Sam offers.

"Black River." The man wears the smile of a victor. "And you won't be able to leave your driveway without a cop on your tail." He leans in till he is inches from Rue's swollen face. "You picked the wrong people to fuck with, pal. You are one dumb mother."

Rue's face has turned white between the rivulets of blood dripping from various places on his head. "Oh, fuck. Who wants that skank?" His voice shakes. "I got what I came for. I'm out of here." Rue starts to the door with all the bravado he can muster though his walk is more stagger than swagger.

The police officer grabs his shirt as he passes. "You're not going anywhere till Sam says you can go."

Rue twists against the hold that anchors him then glances at Lizzie. She can see his fear through his posturing and wonders at his ability to, without fail, put his pride before sense. "No hard feelings, eh?" he says. "Hey. Did you stop to think that if I could find you, don't you figure other people can too? Like, say, your dad? He's really pissed, you know."

Sam pulls herself to her full frame. "If he does find out it won't be because he heard it from you." Her fury is barely contained. "One chance, cracker. This is your one chance. Believe me; you don't know how scary I can be."

There is sudden movement and the trio turn toward the cop. He aims a 9mm revolver at Rue. Lizzie shrinks into the wall while Sam stands guard, her sequinned top twinkling in the hall light.

The cop pulls Rue close and holds the gun against his head. There is a click as the safety is released. "You're even dumber than you look. Do I need to explain the situation to you any further?"

Rue shakes his head. The movement is almost imperceptible. A wet spot grows at his groin.

"Do you think this ugly fuck gets it now?" the cop asks Sam.

"Apologize to her." Sam's voice is so deep it is little more than a growl.

Rue looks to the floor. He starts to say something, but falters. He clears his throat. "Sorry," he squeaks.

"And you are never, ever going to bother Lizzie or Sam again are you?" the cop asks.

Rue shakes his head. He is beaten and Lizzie sees him not as a terror but as the small-time bully he is.

Sam nods and the cop releases Rue with a shove.

Rue flees outside. They listen to the sound of his feet pounding down the pavement followed by the roar of a truck engine. Tires squeal as Rue races up the road.

The cop laughs to himself and pulls his cell phone out of his jacket pocket. "Hey," he says to someone on the other end. "There's a real asshole in a Ford F250 speeding up Windbrooke Lane. Do me a favour and give him some heat." He listens then says, "I owe you one." He disconnects his call. "That little fucker won't be back here anytime soon." He salutes Sam as though he has just had the time of his life, nods to Lizzie and strolls out the door like it's a Tuesday evening like any other. "Friday at O'Callahan's," his voice calls from the sidewalk. "You owe me a cold one."

Sam closes and locks the door and Lizzie runs to her.

They wrap their arms around each other, Lizzie shaking so violently, she thinks she will fall. Sam strokes her hair.

"Don't fret. That little chicken shit won't be back."

Lizzie looks up in wonder. Past the sequins and long hair, beyond makeup and dangling earrings to the face of person who has rescued her. Twice. "I was so scared and then you came—"

"And I always will."

In the butter glow of the lights and the security of Sam's arms, Lizzie exhales.

Chapter Fourteen

They lay in the park under what Lizzie considers their tree, making its shade her favourite place in the world. She reaches for Sam's hand as she struggles against the longing that engulfs her. She searches for something to talk about. Anything, as long as she can listen to Sam's voice. Sam's beautiful voice.

"Do you ever think about your parents?" Lizzie asks. As one who can't stop thinking about hers, the topic holds endless interest to her. "Do you get to a point where you can stop thinking about them?"

"Milk Maid, I no longer have parents. I am a child of the universe." Sam's tone changes from cheerful to sardonic. Her wall is back and Lizzie must choose her next words carefully.

"Tell me about them. About growing up."

Sam sighs. "Now why do you want to go and ruin a perfectly nice day?"

"I thought we were friends. Friends talk. Isn't that enough of a reason?" Lizzie needs words to fill her, to drive the demons out of her mind.

"Friends? You want to be my friend?" Sam's voice is soft and sad. "It has been some time since I've heard anyone say that."

Lizzie grips Sam's hand tighter. So accustomed to keeping her feelings to herself, she wrestles over those she now wants to express. Didn't last night break the barrier between them? She wants to give in to the new feelings she has for Sam, but owning up to them feels impossible.

She replays the events of the previous evening in three distinct acts in her head. The finale, a scene of tenderness is the one she wants to remember yet, try as she might to dwell in that memory, it leads her backwards in time to the second act of rescue, which leads her to the first, the part she has to push aside.

She flounders in the ugliness of it and the pain leaks out. "He raped me," she whispers, shamefaced.

"Rue?" Sam bolts upright. "Last night?"

Lizzie nods. She feels filthy.

"Why didn't you say something? I would have killed him." Sam stiffens; her face is blacker than coal.

Lizzie begins to cry and Sam draws her close.

"I thought I was okay," Lizzie nestles in the safeness of the embrace, thankful for the gift of it.

"I should call Mickey."

"Was that his name? That cop?" Lizzie's fear of the system turns off her tears like a spigot would a flowing tap. "No more police. Rue's gone now, right? You said he won't come back."

"Bullies don't like getting their comeuppance. I don't think you have to worry about him any more. But what he did—"

"It's no worse than what's happened before. I don't want to see him again. I don't want him near me."

"But Mickey would—"

"No! I said, no." Panic soars inside her.

Sam looks thunderous and bites her lips, her internal debate evident. Eventually, she releases Lizzie and asks, "Do you think Rue'll tell him where you are?"

Lizzie's ever-lurking fear flares and gnaws away at her insides. Would Rue do that just to get back at her? He might. It wouldn't be out of character. But he'd had quite a scare, and what would he do if Papa dragged her back to town? Pretend last night hadn't happened? Hope she didn't spread the word about how he was so scared, he'd peed himself?

"They were never close. Rue sucked up and Papa tolerated him because of that. I don't think Rue's going to want anyone to know how badly you humiliated him." Lizzie tries to smile. "But whether Papa will come on his own? If he was looking and since I was easy enough for Rue to find, I guess I'd be easy enough for Papa to find too. Maybe he's not looking."

An uneasy silence comes between them. Sam runs through the possibilities of their situation, but Lizzie stops listening.

Once, when she was little, maybe five or six, she had gotten lost. Her family had gone on a hike around Black Bottom Lake, the source of the river they lived on. When they found a pretty spot about midday, they stopped for lunch and, needing to build a fire to roast their hotdogs, set out to collect dead wood. Lizzie removed her shoes and meandered through the trees, as she loved to do, relishing the springiness of the ground – spongy underfoot from growth and rot and fallen needles. Thick calluses had developed on the soles of her feet from summers spent walking barefoot in the bush and balancing along fallen tree trunks. Her feet were impervious to the sting of twigs and the rotting vegetation that accumulated on the forest floor.

Soon she had gone too far and was unable to find her way back. Raised as she was in the North, she did what her mother had taught her. She sat on the ground and sang songs, waiting for someone to rescue her. She felt calm, certain that her parents would come along. Eventually, she'd grown drowsy in the warm sun and drifted off under a scraggly pine, unable to hear her parents calling for her. It was mid-afternoon before they stumbled upon her nesting spot and were so happy to have her safe they forgot to be mad for the worry she'd caused.

Times changed.

Lizzie's feelings about her father and her current circumstances are more complicated. She both wanted him to want her and to leave her be.

For a man who is adept at ruling over what is his, there is something peculiar about his seeming lack of interest in Lizzie's whereabouts. Certainly, if Rue could track her down, Papa the hunter can. The idea is chilling. What if Rue regains his natural cockiness and decides to tell? Lizzie can only hope he decides that discretion rather than vengeance is in his own best interest. He could usually be relied upon to do whatever he thought was best for himself. This helps to soothe Lizzie and she tells Sam she wants things left as they are.

"If Papa was going to come after me, wouldn't he be here already?"

Sam's lips slide into a bitter grin. "It seems we're both orphans. I'd say that's not such a bad thing given our state of affairs."

Lizzie isn't certain that Sam agrees with how she wants to handle things, but appreciates that she will at least play along. Melancholy settles in.

To dispel it, she leans in to the stroller and plays peek-a-boo with Sarah Jane. The sun climbs; its rays penetrate the ceiling of leaves and brighten the gloom and her mood.

It occurs to her that a sex worker and a cop make strange friends and asks Sam how they met. For once, Sam seems happy to oblige her with information.

"Football." Sam crooks an arm under her head and stares toward the sky. "My old man was so fucking afraid I was going to 'turn out gay,' he forced me into one sport after another. I hated them all – until football. I was bigger than most of them and I was amazing." She grins. "I don't know whether I liked knocking those macho boys onto their asses or whether I loved the game for the game's sake, but man! I did enjoy myself."

"Mickey was on your team?"

"He was. And he was the only person who wasn't bothered by me. Not that I knew exactly who I was at the time – just that I was different. That much I knew. Christ. That much everyone knew. Mickey and I have had each others' backs for a long, long time."

"But he's a cop and you do what you do. Doesn't that create problems between you?"

"He's not that kind of a cop. He couldn't care less about the sex trade. But, even if that were his assignment, I'd still warrant a pass. That's what I like to tell myself anyway."

"So, what kind of a cop is he?"

"He's a detective. Works homicide. He's a good guy. If you're ever in trouble, he's the one to call. Mickey McVie, on College Street. Past Bathurst. Remember that. Just in case. I brought this for you." She pulls a dog-eared business card from a pocket. "Here. Take this."

"I thought I was safe now."

"Life is life, Lizzie. Nobody's safe. You never know when you're going to need a friend like him."

Lizzie takes the card as the image of Sam in her sequins and mini-skirt flying across the room pops into her head. When she looks up, she can't hold back the grin from her face. She's glad to find what little humour she can in it. "It was pretty cool, the way you guys handled things."

"I'm not a guy, but thanks."

"You know what I mean. Plus you acted like a guy. The way you handled Rue. Pretty macho, if you ask me."

"How's your head?" Sam switches topics.

"Sore, but I thought it would look worse than it does."

"It looks bad enough. You white girls sure can bruise."

Lizzie swats Sam's arm. "Hey, at least I wasn't the one with my skirt hiked up over my thighs with my man's bits hanging out—" She bites off what she was about to say.

"Life's like that, Milk Maid."

With those two final words, the nickname it seems Lizzie can't escape, Sam's wall is resurrected.

"I need to get some sleep. I have to work tonight." Sam stands and waits for Lizzie to get up so she can fold the blanket.

On the way home, Sam's face is impassive, her body language stiff and remote. Lizzie had only been joking, of course, but the words that tripped so easily from her tongue were as cutting as if she had honed a blade for its surgical precision. If only she could find a way to tell Sam how she feels without making a misstep.

They are about to exit the park when Lizzie tugs at Sam's hand. "Wait. I have to tell you something." Lizzie's chest tightens. She feels like she can't breathe.

Sam stops and crosses her arms across her chest. Her lips are tight. Her brow is wrinkled.

Lizzie is mute with self-consciousness. Sam arches an eyebrow and looks at her watch. Seconds tick by and she turns to leave.

"Wait!" Lizzie grabs Sam's arm. "Please stop being mad at me. I hate it when you're mad. You're my only friend in the whole world and I think you're amazing and beautiful. I was only kidding around. I didn't mean to point out that you are still a guy. At least—. Oh! I am doing this so badly."

Lizzie feels herself flush crimson, but won't let her discomfiture get in her way. She wants to be brave, so brave. She forces the words out faster and faster until they tumble over each other like a rockslide. "Since last night, it's true that I've been thinking about you differently and I'm afraid to tell you because you get so, I don't know, tense or angry or something. Whenever I say something that you don't like. And I know I don't always get your gender or your sexuality. And it's not that I don't like you, it's just that I think I love you and I wish we could be …"

Sam's composure falters, her arms stretch to hug her own shoulders and tears dance in her eyes. She places a finger over Lizzie's mouth.

"I'm not gay. I'm a woman. I'm not a gay woman."

"But I love you."

"You don't know how much that means to me. To have someone love me, someone as sweet as you. But you have to listen to me now. This cannot be. We cannot be. I'm older than you. I'm going through a process. I've only got one more operation left. You have no idea of how long it's taken me to get where I am. I can't be someone else – not even for you." Sam's eyes are pleading. "Tell me we can be friends."

Lizzie wants to scream. You're a liar. We could have something together. Something better than we've had before. I see it. Why can't we be together? You're still a boy. Oh, Sam!

As usual, Lizzie keeps her thoughts to herself. She bundles them up and hides them in her little black box, the space in her chest where feelings hide. She hears a click as the lid closes, locking up her hurt and confusion, and her attempt at courage crumbles into ruins. Images of Sam run through her mind. Maybe she's got it wrong. Like always.

She screws up her face to staunch the flow of tears that threatens to overcome her. "I am so stupid. Why would I think you'd want someone like me? Why did I ever say anything? Just forget it." She wheels the stroller around and runs as quickly as she dares with Sarah Jane bouncing in her seat all the way to the dockyard. Sam calls out, but doesn't pursue her.

"Sure. You don't have to follow. You know I'll be back," Lizzie mutters bitterly. "Where else do I have to go?"

When she does return, hours later, it is only after she is certain her housemates will be sleeping. She fixes herself some lunch and spends the afternoon in her room waiting for Sarah Jane to wake from her nap.

Shortly before Sam and ZoZo are due to start their day, Lizzie takes her daughter and the bit of money Sam has given her and heads out to find her own dinner. She can't face Sam yet. She isn't sure she will ever be able to.

Chapter Fifteen

When Lizzie was a little girl she wanted to be like her mama: cheerful, married and good with her hands. Mama could do anything. She cooked and sewed and kept a nice house, a tidy house.

Windows were hung with the curtains Mama had made with calico or chintz found in the bargain bins at the fabric store. Most of Lizzie's clothes were fashioned by Mama's own hand and her ancient Singer sewing machine. She was the most patient person Lizzie had ever seen, never losing her temper, not when she taught Lizzie how to sew her first apron or when she taught Papa how to dance at night after Lizzie was supposed to be in bed.

Lizzie loved watching her parents sway together. Mama would put one of their few CDs into the small player she'd found at a pawnshop and hold her hands out for Papa to take. If Lizzie were awake to hear the first strains of music, maybe Hank Snow or Dwight Yoakum, she'd rouse herself and creep to the stairs to peek through the railing at the dance lesson below. A waltz or the two-step. Mama would count while Papa watched his clumsy feet, trying to keep time.

More often than not, he'd make a wrong move or step on Mama's toes. He'd curse at himself and Mama would encourage him to keep trying. She loved to dance and wanted Papa to lead her around the dance floor at one of the Legion dos on a Saturday night.

As much as Mama loved dancing with her cheek pressed against Papa's shoulder it couldn't match the love she had for working in her kitchen. Lizzie could tell from watching the joy on Mama's face as she went about her tasks that they seemed to be no chore for her.

On the days that Papa worked the morning shift, Mama would start her day by cooking two breakfasts. An early one for Papa and later, one for Lizzie. Mama believed in a hearty meal. No cold cereal or hard toast for her family. She was always the first one up and began by making a pot of coffee for Papa's thermos then boiling water for a pot of tea for herself. She drank her first cup of the morning while Papa was getting dressed and the second while she packed his lunch. She waited to eat with Lizzie. It was their girl time.

Often, Lizzie awoke before it was necessary so she could spend a few extra minutes in the kitchen with Mama before getting ready for school. As soon as she heard the screen door slap against its painted wood frame, signalling Papa's departure, she'd pad to the kitchen where Mama would be sitting in her rocker waiting for Lizzie to curl up on her lap. Still sleepy in her pyjamas, Lizzie would stay very quiet for the first few minutes. Mama might read the social section of the newspaper aloud or they might work on a crossword puzzle. If Lizzie was really lucky and Mama was in a particularly carefree mood, she would sing along with the radio. Those were the mornings when Lizzie hated to leave for school.

In the afternoon, when Lizzie returned home, the house was often filled with the smell of baking or preserves. Depending on the season, it might be strawberry shortcake, blueberry pie, pickles or beets. Mama had been such a wonder in the kitchen, she'd make extra and sell her goods down at Red's Grill for spending money. Lizzie can't smell cinnamon without thinking about those times.

Those times.

The time of their lives when Mama could cajole Papa out on the occasional picnic or country hike. The time before Lizzie knew the brutality of her father. Before Mama gave up all the happy things.

Seems like someone else's life.

Things had taken a turn toward bad the day Papa brought home his first pay packet after the sintering plant cut back and Papa lost half his hours. The night he brought home that first small paycheque was the first time he hit his wife. Lizzie hadn't learned about this till later; her parents had thought to keep it secret. Mama must have excused him for it the first time. How could she have known that his frustration would make the change permanent?

Soon enough, Lizzie learned that that one slap to Mama's head must have opened a mental floodgate because the beatings just rained down on her ever since. She'd been made to give up everything she ever loved. How dare she be happy when he was so miserable?

Lizzie misses her mama, not the mama who is, but the one who was and who she might have been if given half a chance.

The mama who is, can't do much more than get through the day. Still, she cooks and takes care of the house, after a fashion, but now works as a cleaning woman for the two motels – neither is busy enough on its own to make the work worth much. But, as Mama said, "These minimum wage jobs keep food on the table and lights on everywhere else. And who am I to turn my nose up at that?"

Lizzie can't remember the last time she saw Mama smile.

Since leaving, Lizzie has tried her best not to think about her. When she does, she pictures her standing in the corner of the kitchen while he hits her, covering her face, not fighting back, whimpering like a wounded dog. She has seen the way he'd punch and punch and punch her in her belly, the soft spot where she'd carried his only child. Like a prize fighter working a heavy bag, he struck with purpose.

It was like she was paying for his inability to provide. He was smart about it though. He rarely left bruises and no one but Lizzie saw the blood on the toilet seat on the days when Mama took to her bed. The neighbours knew what was happening just the same. Their shared rumours filled their greetings and glances with a superior air – an odd blend of pity and scorn.

Mama's response was to turn into herself like she was trying to disappear. Like she'd been waiting for it all along. Her own father had been a cruel man and once his legacy arrived at her door, she must have figured there was no use fighting back.

Papa was ashamed that she'd had to take the cleaning job at the motel to help support the family and Mama paid for his shame. Still, she always made sure there was at least one hot meal a day served by herself or Lizzie depending upon Papa's shift at the plant. It was all the extras that she gave up, the things that made their home special. There were no new curtains in the windows. No fresh baking was set to cool on the kitchen counter. There were no more family picnics. Within a few years, Mama's hair turned steel grey, her skin first sagged then lost its high colour, dark circles underscored her sunken, dull eyes.

The funny thing was, three years ago, when new extraction technology sparked a resurgence in iron ore mining and the sintering plant roared back to full capacity, Papa got his hours back, but the beatings hadn't stopped. It was that more than anything else that Lizzie couldn't forgive. She may have been able to rationalize his anger over his impotence. She could have forgiven him most anything. His continued cruelty required a forgiveness that Lizzie couldn't muster.

It's not likely Mama's life has gotten any better since Lizzie left. She hopes it hasn't gotten worse.

Rocking the stroller with her sleeping daughter inside, she eats her greasy cheeseburger and order of fries, and stares out the window of the diner feeling miserable.

This is the second time she hasn't cooked dinner at the house and no matter how badly she feels, she can't shirk the duties that put a roof over their heads. She has to find a way to refocus on her daughter, her reason for running. Getting sidetracked by love won't help at all.

Chapter Sixteen

Lizzie is cooking pork tenderloin. She is hoping to make up for skipping out on last night's dinner with her first attempt at such a fancy meal.

She has decided that professional detachment is what is called for. She is so mortified by yesterday's declaration of love that if she had somewhere else to go, she would leave. Since that isn't the case, she will do her job and stop dreaming of anything more. Cooking and cleaning and caring for her child. That is her life. Period.

Even with this commitment, her hands tremble as she follows the recipe and she pretends this is due to concern that she might miss out an important ingredient, something critical to the success of her meal. She knows it has more to do with waiting to hear Sam's footsteps coming down the stairs. Lizzie cuts onions and mixes spices to cover the meat before setting it in the oven. While it cooks, she peels potatoes and listens to the women readying themselves for work.

Someone drops something; a radio is turned on. Feet travel back and forth across bedroom floors. This is the busy time of day at the house of the Sisters of Sweet Charity.

ZoZo is the first one downstairs, having not yet taken the time to dress. She has risen from bed late and gives Lizzie a curt nod on her way to the backyard for her first cigarette of the day. Lizzie hands her an oversized mug of black coffee that ZoZo accepts without thanks.

The older woman continues on her way outdoors, her gait stiff, her hair a frizzy wet bush. When she returns, she dumps the coffee into the sink and reaches for a bottle of wine. She uncorks it and carries it and her now-empty mug to her room, passing Sam who enters with Sarah Jane in her arms.

"Picked up a hitchhiker on your way?" Lizzie flashes her best attempt at a grin, but with a dry mouth, the best she can manage is to bare her teeth. She returns to her task.

"We thought we'd keep you company while you cook." Sam holds the baby out for a kiss.

From the periphery of her vision, Lizzie can see that Sam isn't dressed for work. "Doing something special tonight?" she asks.

"I am indeed." Sam bounces Sarah Jane on her lap. "I thought I'd stay home tonight with my two favourite people."

"Really?" Your two favourite people? Since when? Maybe she's changed her mind. No, don't go there. Stop this ping-ponging around. She's just trying to be nice. That's all. And then another thought pulls her in a different and more precarious direction. "It's because of Rue, isn't it? You're afraid he'll come back."

"Can't a girl take a night off without causing a stir?" Sam mugs to Sarah Jane before turning her more serious attention to Lizzie. "I need a night off. It's been an exhausting couple of days."

Lizzie studies her through her eyelashes. She notes the puffiness under her eyes, the droop to the corners of her mouth. She decides, at least for the moment, to let go of her hurt feelings. Dangerous, a little voice warns her. Shush, Lizzie tells it. Shush. Let me have one night of companionship. "Do you think we could go out for a walk, maybe rent a movie?" she asks. "I never get go out at night."

"A walk sounds just my speed. It's nice out, not too hot." Sam moves Sarah Jane to her other leg and adds: "I'm glad you don't leave the house after dark. You may have noticed this isn't the best neighbourhood. Even with the warehouse workers around, it's too empty to be safe after the sun goes down."

Lizzie places the cleaned potatoes in the pan with the roast then starts removing the leaves from the garden-fresh baby carrots.

A door bangs shut and ZoZo stomps back inside, pulling up short when she spies Sam. She snarls. "You're not working?"

"Not tonight. Thought I needed a break."

"Me, I'm tired but I work. ZoZo always works. You, you stay home. This is not fair."

"No one forces you to work, ZoZo. You could try your hand at something else."

"Pffft. What else is there for me to do? No one takes care of ZoZo and ZoZo does not live on minimum wage." She continues to grumble on the way to her room and slams her bedroom door in protest against her perceived injustice of the world.

Sam stares to the distance, saying nothing, her face a mask. Although the two of them seem to have come to some accommodation with each other, Lizzie is surprised that ZoZo is bold enough to criticize so early after her own transgression.

Sarah Jane begins to fuss.

"Here. Let me feed her before our supper is ready." Lizzie has become very comfortable nursing in front of Sam though she is still self-conscious with ZoZo.

They sit at the table, discussing which movie to watch, what groceries need buying this week. The mundane is safe and comforting and Lizzie is glad for the opportunity to let things between them get back to normal.

The oven timer rings and Sam removes the roasting pan with a pair of over-sized potholders. She arranges the food on a white platter and carries it to the dining room, calling ZoZo to the table.

After the meal is eaten, after ZoZo has gone about her evening and after Sam and Lizzie have returned from their walk and kissed the sleeping Sarah Jane good night, Sam takes Lizzie by the hand and leads her to the couch.

"We need to talk."

Lizzie wants to run from the words that she is sure she is about to hear but cannot. She is stuck to the floor. Not a wisp remains of her earlier vow of indifference at the unbearable thought that Sam doesn't want her here. Yesterday was too much. Lizzie has alienated the first decent person she has known in a very long time.

"Come and sit with me."

Lizzie's knees won't bend. Her feet won't carry her.

"You look frightened. Please don't be. Come. Sit."

Lizzie drops to the seat cushion and lowers her head, intent upon worrying a pulled thread on the fabric of a throw pillow.

Sam places a finger under Lizzie's chin and lifts her head until their eyes meet.

"I think we should talk. Don't you?"

Lizzie nods, fighting back tears. Sam sounds so serious.

"I didn't handle yesterday very well and I'd like to apologize for that. I hurt your feelings."

Lizzie nods again. She can't find her voice.

"I want more than anything to be your friend. I haven't had someone to share myself with in many years. I've gotten rusty. I'm not good with this."

Hope prickles at the back of Lizzie's head.

"I care for you dearly. I do. And I'd like you to understand me, my life." Sam breathes in deeply and closing her eyes in an obvious attempt at composing her thoughts. She clasps one of Lizzie's hands, losing it in the two of hers.

"I grew up knowing there was something very wrong with me and knowing that my parents thought I was very strange. I wasn't like other boys, though I didn't understand what the difference was. And then puberty hit and I began to loathe myself. My hairy body, my lack of breasts, my growing penis. It was like my body had betrayed me. Like my soul had been dropped off in the wrong body. I didn't know whose fault it was for the feelings I had. I did know that nobody else seemed to have the same issues I did. There was something wrong with me."

Lizzie aches for Sam's youthful pain, etched now in adult features.

"One day, I stumbled across a documentary on the Internet about the transgendered and it was like eureka! I'd found the answer to my problems." Sam pulls her hands away from Lizzie. Her voice jumps. "I was so happy, I nearly ran over my mother in my excitement to tell her. 'Hey Mom, I'm really a girl. Now we know what to fix.' It's a gross understatement to say that she was horrified. She hauled me to my knees and started praying over me and didn't stop until my father got home from work. If possible, he was more upset than she, yelling at me that I was no son of his if I thought he was going to condone my sinful ways.

"Can you believe it? Sin!" Sam snorts. "It was the lowest point of my life. At least I thought I was about to discover that things were about to get a whole lot worse. My father wanted to send me to military school to make a man of me, mother wanted to send me to the seminary to hear the word of God. While they argued, they let me know how depraved they considered me to be. I wanted to die."

Sam knits her fingers together on her lap and clears her voice. She holds her head high and, in witnessing this gesture, Lizzie grasps Sam's heroic struggle to become herself.

"You don't have to go on."

"Yes, I do. I want so much for you to understand. For someone to understand."

Lizzie closes her eyes and pictures herself leaning over and kissing Sam's cheek. She envisions Sam's arm reaching around her and pulling her tight, She imagines the feel of their embrace.

"When I was sixteen, I tried to kill myself."

Lizzie snaps to attention as Sam offers her wrist, sliding a gold bracelet aside. There are two thin scars, faded from age. "Mickey found me splayed out in the shower in the locker room. Blood everywhere. He called the ambulance and saved my life. Not that I thanked him for it at the time. My attempt to take my life – to put myself in the place of God – became another sin, another example of my degeneracy. My parents, in all their Christian compassion, stuck me in a church-based counselling program to cure me. I left home the following year, knowing it was that or I would surely die." She plays with her bracelet, staring into the distance.

"I've tried talking to my parents since then but it's no use. It's easier on all of us if I stay away."

Lizzie touches Sam's shoulder. There are situations in which she remains unsure about the rightness or boundaries of physical contact, still she reaches out, wanting Sam to know she isn't alone anymore.

Sam regards Lizzie with intense and pleading eyes. "I can't go backwards. I can't be who I'm not. Please don't need that of me."

Lizzie bursts into tears. The insecurities and loneliness she has fought nearly forever are crushing. They overtake her voice.

She holds Sam's hand to her forehead and cries.

That there is no love between them is a lie. It must be.

Chapter Seventeen

ZoZo exits the main floor bath sniffing, her forefinger rubbing her nose just as Sam rounds the corner into the back hall.

"What the hell?"

Sam's exclamation rips apart the calm of the afternoon and Lizzie drops a glass onto the floor. It shatters as though it too has been startled by the blast. Lizzie runs to the hall in time to see Sam take ZoZo by the wrist.

"Are you crazy?" Sam shakes ZoZo's arm. "Right in front of me?"

ZoZo has an odd expression on her face, a blend of audacity and alarm. It is clear she wants to make some point yet is afraid she may have gone too far – a child pushing a parent's boundaries. If I do this will you still love me? And this? And what about this?

"You're the crazy one," she says. "I'm not doing nothing wrong."

Sam reaches around, sticking a hand into one and then the other of ZoZo's pockets. She pulls out a plastic bag. It is the size a jeweller or crafter might use to store delicate items. Lizzie stares at it as Sam waves it in the air over ZoZo's head. "Nothing? What's this?"

ZoZo shrugs. "What do you think it is?"

"Damn it!" ZoZo flinches at the sound of Sam's frustration that is as palpable as is her desperation. Sam's voice drops to a whisper. "Why would you do this?

"It's nothing. You're making a big deal out of nothing. I'm in control."

"Right. You can control it. Doesn't that sound familiar? Discovering the big secret that no one else in the universe knows? Doesn't that sound exactly like what every junkie you've ever known has said? Doesn't it sound exactly like what we used to say?"

"I know what I'm doing."

"Don't you remember how this is going to turn out? The way it did? Don't you remember how bad it got?"

"It wasn't so bad. I'm only using twice a day."

"You're using twice a day? Everyday?" Sam is incredulous. She digs her fingertips into her temples, floundering for the words that will express her fear, turn ZoZo around.

ZoZo locks eyes with Lizzie. Her lipsticked mouth is pulled back in a garish mockery of a grin. There is threat not humour in it and Lizzie shivers in this exposure to unknown menace.

"Leave," Sam says. Her face is downcast, her voice soft in misery.

"That's what I was doing before you interrupted me."

"No. I don't mean just go to your room. I mean leave here. You know our deal and you've pushed too far. You have to move."

"Just like that? You can't kick me out. I pay my rent." ZoZo springs forward, her scowling face close to Sam's. Lizzie crosses the floor to guard Sarah Jane who looks up in innocence from her playpen.

"Don't make this harder than it is. You know what we agreed." Sam says.

"That was a long time ago."

"You have to leave. You can have a few days to find somewhere else, but you have to go."

"This is your fault," ZoZo spits at Lizzie. "Before you got here, everything was fine."

Sam moves between the two, creating a barrier. "If you can't behave, you'll have to leave today."

"So you'll protect her, eh? From me? Well, fuck you! I don't need you. I got friends. Real friends." ZoZo's steps to the side and her gaze flits from Sam to Lizzie and back again. "You love her. That's it. That's why you're taking her side."

"You're being ridiculous. What does she have to do with this?"

"If she wasn't here, you'd let me stay. I know you." ZoZo is apoplectic. She screams in her rage. "You think just because you have her now, you don't need me. You're just a maudit fruit. A fag. She doesn't change anything."

ZoZo storms from the room. Lizzie and Sam stare at the ceiling, as if they can see her through it and listen to her throwing things around her room. Minutes later, she clomps down the stairs, a large canvas bags in hand.

"Fuck you," she says. She has been crying, mascara tracks are smudged across her purple face giving her the appearance of a demonic clown. She opens the front door as a taxi pulls to the curb. She turns to Lizzie. "You better watch your back, Bébé. Nobody fucks with ZoZo."

"But I haven't done …" Lizzie stammers as the door slams closed behind the departing woman. She lifts a fretful Sarah Jane. "I had nothing to do with anything. Why is she blaming me?"

She turns to Sam and in the slump of her shoulders and sad expression, realizes that ZoZo's words have stung. Lizzie wonders whether any of it is true, specifically the part about Sam being in love with her.

Seconds tick by and Sam lets out a bruised sigh before answering. "Because she can't blame herself. That and I think she's jealous of you."

Lizzie can't imagine how she, a person with so little, could evoke such feelings and expresses as much to Sam.

"You've got your whole life ahead of you. Time to change the way things are. Time she must feel she doesn't have."

"She's not that old." Lizzie thinks of Mama and her inability to picture a different future for herself and finds a glimmer of understanding for ZoZo and her anger. She wonders what sort of an upbringing ZoZo had. Could it be that Lizzie and ZoZo aren't that different from each other? Could it be that the difference between them is as simple – and as complicated – as having the ability to envision different paths for themselves? A frisson of self-satisfaction at her higher goal of runs through her.

Yes, Lizzie reminds herself, but you would have failed at yours if Sam hadn't come along.

Dear Samantha.

Lizzie looks at her, the person she loves. "You don't believe what she said, right? You know you aren't what she called you?"

Sam crosses her arms over her chest. "I try." She walks to the sofa and sinks into the cushions. "It always comes back to that though, doesn't it? My body." She runs her fingers over her short, tightly curled hair. "I'm so tired of it all."

Lizzie sways her daughter on a hip. She wishes she had a magic wand that she could wave and make Sam feel better.

She sits next to Sam. The three of them rest against each other and Lizzie closes her eyes.

There is no magic in the world that can fix this.

Chapter Eighteen

Sam stares at the letter delivered that morning by Canada Post, reading and re-reading the contents. She chirps and bleats partially formed language, the sounds of incredulity and anguish. Her hand covers her mouth as though to hold back the words that will make the message real. Disbelief and misery transit to anger, emotions carving their intensity upon her face until they build to a crescendo and tumble out in a howl of despair. Sam crushes the letter into a ball and snaps it into the garbage can under the kitchen sink.

Lizzie stands a few feet away, watching Sam in alarm. She takes one step forward and then retreats. "What is it?" she asks.

Sam hands squeeze her temples, heaving dry sobs. She stumbles across the floor and up the stairs.

Has someone died? Death doesn't arrive in a regular-delivery envelope. Surely, that would come by phone. Sam's mother? It must have something to do with her. Lizzie plucks the envelope from the living room floor. The return address is from a clinic in Montreal.

Lizzie is torn between wanting to know and wanting to respect Sam's privacy. She walks to the garbage can five times in five minutes, debating with herself. She reaches for the balled-up paper. She should at least remove it from the trash so it isn't dirtied. Sam might need it later. She places the letter next to the trash and closes the cupboard door.

Hours pass and dusk gathers yet Sam remains in her room. Lizzie's eyes travel across the ceiling in lockstep with Sam's footfalls as she paces her bedroom floor.

Tension grows. Lizzie's nerves stretch until they become over-thin and brittle. Even Sarah Jane is not immune and she fusses unless carried. Lizzie perches her daughter on a hip and retrieves the ball of paper from the cupboard, determined to read it. She hesitates then pushes the wad into the front pocket of her jeans where it pulses as though it has a heartbeat of its own. Lizzie feels its imagined heat on her thigh and, tempted though she is, she refrains from reading it. Sam must tell her. That is important.

Lizzie is anxious and waits impatiently for Sarah Jane's bedtime and when it arrives, she rushes through the evening ritual. Sarah Jane resists her mother's mishandling, intensifying Lizzie's need to get the child to bed. A full hour after her bedtime and with an extra nursing in her belly, Sarah Jane finally succumbs to over-tiredness.

Lizzie's nerves jangle and hum. She takes a deep breath as she tiptoes backwards from the crib, willing the baby to stay asleep. She turns and glides to Sam's door where she presses her ear against the wood, hoping to hear something from within. Silence. Lizzie raps timidly. There is no answer. She knocks harder. "Sam?" There is no answer. Lizzie tugs on the locked knob. "Sam. Come on. Open up. You're scaring me." She thumps on the door with the heel of her palm. "Sam!"

There is a muffled sound and the door opens.

Sam's eyes are puffy and her clothes are wrinkled and twisted.

"What is it? That letter. What did it say?" Lizzie's eyes search Sam's for answers and her hand cups the bulge in her pocket to protect Sam from its malevolence.

Sam steps away from her door, allowing Lizzie to enter. She proceeds to her bathroom to wash her face then sits on the edge of her bed. "They rejected me."

"The clinic? I don't understand."

"Yes, the fucking clinic." The words are spit from her mouth syllable by syllable. "I don't meet the criteria. Goddamn it! It was supposed to be this year."

Lizzie kneels before Sam and taking her hands in hers, peers into her face. "You have to explain. I don't know what you're talking about."

"According to them, I can't prove that I've lived as a woman for a year."

"But I thought you'd been living this way for a long time?" What hasn't Sam told her?

"I can't tell them I've been a hooker, now can I?" Sam's sneer is washed away by despair. Her eyes beseech Lizzie to understand. For a lifeline. "I need proof of employment at a place where someone – a boss – can say I've presented as a woman. Somehow, I don't think hooking qualifies as 'employment.'" Her fingers air quote the word and she cackles unhappily. "And who would verify that anyway?"

"But you've already had surgeries."

"Yes! Yes! Yes!" Sam jerks her hands away from Lizzie's and runs them over her hair. "Ugh!" She flings her arms from her head.

Lizzie waits. What to say? What to do?

Finally, Sam breaks the silence. "This has additional requirements. It's covered by Medicare and they make the rules. The fucking rules. I only needed to save enough to tide me over during recovery. Fucking fuck. Now I'll have to save even more and see if I can do it in Thailand."

"Then that's okay? You'll go next year."

Sam eyes flash with anger.

"What did I say?" Lizzie's heart jackhammers.

"Let's pretend for a minute, shall we?" Sam's voice cuts, slicing at Lizzie for her stupidity. "Let's say you woke up tomorrow morning and felt exactly like yourself. You have the same thoughts you had when you went to bed. You feel the same way about yourself, your place in the world. Nothing has changed. You run your hands over your body and leap out of bed in horror. Your body isn't yours. It's changed. You have hair where you shouldn't have hair. Your breasts have been replaced by hard pectorals. What else? Your hips have vanished. Ah, and the coup de grace. You've grown a penis."

Sam comes to her feet. Her voice is animated, thick with passion. "You run to the mirror. You must be dreaming. This can't be real. The face staring back at you isn't yours. You go crazy. You tell your parents there's been a big mistake. Your doctor. Only nobody listens. You actually begin to believe in your insanity. Your head could explode trying to conform. Years later, you brave the discovery that you have to be labelled with a mental disorder so that you're eligible to get your own body back. Your own goddamned, fucking body! But you bear it. The years and the pain. Being shunned. Hearing your parents wish you dead."

Lizzie's insides twist for Sam's pain, but Sam isn't finished.

Her voice drops. "You know what? That isn't even the worst of it. True hell is living with the knowledge that in spite of what you've endured and what's still ahead, that at any time, some committee of no-doubt straight and brilliant experts – people who don't really know anything about you or what this 'mental condition' is like – might decide you aren't quite right. That you don't measure up to some fucking condition of gender that you had no hand in setting." Sam bends nearly in two until her face is inches from Lizzie's. "And you'll have conversations like this trying to justify yourself for the rest of your life."

Sam breathes hard; her eyes crackle and jump. Then, the prick of her situation deflates her and she slumps, emptied, onto her bed, her misery washing over them both. "But it's only one more year, right?"

Lizzie realizes her mouth is hanging open and closes it. "I didn't mean …" She doesn't know what to say. "You have to understand—"

"I'm tired of understanding, Milk Maid. I want to be understood."

There it is: the barrier between them back in place like it had never been down. Lizzie curses herself. "Please forgive me. You're right. I don't always say the right thing or get whatever I'm supposed to understand, but I want to. That's got to count for something. Doesn't it? Please tell me it does."

"I'm tired, Milk Maid. So tired." Sam stretches out.

"You haven't eaten. Let me bring you some supper."

"I'm not hungry."

"You have to eat—"

"I don't have to do anything for you or anyone else. Just go."

Lizzie takes a single step forward, reaching for her friend, but she isn't there anymore. A stranger rolls away from her and Lizzie walks from the room.

Stopping in the hall to close the door, she feels useless and, once more, alone. No, she tells herself. Sam needs me. If I have to deal with her being angry with me then that's what I have to do.

She throws her shoulders back and strides into the room before timidity can overtake her.

"I'm not leaving, Sam."

There is no response and Lizzie worries that she's made the wrong decision. Don't chicken out.

She slides her body gently onto the mattress and shimmies next to Sam's still body. Hesitating for only a moment, she wraps her arms around Sam and feels her chest heave. Sam grabs hold of Lizzie's hands and hugs them to herself. She cries and Lizzie holds tight till morning, the discarded letter wedged between them no longer an object of curiosity.

Chapter Nineteen

Sam keeps to her bed. She isn't working; she isn't eating. She is listless and prone to tears. She calls to Lizzie's mind a Georgian heroine suffering the vapours. Thinking of invincible Sam this way would be comical if her situation weren't so tragic.

Lizzie establishes a command centre in Sam's room, a room set up much like Lizzie's though with unmistakable differences. The bed is king-sized rather than queen and a chaise the colour of fresh cream lounges in the place of a reading chair. A violet cashmere throw is draped over its arm. The walls are painted plummy taupe and antique silver accessories present a brilliant counterpoint. A rectangular-shaped, cut-glass mirror hangs over the dresser. The drapes are grey taffeta. Where the other room is light, this one is dramatic. It is a room designed for brooding.

Lizzie lugs the television and DVD player from the main floor and erects Sarah Jane's playpen in a corner. She can't control Sam's depression but she can control her solitude.

As she imagines she would treat a girlfriend with a broken heart, Lizzie brings ice cream and chocolate. She rents a half dozen movies – chick flicks and comedies – then drags the chaise closer to the bed, feeling like a spinster sister who should be cross-stitching a sampler or tatting lace. She forces Sam to play cribbage and Go Fish and to help her with the daily crossword puzzle. Sam is much better at the latter than Lizzie, something Lizzie hopes will lift her spirits. They speak very little.

On the second day, Sam breaks the silence. "Have you ever been in love?" she asks.

Lizzie has just returned from putting Sarah Jane down her afternoon nap and the question catches her off guard. "Love?" She chews the inside of her mouth, pondering how to answer this loaded question. What can she say to the person who doesn't want to hear the truth about her feelings for her?

"No," she says, mentally crossing her fingers against the lie. "You?"

Sam smiles wistfully. "Once. It was a few years ago." She takes in the room. "We bought this place together. Fixed it up. He was quite uninterested me as a woman."

"What happened?"

"These." Sam indicates her breasts. "I grew these."

"How long ago was this? Where is he now? Are you still in touch?" Anxiousness rises in Lizzie like mercury on a hot day. Her position is a delicate one, physically and emotionally. Would Sam tell her to leave if her lover returned?

"He's gone. Found a job in Vancouver. I guess that's about as far away from me as he could get. I got the message loud and clear."

"What message?"

"That I was too queer even for a gay boy."

"Are you still in love with him?" Lizzie tries to look her most encouraging, feeling her most discouraged.

"No. Not any more."

"Why did you ask? About me being in love."

"Just popped into my head. The irony of losing him to my femaleness only to find out I might never get there."

"If you want it, you'll get it. There's always a way." Lizzie responds the way she was raised to respond. What else is there for her to say? That Sam may never be the person she wants to be, the person she is? That Lizzie doesn't have the first clue about what being Sam is like? That she's not even sure how she feels about Sam completing her metamorphosis?

Sometimes saying the trite thing is the only kindness one can offer.

"If you say so, Pollyanna."

"I see you've moved on from Milk Maid. It's a nice change."

Sam smiles wanly and pulls the cashmere throw over her, closing her eyes.

The conversation over, Lizzie pops a movie into the DVD player, hoping to take her mind off love and Sam and the past.

She cannot. While Sam slumbers, Lizzie drifts to thoughts of her own meagre history of love. Pathetic. Rue didn't love her, not one little bit. He loved having been the first to conquer her. That's what he loved, owning her.

Getting away has certainly given her some perspective on him. She sees him standing god-like on that stage at The Fire Pit singing, his eyes closed, his body rocking sensuously with the music.

Being underage, it wasn't something she got to see very often. The bar manager let her in a few times, but warned her not to make it a habit. When she'd go, she'd see the other girls with their low-cut blouses and high-cut skirts squirming and giggling for the band's benefit.

Come to think of it, some of those girls were younger than she'd been. Girls still in high school just like her. Girls whose parents believed that marriage after grade twelve was the best opportunity for their daughters. Other girls who snuck out if their parents didn't share this belief. It was a man's world in that blue-collar town. For the most part, girls took – and accepted – what they could get.

It seems that only Lizzie had been denied open access. Rue must have told the manager not to let her in. How stupid she had been not to realize it then.

She wonders how many other girls he'd slept with while they were together. Her chest burns with hurt and jealousy.

The Pit was popular due in part to the popularity of Rue's band. The bar was one of four in Black River, all profitable and catering to the hardworking men who made their livelihoods from the dangerous underground or the forestry industry. Women didn't really figure into bar management's plans with the exception of ladies' nights and even those were established to entice the male clientele.

The bar was dark, panelled in ancient wood, sticky from years of absorbing the miasma of its customers. Half a dozen pool tables squatted kitty-corner behind the stage, a scarred, parquet dance floor opened up before it. The chairs and tables that filled the room were also wood, the kind that would break in a fight rather than chrome that just might kill someone.

The stench of old beer had become so overpowering that the carpet had been torn out one year previous, leaving the more practical concrete surface behind.

With the exception of the bars or dance clubs she'd seen in Hollywood movies, Lizzie figured they all must be the same. She had no experience with anything other than those built for serious drinking, fighting and getting laid.

If The Pit was a henhouse, Rue was head rooster and he loved every second of his fame.

How had Lizzie ever been so taken with him? She regrets this supposed great love that she now considers a childish infatuation. An infatuation that resulted in a child. No such thing as an adolescent mistake and the allowance of a do-over for her.

Lizzie had been caught up in the thrill of Rue wanting her and the pride of knowing she was the one he had chosen. For the first and likely only time in her life, other girls were envious of her. Lizzie, the quiet girl who thought of herself as stocky rather than sexy, who came from a home that wasn't part of the social registry, and who, until little more than a year ago, had doubted she had what it took to get anywhere beyond being pregnant and married – like hundreds, no, thousands of female relatives before her.

She was so silly, waiting in a fever for his calls, sure they'd never come, sure that he couldn't want her the way she wanted him. Sure too that she'd die if he didn't. When the phone rang, she held her breath in agony, praying for the sound of his voice be at the end of the line. When it was, she'd be so overwhelmed she'd do little other than giggle as though everything he said was the cleverest thing she'd ever heard.

She was cocooned in daydreams about him, separated from the world around her in cottony delirium. She hadn't imagined that a time would come when she wouldn't be completely in love with him.

The haze lifted in time for her to hear the guidance counsellor's presentation on preparing for university. It was that talk that built on the idea she had, only weeks before, conjured as being a possible future for herself.

Three days after this bit of inspiration, Lizzie, annoyed at being left behind once more as Rue hung out with his band mates, set an appointment with her counsellor and began a plan to get her marks up. Her marks hadn't been poor, but neither were they outstanding and she had a goal she wanted to make certain she'd reach.

Not long after that – her love killed by Rue's violence and stupidity – she tried to break things off.

Lizzie shakes her head to clear her memory of that evening – the night that ended what remained of her naïve notions of love.

Her thoughts turn to Sam. She wishes she were awake. She'd like to talk to her, to tell her that she is beautiful and perfect, that she doesn't have to change.

Lizzie bites her lips, torn as she so often is between supporting her friend and wanting to have what she wishes for herself.

Sam stirs, muttering something Lizzie can't make out. She leans in, cocks her head to one side. "What?" But Sam rolls away, tossing the blanket from her.

Lizzie sighs again and pushes up from the chair to check on Sarah Jane.

Chapter Twenty

The twirling mobile serenades Lizzie and Sarah Jane with tinny sounds of the rainforest as they recline in the backyard on lawn chair and in playpen.

It's still morning, the sun far from its apex, but the heat is already building, the humidity climbing. Indolence and boredom makes Lizzie antsy.

"Get out and learn the bus system," Sam suggested.

But Lizzie has been too wary to venture out on her own again. Intimidated by her earlier trial and having only a too-warm corduroy baby pouch to transport her daughter, she is stranded.

For now, she rests, listening to the cicadas and the cracking sound of grasshoppers leaping about the tufts of dry grass.

The yard isn't much of one. A wooden privacy fence, suburban and incongruous against industrial surroundings, edges the tiny plot that was once part of a larger parking lot or loading zone. Not much more than a postage stamp, Granny Gee would have said. Any space too small for a garden was too small to count, according to her.

A strip of soil measuring about six feet by ten is evidence of Sam's attempt to rid the yard of the macadam. Jackhammering was desperately difficult and Sam gave up, not interested in building those kinds of muscles. She planted some perennials in the new soil and let them survive through the seasons as they could. The rest of the yard remained blacktop. By noon, it would be an oven.

Lizzie sips from a glass of iced tea and pretends to read a magazine. Her eyes wander from the sun's glare on the page to the kitchen window, to a butterfly resting on a flower, to her daughter.

There are things she could be doing. Useful things. Laundry, vacuuming. She could bake something special for this evening's dessert. The flowerbed would benefit from a thorough weeding. She could be reading something to advance her education, something from the reading list for the university's first-year English class that she printed from the school's website – a list she has sworn to get through by Christmas. A list that, when finished, will make her feel like she isn't wasting her life, going nowhere, turning out to be the nothing Rue said she was.

Instead, she swings one leg over the side of her chair in aggravation, strums her fingers on the sun-bleached plastic arm.

"Agh! There's nothing fun to do!" She springs up and looks about her. There isn't anywhere for her to go. There is no one for her to see. No girlfriends to talk with or shop with or linger with in coffee shops. In short, aside from the daily cycle of baby care and meals, there is no schedule for her to keep.

She glances at Sarah Jane who seems content with her mobile and the clouds. A robin swoops overhead and catches the child's attention. After the bird vanishes over the fence, Sarah Jane returns to cooing at the plastic menagerie circling above her head. Something excites her and she pumps her arms and legs in some sort of juvenile fit.

Lizzie laughs at her. She sinks back to the chaise lounge and closes her eyes. For now, the sun feels good on her skin.

A whiff of something travels over from the fish plant. An unmistakable and pungent scent. Vinegar. Like Mama's pickles. And Granny Gee's.

Granny Gee's kitchen was a wonder. Small and efficient like its owner. A single rectangular porcelain sink sat in the middle of her working counter. It was marred by two black chips where she had twice dropped heavy pots loaded with some foodstuff or other. The countertops were yellow. Soft, buttery yellow. Buffed nearly through with years of cleaning. An electric range stood next to the wood oven she'd inherited from her mother.

When Granny Gee put up her preserves, the kitchen could hit one hundred degrees or more. She'd drench a rag in ice-cold water and wrap it around her head to stay cool. Sometimes, she'd stick one under her breasts at the bottom of her bra. "It's a furnace under there," she'd cackle.

Before Mama had made her mistake in marriage, Granny Gee had her own chance at love and married a cruel man. They had fought like wild things, their hatred for each other a spreading infection, until Gramps's spite had faded in his senior years, leaving him snarling and toothless. Granny Gee took pleasure in ignoring him almost completely. When he died of cancer – his meanness rotted him from the inside out she said with satisfaction – he died without her at his side. "No need of hypocrisy. I hated that son of a bitch and he deserved to be hated."

Granny Gee had enjoyed more than a decade on her own, doing what she wanted when she wanted and trying to get her daughter to leave her own good-for-nothing husband. But Mama would never leave. When Granny Gee pestered her for a reason, Mama would shrug and say that it was no use, or that maybe someday he'd stop. Sometimes she'd get angry and say that people in glasshouses shouldn't throw stones.

Up to the end, Granny Gee contented herself with her garden and making enough preserves to supply other families. Those who had fallen on hard times would find freezer bags full of string beans, jars of jam, baskets of potatoes on their doorstep.

She knew it was old-fashioned, the notion of helping your neighbour, but she also knew that some traditions were worth keeping.

So, though she no longer needed to sustain her own family over the winter, Granny Gee sweated in her kitchen and toiled in her garden, reaping contentment from her labours. She lined up regiments of sterilized glass jars on the sturdy pine table that sat in the centre of the kitchen and ladled her preserves into them.

Lizzie loved that table. It was older than she. Older than her mother. Years of use had given it a deep golden patina. It was scarred from carving bread, by the bottoms of pots too hot for wood, and by the grooves left by ballpoint pens during years of homework and bill paying. When she visited her Granny, Lizzie would often sit at that table tracing the engraved swirls with her finger, imagining her mother as a young girl dreaming about her own future.

Had they had similar dreams? Lizzie believes this is true as she pictures herself doing the same things Mama used to do. Homey things designed to make a family happy.

Poor Mama.

Was Lizzie's flash of recollection on the bus of something real or imagined? Was it behind the reason Mama stayed with him?

Lizzie closes her eyes and conjures a dream not so different from one she had in childhood. She envisions her fantasy family then, like a kaleidoscope rotating from a pinprick of colour to a full screen of vivid imagery, she imagines beyond a home life to an independence of her making, a successful career, a partnership with a man who would love her entirely.

She pictures tender lovemaking and tries to conjure her lover's face, but cannot. As her arousal grows, the featureless orb prevents her from reaching a satisfying conclusion. She wants the explosion, the satisfaction of orgasm. She plays the final scene over and over, trying to force a face to appear. Again, she fails.

As the heat of the day lulls her, Lizzie drifts deeper into her fantasy, adding details, reformulating her job, her clothes, her hair, her home. She pictures herself a geologist, searching for some new fuel. She wins an exploration contract and arrives home at the end of a satisfying day to celebrate with her family. A nanny greets her at the door, Sarah Jane in her arms. Lizzie kisses her daughter then, after promising to return quickly, glides to the master suite where she changes for dinner. She removes her suit and, as she faces herself in a full-length mirror, her husband approaches from behind and nuzzles her neck. He runs his dark hands over her smooth stomach and cups her breasts.

Lizzie's heart beats faster. She runs her hands over her breasts while her dream self stares into the mirror, willing a face to emerge. She sees the top of a head covered in curly black hair. The head rises from behind her over her shoulder toward the mirror and she waits.

Nothing. No face.

Her fantasy dissolves.

Chapter Twenty-One

Summer is upon them with the intensity of a forest fire. Lizzie, unaccustomed to such heat limits her forays to the into the world even further, venturing out only in the early morning hours or before dusk. She spends days tidying and cleaning and playing with Sarah Jane. In addition, Sam has given her open access to her bedroom and the library housed within. Books fill many of Lizzie's free hours. Thoughts of school tantalize her but she pushes them to the back of her mind.

"Next year."

Sarah Jane is growing fast. She survived her two-month inoculations with nothing more dramatic than a volley of tears. Her cheeks are twin spots of brilliant rouge from teething and drool fills the lines of baby pudge around her neck. She is able to roll over and support her own head.

As the baby learns new skills, Lizzie expands her knowledge of the art of cooking with the help of Nigella, Martha and Jamie. Her satisfaction in producing a meal brings to mind images of her mother. These are bittersweet and remind Lizzie of the way she wishes life had remained.

When Sam is not working, the two are inseparable. Lizzie is convinced this has been made possible by ZoZo's absence. That horrible woman would have had plenty to say had she been here to see how close Lizzie and Sam have become. This companionship is a new experience for Lizzie who eats it up greedily, afraid that, like her own family's happiness, it might end too quickly. She craves Sam's company while understanding that the less Sam works, the further off her final surgery becomes.

This morning, Sam's dazzling work attire does not match the tired mien of the face above it. She slips off her shoes and carries them to her room. She will not speak until she has showered, removed her wig, changed her clothes. This decontamination ritual — the daily birthing of a fully-grown swan — provides her with a life beyond the circumstances of her profession.

As Sam ascends the staircase, Lizzie starts breakfast. Today, she makes omelettes with smoked Gouda. There are fresh strawberries with vanilla yoghurt on the side.

She removes the rind from the cheese then grates half the block. Her progress is slow as the cheese bows against the holes of the grater. She whisks eggs and adds a drop of cold water, a dash of salt and pepper, a teaspoon of onion powder. When the shower goes silent, she adds the eggs to the already-warm frying pan and turns on the coffeemaker.

Sam and Lizzie eat together. As the meal proceeds, Sam's day self, her true self, Lizzie believes, re-emerges. Lizzie sees both as two sides of the same persona, in awe of the powerhouse that is night time Sam, she cannot spend enough time with the beautiful daytime Sam.

Lizzie is curious about Sam's work, a world she knows nothing about other than what television dramas have shown her. She has attempted to learn about Sam's other life once or twice, stumblingly, ineptly.

"The world is a strangely hypocritical place filled with closeted assholes," Sam said in a tone so guarded and flat that the window to that topic slammed shut. The response gave only a glimpse of what lay beyond without providing much understanding. Lizzie is left with her questions along with others more complex than she can articulate.

When breakfast is finished and the kitchen is tidied, Sam announces a trip to a flea market. "See if we can find a used carriage for Sarah Jane."

"I'll be ready in two minutes." Lizzie races to her room and throws baby essentials into the diaper bag, brushes her teeth and grabs the old baby carrier.

"Let me take her," Sam says strapping the pouch to her chest. Lizzie lowers a drooling baby into the hollow. Sam removes a tiny facecloth from the diaper bag and wipes Sarah Jane's wet chin before tying a sunbonnet over her downy head. "To the subway. Pay attention to the streets. You have got to learn your way around without me."

"It's not like I don't want to," Lizzie says. "The city is just so confusing."

They take a bus that will take them to a streetcar that will drop them off at a stop for a subway line heading west. She stares out at corner stores with windows covered in cardboard signs heralding New Video Releases and Lotto Tickets For Sale and publicizing the availability of Coke and twelve-packs of bottled water. She watches the street signs and tries to picture an overview of the city in her head. Within minutes, Lizzie is lost in a tangle of streets with dusty corners and tired tenement buildings. The only thing Lizzie can be sure of is south. As long as she can see the CN Tower, she knows that much. Otherwise, the city remains a jumble.

She fans her face already slick with sweat in the stagnant air of the bus. Her ears prick up at the recorded broadcast that announces the name of each stop as they approach it. Maybe learning bus routes won't be impossible after all.

Lizzie lifts her hair off her neck and pulls it into a knot with elastic band. She is instantly cooler without the layer of insulation.

She worries about Sarah Jane swaddled as she is in the baby carrier. She unties her baby's hat then pours cold water from a bottle onto a washcloth. She wipes Sarah Jane's face and neck then offers a drink to Sam who whooshes a mouthful around her mouth to cool her gums before swallowing. "It's hotter than Hades in here." She unzips the front of the baby carrier to expose Sarah Jane's legs and lifts the pouch away from her body to release the captured heat. A wet rectangle in the shape of the carrier marks the front of her sleeveless bamboo shirt.

Lizzie feels ill and holds the still-cool cloth against Sarah Jane's head. She is relieved when they come to their destination minutes later.

"Let's avoid this and walk home from here on the way back, okay?" she asks Sam.

"Or take an air-conditioned cab."

"Even better."

They hop onto a streetcar that descends into an underground terminal. Lizzie feels the walls closing in on her as they enter the bowels of the subway system. The ceiling is only inches higher than the train that rushes by in the opposite direction and creates a tornado around them. They have only a two-minute wait before their train arrives and, upon entry, Lizzie is delighted to discover that it is air conditioned and quite comfortable.

"What a relief!" She plops onto a bench. Sam sits at her side. Lizzie reaches over to kiss Sarah Jane. "Isn't this better?" Her rescue from the unbearable heat of above ground makes her giddy and she tosses her head back and giggles. "God. That was awful. I don't know how you stand living here in this awful humidity. I really don't."

Sam smiles as she straps Sarah Jane's bonnet back in place.

Lizzie looks around her. She takes in the blur of the lights that run along the sections of the subterranean tunnel. She watches Sam supporting Sarah Jane's little head and bending to murmur into her pink ear.

Lizzie glances at the faces that surround her. Couples chat; a man reads the

Sun. A woman jerks her gaze away. A middle-aged man purses his lips in disgust. Lizzie turns her attention to the back. Most travellers are lost in their own thoughts or the music on their MP3 players. She meets the eyes of a boy her age. He raises his eyebrows and smirks.

Lizzie peers at Sam in alarm, but she seems oblivious and involved with her charge. Lizzie's chest tightens and she whips her head about, a scowl on her face, daring anyone to say something – anything. She knows what they are thinking. While she has come to see Sam's appearance as unremarkable, here she comes face-to-face with the cold hatred so-called regular people have to anyone different from themselves.

She is enraged that anyone would think themselves superior to Sam, that they could so openly display their bigotry. Aren't city dwellers more sophisticated than this? Urban/urbane. Isn't small-mindedness the province of small towns?

She slips her arm into Sam's as she might with any best friend and stares straight ahead. Her cheeks burn with indignation and more than a little trepidation.

Ignore them, she tells herself. Ignore them.

She is jolted against Sam as the train pulls to a stop then lurches ahead as it rushes to the next station. Passengers disembark and others take their seats. Lizzie will not look at them. She knows they will be the same as the last bunch and she will not give them the satisfaction of acknowledgement.

A twinge of guilt niggles the back of her mind and she closes her eyes in remembrance. How long ago was it that she thought the same thing?

With her eyes still closed, she rests her head on Sam's arm, fighting the urge to look at those around her. It seems ages before Sam tells her they are at their destination. Lizzie stands and keeps her eyes fixed on the door. She passes faceless people with whatever grace she can muster as they leave the subway behind.

"You'll need a thicker skin than that to go anywhere with me," Sam says as they walk the last few blocks to the flea market.

Lizzie is taken aback. "You saw them?"

"I've been seeing them for years and years. I don't let myself think about it."

Lizzie shakes her head, marvelling at human capacity for ugliness and hate. These people are no different than Papa or Rue.

Downcast, she walks beside Sam, her eyes on the sidewalk following edges and cracks as they pass over it, the intensity and white-hot glare of the mid-morning sun melting her defences, making her feel weak. Shining its spotlight on the elements of Sam's incongruous physique. Lizzie longs for the calm of shade, the cool caress of night. The moon is so much kinder to Sam than the sun.

"There it is."

Lizzie looks ahead at the tents and buildings in the near distance that make up the year-round market. It seems to go on for blocks, a far cry from the flea market in the basement of St. James Anglican Church in Black River, and as they draw near, the streets become evermore filled with pedestrians. Lizzie wants to flee. There isn't a place on her body where sweat isn't running in rivulets. Her feet are already swollen and she is parched. Her spirit is small and defeated.

"I better nurse her before we get over there."

They find a bench and Sam tents a crib sheet over Lizzie's shoulder and Sarah Jane's for privacy. Lizzie wipes at the film of sweat building between her warm torso and Sarah Jane's. The baby pulls away, fussing and rubbing her face.

Lizzie wets another cloth and rubs it over Sarah Jane's semi-nude body. She holds the bottle of water to the child's lips and tilts it ever so slightly toward the tiny mouth. A trickle goes in and Sarah Jane swallows. Lizzie tips the bottle again and again Sarah Jane accepts a mouthful of the cold liquid.

"Look at that," Sam exclaims. "She's actually drinking."

Sarah Jane takes three more mouthfuls of water and blows air between her wet lips. She giggles, quite delighted with her new skill.

"Mama said I started drinking from a glass when I was only two months old so I thought I'd give it a try. Seems an odd thing for someone so little to be able to do, but in this heat she must need something cold."

"This kangaroo pouch is too hot for a day like today," Sam says. "Let's find a buggy and get back home before one of us gets heatstroke."

Chapter Twenty-Two

Sam is not working tonight. "As an entrepreneur, I can do that," she says. She speaks with irony as though it is a joke, but Lizzie knows how Sam's alter ego wears on her.

Tonight, they will venture out-of-doors together again, this time for something fun – a jazz festival. They hope Sarah Jane will sleep through it.

"If she fusses, we'll just come home." Sam has assured Lizzie that she won't be disappointed if their excursion fails. She simply wants a night out like an average person. "What could be more ordinary than not finding a babysitter?"

Lizzie is as nervous as a brood hen and as she pulls on a summer dress, she steels herself against the coming onslaught of public scrutiny. It isn't only what they might face out there that has her on edge though. Something else gnaws at her, something she can't identify.

She tugs at the buttons that run down the front of her dress, hoping for more give. Above her waist, the dress is tight over her engorged breasts. She wishes she had something new to wear, but must be content knowing that the cornflower blue of the cotton brings out the colour of her eyes. She pins her hair off her neck and reaches for silver earrings, something she hasn't worn since the baby. Her hand shakes in anticipation as she targets the piercing with the end of the hoop. Her mascara is old and cakes in the brush, but she manages enough for her too-blonde lashes. She runs pink lip-gloss over her mouth and pouts into the mirror. "Yeah. You're gorgeous." She rolls her eyes and slips her new, corner-store flip-flops onto her feet.

She straightens, takes another look into the mirror and gasps, her feelings of discomfort now identifiable. Tonight feels like a date. The flutter in her stomach, the extra care she is taking in her preparations.

"Stop it," she tells herself. I can't think this way. We are girlfriends going out for a couple of hours. Girl. Friends.

She sips a handful of cold water and wipes most of her lip-gloss onto a towel when she dries her mouth.

Get a grip. Stop these feelings. Right now.

She takes a deep breath and goes downstairs. Sarah Jane is already asleep on the reclining seat of the stroller and Lizzie pins a draped sheet around the canopy to keep festival lights from flashing in the child's face.

The air remains humid and it hits them like warm soup as soon as they exit the house. Sam is in beige capris and within minutes, her sleeveless orange blouse is wet under her arms. Lizzie feels a sweat running down her spine, soaking the waistband of her panties.

"I'll be glad when this weather breaks," Sam grumbles, fanning her armpits with both hands.

"I'll take the black flies from home over this any day," Lizzie says. "I'll never learn to stand this."

The festival is nearby, only a few blocks beyond the warehouse district so they stroll, taking their time in the heat.

It doesn't take long before they hear the first strains of music and Sam expounds the mastery of some trumpet player they are about to encounter. Lizzie doesn't care about the musician or about the music. She is happy just to listen to Sam talk about something she seems to love and glad that in the dark, Sam's physical characteristics less conspicuous. Even her height is less shocking in the shadow of night. Her feet and hands don't appear to be as huge. Her physique is softer.

Sam wears large golden hoops in her ears, simple and warm against her skin. Her close-cropped hair shows off her luminous eyes and marvellous cheekbones. As they pass under streetlights, Lizzie catches her face in full animation as she explains the origins of jazz.

The crowd is heavier now as they make their way toward the first venue. Police officers patrol the area on foot. A horse clip-clops by pulling a carriage; a driver sits on the high front bench; a young couple with their arms wrapped around each other sit in the back. Lizzie likes the sound of the horse's shoes on the paved road. It makes the city a little friendlier.

A trumpet bleats, cutting through the buzz of the crowd and Sam manoeuvres them in its direction. They find seats at a patio and order drinks, an iced tea for Lizzie and a beer for Sam.

They sip and listen to the band playing inside the pizzeria that serves as a stage tonight. People fill the street, some stopping to listen, some on their way to another location to hear a different band.

The patio is quickly filled and two men ask if they might share Lizzie and Sam's table. Sam agrees, her voice suddenly playful. Lizzie's stomach twists. Her heart beats faster; her fingers bounce on the handle of the stroller. She fights the urge to vomit.

Sam talks with the young men who order a round of drinks. She sparkles in the glow of their attention. One of the pair asks Lizzie her name, but she can't answer. Her throat has gone dry.

Lizzie touches Sam's arm, but for once Sam's interest is elsewhere. She pats Lizzie's hand without looking at her as she laughs at something someone has said.

The men make Lizzie nervous. Memories of Rue and the power and needs of that sex threaten to drown her. Her nostrils flare and she swallows rapidly as she fights to keep such thoughts at bay. They will be gone soon. She repeats this like a mother's promise to her child-self. Sam is only flirting, harmlessly flirting, just like any other woman out for a bit of fun.

I can wait this out. It will be over soon.

Lizzie lets her mind drift high above, far from the music and people around her. She gazes into the inky sky recalling another night such as this. A night spent listening to music – a time that Rue invited her to watch him play.

Lizzie sat at a table with one of her girlfriends, sipping beer and feeling like she was queen of the ball – a queen who might lose her crown any minute. It was after the band's first break, sometime during the second set. She remembers this because, at the time, she had been thinking how loud the crowd had become as the night went on. She had to shout to be heard by her friend and soon gave up on conversation.

A guy approached her and asked her to dance. She said no but her friend snagged the boy's by his forearm and pranced with him out to the dance floor.

Sitting by herself, Lizzie locked eyes with Rue and felt like he was singing to her alone. She hadn't noticed the advance of a boy she knew from school until he was seated beside her. She was startled and he laughed. She had laughed too.

He'd brought her a beer and leaned in close to ask her how she liked the music. Lizzie was about to tell him that the lead singer was her boyfriend when Rue came flying off the stage and toppled him to the ground.

Rue had surprise and what Lizzie would soon learn was a cruel-streak on his side. He pummelled the helpless teen until the bouncer pulled him off.

Lizzie had run bawling to Granny Gee's that night. Granny Gee made her some cocoa and patted her back and told her to stay away from bars. She told her to stay away from Rue too, but Lizzie hadn't listened.

She listened instead to Rue with his hypnotic eyes and his claim of protecting her from the douche he had thought was bothering her. She let herself be caught up in the romantic notion of a manly display.

What a stupid little fool she'd been. The excuses she'd made for him.

More recent events in her life crash upon her. Rue barging into her home. The brutality. What might have happened to her and Sarah Jane had Sam and Mickey not arrived in time?

She shudders and Sam looks at her with an expression that asks whether she's all right. Lizzie shrugs.

Seeing this, one man says, "Hey. We didn't mean to intrude." Signalling to his friend, they grab their mugs of beer and mutter something Lizzie couldn't hear as they walk away.

"That was fun while it lasted," Sam remarked. "What's wrong?"

"I was thinking about Rue. About when he came here …"

A bolt of insight strikes and Sam lets out a moan. "What have I done? I'm so stupid. Of course, you would be upset around men. Please forgive me."

Lizzie shrugs again. "I don't know why…"

"Post-traumatic stress. I should have known. Let's get out of here. Do you want to go home? How about we walk?"

They push through the audience to the street, the stroller parting the crowd for them. Sam curls her arm around Lizzie's shoulder to draw her near. "It was fun to be a girl for a few minutes. I wasn't thinking. Are you angry with me?"

Lizzie leans into Sam and shakes her head. "I didn't know I'd feel like that. I haven't thought about it since that night. Not really. I …" She shakes her head. "I guess it bothered me more than I wanted to admit. It's not like it was the first time he was rough with me. You know? I thought I could forget it."

"Maybe you should reconsider charging him. He should pay for what he did."

"I'm not sure. Maybe…"

They stroll along the road, listening to the sounds of music grow and then fade as they approach and then pass by one venue after another. Stores and restaurants, like the pizzeria, have been converted into stages for the three-day event and the streets are filled with smiling, laughing, dancing people.

Away from direct male contact and thinking about Rue, Lizzie relaxes. Her flight impulse recedes. Individuals can threaten; a faceless throng is impersonal, removed from her. She doesn't have to meet someone's eye or respond to questions that in spite of their simplicity cause her thoughts to jumble and her tongue to tie. Walking with Sam at her side and attentive once more, Lizzie is safe.

The music runs though her and she strums her fingers on the stroller handle, this time in sync with the beat. It is good to be out at night rather than being cooped up in the house. She is with a friend, having a good time.

"Hey, that's him." Sam grabs Lizzie's arm and directs her toward a club that is hosting the night's main attraction: a legendary pianist from New Orleans.

The audience has flowed out from the bar and spilled onto the street. Sam leaves Lizzie and pushes her way indoors, emerging some time later with two plastic drink cups in hand.

She grins. "Just listen to him go." They stand at the edge of the crowd and Sam rocks back and forth, clapping her hands along with everyone else.

Lizzie watches and smiles, happy that Sam is happy.

The next song begins, a spirited, blues-infused number.

"Let's dance," Sam says.

Lizzie hopes the darkness camouflages her blushing cheeks. "Here?" she squeaks.

Sam holds her hands out in front of herself, swaying and moving her feet. Lizzie joins in. She keeps her eyes lowered, not daring to look up at the others who are undoubtedly staring at her. Sam laughs and Lizzie peeks out from under her lashes to see couples around them dancing as well. She giggles at her own timidity.

As the song winds down, Lizzie hears Sarah Jane crying and lifts her up. The baby's attention is grabbed by the music and the people. Her head moves this way and that in an effort to take everything in. A slow song begins and Lizzie sways with her baby on her hip. Sam joins in, wrapping her arms around them. Lizzie lays her head against Sam's breast, feeling content and safe.

They move together, Sarah Jane blowing bubbles, the adults holding each other close.

Sam searches Lizzie's eyes questioningly. Lizzie sees her hesitation, but from what, she doesn't know. Sam's lips part and Lizzie tilts her head back falling deeper into the embrace. She reaches up on tiptoe and grazes Sam's lips with hers.

Sam freezes, stopping Lizzie in her tracks. Seconds tick by; the adults not moving, not breathing, Sarah Jane's head tilting this way and that as one thing or another catches her attention. Lizzie is afraid of what might come next. She waits until her lungs fill with fire. Still she waits and when Sam's body softens, she exhales. The crisis has passed. Perhaps they can agree that nothing happened. Almost, by all reckoning, only counts in horseshoes and hand grenades. And this almost-kiss was as near to being nothing as it was to being very nearly everything.

Sam moves and they take up the dance and Lizzie wonders if the faint "Fuck, me" she hears uttered with despair is only part of her imagination.

Chapter Twenty-Three

Sam arrives home later than usual and is quiet during breakfast. Her responses to Lizzie's stabs at small talk are curt. They finish breakfast in heavy silence. Lizzie failing to breach the barricade Sam has erected since the jazz festival days ago.

They clear the dishes. Sam does not look at Lizzie, her gaze focusing myopically on the task at hand.

Lizzie bangs a pan on the counter. "Sam, c'mon. This is so unfair. Please talk to me."

Sam purses her lips. "I can't."

"But why? We're supposed to be friends. Friends talk. Look, I'm sorry, okay? I didn't mean to ..."

Sam holds her hands in front of her face to ward off more words, to shield herself from the barbs of their intended and unintended meanings.

"I can't." Leaving the dishes for Lizzie, she escapes to her room. Hours later, Lizzie hears the front door click shut as Sam leaves the house, presumably for her weekly appointment with her psychiatrist. It's a standing appointment she has kept for years and is required to allow Sam her final surgeries.

Lizzie nurses Sarah Jane then lays her in her playpen and fetches a book to read. She stands in Sam's bedroom doorway, taking in the room and looking... For what? Evidence of Sam's mental state? Clues that things will get back to normal soon? How could a room possibly give her this?

She trails her fingers along a row of books her eyes blurring over titles as she strolls, swinging one leg out in front of the other in a semi-circle. She runs one finger and then her hands along the wood, removing dust. She arrives at the bedside table and, lifting each item from its surface, hand-dusts, wiping the white fluff onto her shorts. She picks a slim volume from the table and turns it over. It has no title.

She hesitates, then flips it open. It falls to a marked page with today's date.

"I'm in trouble" is all that is written. Lizzie slams the book shut and returns it to its place, ashamed that she has snooped.

She retreats to the wall of bookshelves, shaking. Her spying has provided her with the sort of tidbit she was looking for and now that she has it, she isn't sure how to deal with it

Forcing her attention to the rows of books, she wants to pick one to justify her presence in the room she can access only because of Sam's trust. Maybe she can pretend she has done nothing wrong in betraying that confidence.

In the same way she pretends she did nothing wrong with the kiss. The almost-kiss, the not-really-a-kiss, she repeats to herself.

She selects a book and flees the temptation of more spying. She grabs a bag of chips and a can of pop and plunks onto the couch, cracks open the spine of the book and listens to Sarah Jane burbling to herself over the monitor. Her eyes float repeatedly over the same lines of text until she concedes defeat and stares into space, waiting for Sam's return, wondering how much harm she has done.

"I'm in trouble."

The words play in Lizzie's head. She fantasizes about their meaning. Could it be that Sam loves her? That she might forego her surgery? That they might live together as a couple?

With the book flat against her stomach, Lizzie leans back, stretches her legs in the air then rests her feet on the coffee table. She closes her eyes and smiles. Maybe that's what Sam is talking about with her psychiatrist right this very minute. Childish anticipation squeezes a sigh from her.

Why couldn't they be together? She knows Sam cares for her. She could still be a man. Her penis is intact. Her breasts are so small they're barely noticeable. Though, in truth, even if this were not the case, Lizzie wouldn't mind them. They make Sam softer. More maternal and nurturing. Less aggressive than the men she has known.

She pauses, bewildered. As always, her feelings about Sam are difficult to navigate.

Who is she in love with, exactly? Sam the woman? Sam the man? Or just Sam? Sam regardless?

Lizzie claps her palm against her thigh. What the hell is she thinking?

She's turning out to be just like everybody else, telling Sam who to be, what to do. To give up being who she is.

She scowls at herself. "You're disgusting. You're just out for yourself. You're no better than Rue."

She begins to cry. "What am I going to do?"

Lizzie needs to escape her the jumble of her feelings though she has nowhere to go, no one to talk to. Regardless, she showers and brushes her teeth and changes into her nicest dress – the one she wore to the Jazz Festival. She packs the diaper bag and when Sarah Jane wakes, loads her into the stroller. She has to find something to do with herself. Sitting at home, hanging onto Sam isn't good for her.

She needs a job. Something that will take her out of the house, maybe even find her a new friend or two. Something that will break her reliance on Sam. Give her some perspective, a distraction from her emotions.

Still, if she finds work what will she do with the baby? Daycare? Lizzie doesn't know if those places accept infants and even if they do, they can't be cheap.

But it's time to find out. She's almost eighteen. An adult.

It's time she started acting like one.

Lizzie marches up the road, pushing Sarah Jane to the shelter of a bus stop. She studies the route map posted within. Its jumble of coloured lines and microscopic numbers is worse to figure out than the street map Sam had used to try to orient her.

She's overwhelmed by this foreign land. A surreal place where she can't find her way, where day is turned to night, and she remains apart from all but one. The urge to get to a place where people don't stay up all night and sleep all day, somewhere people have normal jobs and regular lives, encourages her on. She finds the red "you are here" dot and holds a finger to that spot. She traces a route west to Yonge Street.

Ten minutes later, she boards a bus and finds an available seat directly behind the driver. The row faces sideways, providing space to pull the stroller close and out of the way of other passengers.

A man sitting across the aisle stares toward the front and mutters to himself. Two people to Lizzie's right are doing the same. She blinks nervously. The man guffaws and it dawns on Lizzie that she isn't surrounded by lunatics after all. Just regular people with cell phones and wireless headsets. She bites her lips to stop from laughing out loud. Like she's never seen such things before.

As the bus lumbers up Yonge Street, she watches the multitudes walking, scurrying, skateboarding, jostling and being jostled. There is excitement in the bustle, in so many rushing to attend to their affairs. The blur of motion and splashes of colour reflect and refract off of the mirrored windows of the new high-rises, gleaming in the sunlight. These individuals, curious whirlwinds of self-importance, add vitality to the streetscape.

All this dazzle is in sharp contrast to the carbon-encrusted brick facades of the stately, older structures. Banks and shops that have an air of old money and a disdain for their newer counterparts. They wear their age with pride. She sees a doorman in front of a bank. He wears a blue great coat and jaunty cap. "He must be sweltering in that get-up," she whispers to Sarah Jane. "It's a wonder he doesn't pass out."

The Eaton Centre comes into view and she debarks. She walks under an imposing mobile of a flock of Canada geese, which, she reads on a plaque, are made of fibreglass.

She is small; she doesn't belong here.

Be confident, she admonishes, throwing back her shoulders. Attitude is everything. You're as good as any of them.

She strides over to a floor plan. There are hundreds of shops and she plans on hitting them one by one. She's going to land a job. Yes, indeed.

She glances down at the fabric of her dress pulling across her breasts and at the plastic flip-flops on her feet. Who is she going to fool, looking like this? Looking exactly like who she is: a nobody from Upper Nowhere. She flees to the nearest restroom where she stares into the mirror, pulling at the front of her dress, rounding her shoulders forward to draw herself in. Two hundred and fifty stores and restaurants are a lot of opportunity to walk away from. There is nothing to do for it. She washes sweat from her face, re-applies her lip-gloss and takes a deep breath.

Tossing her hair back and holding her head high, she readies to tackle every single outlet.

Approaching the first shop, she asks if they are hiring.

"Do you have any experience?" the clerk asks with an air of contempt.

"Not at a store, but I –"

He thrusts a job application at her. This is a waste of time his expression seems to say, but she fills in the small boxes on the form and hands it back to him with a nod.

Without a resume, it takes more time than she had figured to complete the applications. After her first experience, she is grateful for every friendly face she encounters. So many are not. They may be at the bottom of the salary ladder, but they, at least, have jobs and are higher up the food chain than she.

Employees in women's clothing shops are the worst. Lizzie regards their expressions of condescension for her out-of-date clothing and the childish braid that runs down her back. They beam fake smiles from beneath cold eyes, but it doesn't matter. Someone somewhere will give her a chance. One is all she needs.

Lizzie clenches her jaw and thanks them for their time, pretending she doesn't see what they think of her. She huddles at the far edges of counters, away from the cash registers, filling out her personal information. She holds her arms close to her body to be as unobtrusive as possible, to not interfere with customers purchasing their goods.

Hours slip by during this demoralizing business of job hunting. By the time she hops a bus for home, she feels worse off than the unsophisticated girl they have tagged her.

It's rush hour and the ride is a long one, much longer and more crowded than the ride in. There are no available seats so Lizzie stands, one hand on the stroller handle, one gripping a pole for balance against the lunging of the bus.

Sarah Jane, who has been a model of infant perfection all afternoon, starts to whine. She thrusts her head against the stroller, pushing her torso away from the sea. Her lower lip protrudes. Lizzie looks about wildly for a place to sit, knowing her baby is hungry. No one makes room for her. She can do little more than squat next to Sarah Jane and try to soothe her with words. Tears spring in Sarah Jane's eyes. Within seconds, her crying turns into a howl as though she can't believe her mother's cruelty in letting her go hungry.

Off the bus, Lizzie races home. "Holy cow, kid. Calm down. We're not that late."

They settle in to nurse and Lizzie cocks her head to listen for sounds of Sam. The house is too still and she wonders if Sam is napping after her therapy session.

The thought of Sam and their current situation further saddens her. This is not how she wants things to go – to hurt the person who has given her so much. How is she to reconcile this with what her heart wants? Does she even know what her heart wants?

Is this longing she feels love? True love? Or is it some sort of heroine worship? Lizzie shakes her head. How can she know for sure? Love is worth fighting for, if that's what it is. But what if she discovers it's not? Hadn't she once thought she loved Rue?

Remember that, you stupid girl? You were so sure of it and now you're not sure of anything. Waffle, waffle, waffle. That's all you do anymore. Can't make a decision about anything. School, Mama, and now this.

She has to do something to make things right with Sam. But what? And what if Sam's upset enough that she wants Lizzie out? The idea of not living here is unbearable.

Why is that? Is it only because she'd be alone and defenceless? Is that all Sam is to her? A protector?

Lizzie pictures Sam's beautiful face, her cropped hair, the thread-like scars on her wrists. She imagines the warmth of her arms and something tingles inside.

What is she going to do? What can she, should she do?

Sarah Jane pulls away and Lizzie carries her to her playpen. She stops to listen for sounds of Sam. There are none.

The afternoon has worn her out, but it's time to start dinner. She chops and grills vegetables and boils water for rigatoni. She mixes everything together with spices and cheese and slips the casserole into the oven.

It's nearly seven o'clock and Sam should be up. Lizzie goes to her room and finds the door ajar and the room empty.

Had Sam started her night early without saying anything? Lizzie feels weak. Her knees actually shake. Sam has never strayed from her rules. That's how people in her line of work stay safe, she has said. If something is out of the ordinary, people need to know they should look for you.

Maybe she just needs some time alone.

Lizzie runs down to the phone and dials Sam's cell. The call goes directly to voicemail. The phone is either off or the battery is dead. Two options that Sam has never, ever allowed to happen.

Lizzie imagines Sam hurt – or worse – then chides herself about becoming hysterical. She bathes Sarah Jane, rocks her to sleep and tucks her into her crib. She removes the casserole from the oven, checks the phone for a dial tone, looks down the street, returns to the phone and recalls Sam's number. There is still no answer. She considers calling Mickey, but it's only nine. Sam might still show up to change for work.

Lizzie paces the floor then tries to distract herself with television, surfing channels up and down.

She alternates between worry and anger. She warms a dish of pasta and eats in front of the television then washes her dishes and peers out the front window. Her reflection stares back at her. She stands still, waiting, hoping to see

Sam walk down the street, until a sense of being watched steals over her. She is a target, standing alone in sight of anyone who might be watching.

Lizzie forces a laugh at her own paranoia, but it falls flat as she remembers how Rue watched and waited for Sam to leave. She closes the drapes and stretches out on the couch, watching a documentary on birds of prey, determined to stay awake until Sam returns.

Her eyes sting from fatigue and water when she rubs them. Acid rises in her throat and burns.

Sam is okay. There is nothing to worry about.

Her eyes are heavy and she tumbles into sleep.

Chapter Twenty-Four

It is morning and Sam returns home as if nothing out-of-the-ordinary has happened. After a quick and silent meal, she retreats to her room, leaving Lizzie alone for the morning walk. Lizzie heads out, frustrated and at a loss about how to fix things.

It's only seven yet the temperature is already warmer than it would be at its highest in Black River; the humidity is suffocating. There is no breeze and Lizzie's T-shirt sticks to her. She can't bear this dripping heat. Her clothes feel like plastic wrapped around her, suffocating the pores of her skin.

At the park, Lizzie removes Sarah Jane's sundress and diaper, letting the child lay naked under the shade of the trees. She doesn't care if Sarah Jane pees on the blanket. She wants them both to enjoy their hour in the park. The heat has affected Sarah Jane too. The child has a raised rash on her face that the doctor says is from immature sweat glands. It's not as serious as it looks, which is good, because it looks painful.

It's degrees cooler on the ground and Lizzie breathes in the less-oppressive air with relief.

She lies beside her daughter and the child turns her head toward her. In a low voice, Lizzie sings a song and Sarah Jane gurgles along with her.

Sarah Jane becomes drowsy. Lizzie watches her fight against heavy eyelids. Within minutes, she loses her battle and falls asleep. Every now and then a limb jerks as she dreams.

Lizzie stares at her child, wanting to be a good mother. She questions her ability, thinking of her impatience with being tied down and lack of independence.

There is something else she has noticed about herself that is concerning. The intensity of her anger when something goes wrong. When she isn't crying, something she attributes to having had a baby and a surge in some post-natal brain chemical, she is hitting something. A pillow, her leg, it doesn't matter what. What if something turns into someone? Is that how things with Papa began?

Not to mention the stress of her tenuous living arrangement. Without Sam, Lizzie would have perished or she'd be back with Rue. She shudders at this last thought before a new anxiety flutters over her heart. The new Sam. Relying on someone whose behaviour has become erratic is at best foolhardy.

Once more, she is stuck without the means to improve her lot. She is no closer to being able to fend for herself today than she was two months ago.

Lizzie traces Sarah Jane's profile with her forefinger and the baby wrinkles her nose, but remains asleep.

What is Lizzie going to do?

Her mind floats, trying to land on a solution. There is nothing and then, an image of Mama appears. That's where she should begin – answering Mama's email. She determines to take a bus trip to a library in Scarborough or Mississauga. Maybe go as far as Belleville.

That leaves the question of Sam.

As the sun crawls upward, Lizzie decides it's time to go home. She lifts her sleeping baby and places her in the stroller, careful to avoid bumps along the pathway as best she can.

Sounds of laughter greet her at the door, laughter that is cut short with the closing of the door. The sudden silence seems portentous and is made more so when a familiar cackle cuts it in two. Her stomach in knots, Lizzie walks into the main area to see ZoZo sitting at the dining room table with Sam. Sam will not meet Lizzie's gaze and a self-satisfied smile lifts the corners of ZoZo's narrow lips. She looks every inch the cat that has licked up all the cream.

Lizzie says nothing. She cannot.

She nods a hello then carries Sarah Jane up to the crib and sits on the rocking chair, wondering how to deal with ZoZo's presence. As she rocks, her body cooling in the air conditioning, curiosity gets the best of her.

She returns to the main floor and greets ZoZo. Her voice sounded strained, reserved. This isn't the impression she wants to make. She smiles a phoney smile, hoping they can't read her mind, that they don't know she wants to ask what this horrible woman is doing here. She sits across from Sam. "You're up so early. Or have you not been to bed?"

ZoZo interjects, "I just dropped by out of the blue. 'Surprise!' I said when she opened the door. What fun, yes?"

Sam nods although ZoZo is the only one smiling. The atmosphere is bleak.

Sam could easily pass as a mourner at a funeral.

In spite of the cool air inside the building, there are beads of sweat on Zo-Zo's upper lip as though it's a strain for her to be friendly. She picks at a hang-nail until it bleeds. "You two aren't much of a party."

"I should be sleeping," Sam says.

"Eh, well. I won't keep you. I'll lay my cards on the table."

Here it comes.

"I want you to give me my old room back. You know, it can be like old times. You and me working, this one playing housekeeper." ZoZo stares at Sam, trying to connect. It isn't Lizzie's approval she needs.

"I don't think so," Sam says. Her voice has lost its normal certainty and she avoids looking at ZoZo.

Lizzie's stomach sinks. There is something between the two that Lizzie can-not name. It crackles between them, not in joy – it feels too sharp for that.

"Don't be stubborn," ZoZo cajoles. "I told you I quit. No more blow for me. I told you if I wanted to quit, I could and I did. It was easy. Like that." She snaps her fingers.

If this were a movie, Lizzie thinks, ZoZo would be the devil come to take a soul. Maybe that isn't so far from the truth. That mane of red hair, those bones that jut out in angles around her. Her cruel laugh. Yes, there is some-thing devilish in her.

Sam pushes away from the table. Her movements are slow, like she has dif-ficulty setting herself in motion. "I'm sorry. I can't."

ZoZo's head begins to shake on her snake-like neck. "You can't? You can. You will. I am too old to be out there alone. You're sending me to die. You know that." She reaches across the table, but cannot reach Sam's hands. "I helped you once, remember?"

Sam crosses her arms. "The way I remember it, we helped each other. I gave you somewhere to stay."

"Yes, yes. Of course." ZoZo raises her hands in a truce. "Whatever you say."

"I'm sorry."

"Please." Her desperation hangs heavy in the air.

In an instant, Sam reaches forward and grabs one of ZoZo's hands in hers. She presses ZoZo's fingerpads away from her nails then rounds the table and grabs her by the jaw, opening her mouth. "Look there. Don't tell me you're clean. You're injecting. Just like before." She throws ZoZo's hand aside. "How many times a day is it now?"

ZoZo glares at Lizzie, hate and fear burn inside her. The smell from her is of sulphur. "It's her fault!" she screeches, pointing a claw-like finger at Lizzie. "Why did you let her come here? We were fine till then."

"This is about you, not her."

"Always you have to help the lost ones. Take this one home for a meal, a few days. That one. Still, they were nothing to you. They went on their way. What's so special about this one, eh? She controls you, feeds off you. Why can't you see?" ZoZo leans against Sam and wraps her arms around the tall woman's neck. "It's her fault. She made me so crazy I had to do something."

Sam pulls ZoZo's arms off her and moves away. "Quit it. You sound crazy."

"It's not me. It's her. You don't care about me no more. Nobody loves ZoZo." She bursts into tears.

Sam looks stricken at the state of her one-time twelve-step partner. "I can't be around you. You know what will happen to me – the same thing that's happened to you."

ZoZo takes something from her pant pocket, a small plastic bag filled with white powder. "Look what I got." She waves it in the air.

"Stop it!" Lizzie jumps between Sam and ZoZo, terrified that Sam might be tempted.

"Mind your own business, you Goddamn bitch," ZoZo growls. "If this has nothing to do with you, then fuck off. I know she wants it. We all want it. We can go through twenty programs – the desire never goes away. Right, Sam?"

"Get. Out." Sam has pulled herself to her full height, a most formidable opponent, but there is something wild in her eyes and Lizzie knows Sam needs her size to do what her will cannot – fend off the pull of the powder.

ZoZo saunters toward the front door. "You want it. I know you do. That's fine by me, Bébé. When you can't say no, you'll call ZoZo. Then you'll need me." She closes the door softly behind her and Lizzie flies to the window to be sure the woman is leaving. With her eyes, she follows her down the street then turns to find Sam sitting, her forehead resting on the table.

"She's right, you know," Sam says. "I wanted to rip that pouch out of her hand so bad."

"But you didn't."

"Just barely."

"You aren't like her—"

"I am exactly like her." Sam stands and drags herself across the room and up to her bed leaving Lizzie to worry about Sam's state of mind and about her own future.

This new world that had felt so safe is tumbling down around her and Lizzie has no inkling as to what to do to prop it up.

Chapter Twenty-Five

Lizzie wakes with a start. Disoriented, it takes a moment for her to realize she is on the couch once more.

She rubs her face and rotates her neck, stiff from having her head canted all night on her arm. She reaches for the remote and turns off an infomercial for a new meal replacement product in time to hear a peep from the baby monitor. Sarah Jane is waking too.

Has Sam come home?

Lizzie pads upstairs. Sam's room is empty. Lizzie continues to her room, her soothing blue room, her mood weighted down by lack of sleep and discouragement. Sam has been missing for nearly twenty-four hours – something she wouldn't have tolerated of anyone else.

Sarah Jane twitches in her crib, but her eyes are still closed, giving Lizzie time for a shower.

As she towels herself dry, she hears Sarah Jane moving around. Something rattles against a fist or a foot or the side of the crib. It falls to the floor.

"Mommy's coming, baby girl," Lizzie sings from the bathroom. She dresses then tends to Sarah Jane's morning needs.

More than an hour has passed. If Sam had worked last night, she would be home by now.

Lizzie can't get a grip on what is happening. She carries her daughter downstairs and sways her on her right hip as she tries Sam's cell phone. There is no answer. With a heavy sigh, she places the phone in its cradle and turns to the kitchen to start breakfast.

Moments later, Sam enters sporting a grin that stretches across her face. Her eyes twinkle.

"Hello!" she calls. "I'm home."

"I can see that." Contrary emotions wrestle inside her. Anger again wins and she blurts: "Where have you been? Why haven't you called or answered my call? How could you let me worry like that?"

Sam is dressed in her usual work attire. She swoops over to Lizzie and clasps her by the hands, waltzing her around the furniture.

"Stop it," Lizzie demands. She feels the brittleness of anxiety inside her and wants to give in, wants everything to be better. "You owe me an explanation."

"Not now. I'm in a good mood."

Lizzie's pride holds onto her righteousness. "Tell me what's going on. I deserve that much."

Something changes in Sam's face. Lizzie tries to read this new expression – the tightening of her muscles, the edginess in her eyes. She can't and this scares her. The hardness scares her.

"I've made some decisions for myself and I'm happy. Let me be happy."

Lizzie doesn't think what she is looking at is happiness. She opens her mouth to protest, but thinks better of it. "What have you decided?"

"Ah, for now that's for me alone, Milk Maid."

"God, we're not back to that, are we? Look if this is about the other night, I'm sorry. I didn't mean to … A realization of the truth compels her to be honest. "I guess I did mean it. Yes, I did. In the moment. It's how I feel – felt." Alarm makes her voice shrill. "I take it back. I take it back. I'm just screwed up sometimes and I—"

"Bygones and all that." Sam smiles. Her eyes dance dangerously. "So, what's for breakfast? I'm starved."

The room slips out of focus. Lizzie closes her eyes against the knowledge that something is coming, something bad over which she has no control. It's a situation with which she is all too familiar.

She listens to Sam's fake-happy voice promise not to do it again.

"You have my word," Sam proclaims as her feet pound up the stairs. "I'm going to shower and then I need some food."

Lizzie goes to the kitchen, empties a can of beans into a pot on the stove and slides multigrain bread into the toaster. She cracks three eggs over a hot pan. Two yokes break when she flips them.

Sam seems not to notice the hard eggs, the cold toast or Lizzie's silence as she chatters like a magpie. Lizzie's arms are leaden as she moves the food about her plate.

After the meal, Sam retreats to her room to sleep. Lizzie stays indoors, waiting. She tells herself that Sam is overtired. That she's totally fine. That when she gets up, she'll be back to normal.

Lizzie's hands tremble and her stomach rolls into knots as she dusts tables and shelves that don't need dusting and strips linens from her bed that don't need washing. She doesn't believe that things will be okay. This feels too much like an ending. She waits impatiently for Sarah Jane's nap time, aching for some sleep of her own.

When the time comes, she dreams she is in Black River at her Granny Gee's house. They are working in the kitchen, pickling something. Lizzie can't tell what it is. They are in long dresses, the sort of frocks worn by early settlers although Lizzie's is torn and the bottom is ragged and caked grey with clay. Someone bangs at the door. Something in the sound scares Lizzie and she calls to her grandmother who ignores her. A man's voice shouts to open the door. Lizzie tries to move, but her feet are heavy, her movements are slow. She tenses her muscles and urges herself on, attempting to move faster but fails. She calls once more for help from her grandmother. The older woman seems not to hear although she stands only feet away. Someone is crying. The sound is pitiful and tears at Lizzie's heart. She knows someone is hurt and she has to hurry. Why can't she move? She tries over and over to reach the door's deadbolt but can't stretch far enough to grab it. She imagines blood and chains waiting for her on the other side. She knows only she can save whomever is dying, his blood seeping through the slats of the wooden porch. Granny Gee sings a country ballad, continuing with her chores as though nothing untoward is going on. Lizzie cries out, "Help me!"

She awakes with tears on her cheeks and knows Sam is gone.

She rolls onto her side and grabs a pillow to her chest sobbing till she can't breathe, till her eyes are swollen to slits with grief, till she wishes she were anywhere but here. Even if that were back home. She has done something terrible, something she can't undo.

"I take it back," she cries into her pillow.

When she rouses herself from bed some time later, she checks Sam's room. The door is locked as it hasn't been in weeks and Lizzie sighs.

She carries Sarah Jane downstairs. Caring for her child gives her no pleasure today as she goes through her actions by rote. She props the child inside the stroller, padding her with receiving blankets. They walk the neighbourhood in the heat of mid-afternoon, ending up at the park. Lizzie meanders along the trails, aiming for the lakeshore and the dockyards. There is no real goal in arriving there. The hustle of the stevedores is merely something to watch.

Lizzie can't bear this aimlessness of hers. She finds a bench next to a grove of aspens that face a busy pier. She sits and stares, registering nothing but the flow of movement in front of her.

What has her life become?

For a girl who had plotted and executed an escape – as grand a thing as even Steve McQueen, Granny Gee's favourite, could have acted out – she has fumbled her arrival. The plan, or lack of one, nearly meant disaster once and looks like it may yet.

Sam's intervention had saved her. From this, and aside from motherly duties – which Lizzie had to admit were limiting in a way she had never thought possible, rewarding too, but every coin has two sides as Gran would have said – Sam has become her whole life. That she has shelter and other necessities is due only to Sam's goodwill. It is quite a situation she's gotten herself into. The million-dollar question is how she might get herself out of it.

In the past, school had been her salvation. It had been the thing she thought would launch a new life. The romance of it! Classes in the fall, leaves in full colour. New books and a study group.

And a baby.

That's where the dream falls apart. How will she ever be able to take on studies with an infant to care for? She can't see beyond this and her fear of losing her child stops her from asking for help. It stops her from grabbing hold of the future she wants.

Her eyes rest unseeing on the horizon as she rocks the stroller mechanically. A breeze from the lake caresses her face, blows fine hairs from her ponytail.

My life can't be this forever. She lifts her daughter from the stroller. "This isn't what I wanted for you. Nothing is turning out the way I want. I wanted so much to be different. To be better. For you"

Even with despair nipping at her, she knows she has changed. The differences aren't dramatic, but her old life – the one that she lived only a handful of weeks ago – seems long ago. She is different, isn't she? She has a child after all. That must mean something in terms of change.

And yet the other things remain the same. Her fearfulness, her loneliness. She has escaped her physical past but not the metaphysical.

Lizzie flicks a stone with the tip of her flip flop and it skitters across the walkway. She wishes she could shrug off her despondency as easily.

Life would be so much easier without a child.

The thought takes her by surprise. She is flooded instantly with guilt for having that inside her.

What kind of a mother am I?

She pulls Sarah Jane close and strokes her smooth cheek. "Don't you worry about anything," she says.

She settles back on the bench and continues fretting until, reaching through the shade, the afternoon sun turns her skin pink. Lizzie opts for the coolness of home and returns there, so caught up in her thoughts, she doesn't notice Sam waiting for her until she reaches the front stoop.

Their eyes meet and Sam grins wolfishly. "Let's go out to eat. I bet you could use a break."

Lizzie squints, examining her supposed friend. Sam isn't herself in tone or language. Lizzie looks closer. Sam's eyes are bright; her hands skitter across her lap then to her hair and back again. She shoves them between her knees but they have a will of their own and are soon rubbing her thighs, picking imaginary lint from her shirt or pinching the non-existent crease in her slacks. One leg, crossed over the other, swings up and down, a hinged gate in a high wind.

Lizzie vacillates. The landscape is moving too quickly. Things aren't in focus. Why would – how could – a kiss, nothing more than skin brushing against skin, cause her life to unravel.

"Well?"

"Give me thirty minutes." Lizzie retires to her room to nurse and change Sarah Jane, contemplating Sam; her unease growing. Why can't they put it behind them? They had talked about such things before. Why not now? It isn't just Sam's jumpiness that's new. There's something else. Something that Lizzie can't quite put her finger on.

She repacks the diaper bag, brushes her teeth and changes into her blue dress.

As she reaches behind to pull the zipper, the image of Sam in a shirt and pants grabs her by the throat.

Sam is dressed like a man.

Lizzie cannot move. The enormity this staggers her. Somewhere deep inside a bit of insight flashes its brilliance and is as quickly extinguished.

Sam calls to her. "Hey! Are you coming? I can't wait all night."

Lizzie jumps. "Just a sec." She gathers Sarah Jane and her things and heads out the door where they wait for Sam to lock up.

As Sam walks toward her, Lizzie sees that Sam isn't wearing actual men's clothing. But she's not dressed in her usual style either. The short-sleeved shirt is loose enough to mask her small breasts, giving the allusion of pronounced pectorals. Her pants are shapeless linen and are as androgynous as the beige espadrilles on her feet.

Lizzie says nothing. She tells herself that she is reading too much into a change of clothing. It's nothing. Nothing. Didn't Sam say she is happy?

Sam leads the way through labyrinthine streets to a sports bar some blocks away. Lizzie has trouble keeping pace and Sam is waits, standing at one of the few outdoor tables, for Lizzie to arrive. When she stops, she is annoyed, sweaty and breathing hard.

Fortunately, the sun has dipped to the west leaving the area in shade. Maturing trees provide a green screen, separating them from the parking lot. The temperature cooperates by dropping a degree or two from its mid-afternoon high.

The waiter brings ice water and menus. He relates the daily special – a Montreal-style smoked meat sandwich. Lizzie only half listens before tuning out. She is unexpectedly weary. If only she could lay her head on the table and sleep. Her eyelids droop and then close, lulled by the hum of a bluebottle fly.

Sam exchanges a few words with the waiter who departs with their drink order. "Something wrong?" Her voice is off-kilter like a pubescent male's sliding out of one register and into another.

Lizzie shakes her head and sips her water. "Just tired all of a sudden. I guess I should have stayed home."

"You're home all the time. I thought you'd like to get out."

"You're right. I should." Danger sizzles in the air. "I do. Really." Lizzie all artifice, must placate. "My body's being contrary."

"Your body? We could talk." Sam's laugh is booming and bitter. She slaps her hand on her thigh as though her joke is funny then her attention drifts into the distance.

The drinks arrive. Sam throws back a double shot of tequila and has a mouthful of beer before the waiter has a chance to give Lizzie her ice tea.

"Someone's thirsty," the waiter jokes.

"It's a thirsty kind of day, don't you think?" Sam asks.

"Absolutely." The waiter takes their food order and promises to return post-haste with another shot. That was the way Sam put it: post-haste.

Sam picks at the label on her bottle with jittery fingers. Pick, pick, pick. She peels it off, shreds it into strips then tears each strip into pieces of square confetti.

As Lizzie watches, her mood sinks lower. Sam's demeanour is not her own.

Her outfit is all wrong. Had this been anyone else, Lizzie would admit these two things don't amount to much. But it's not anyone else. It's Sam and Sam has worked so diligently to create her own calm, reflective nature that a change means something significant. Lizzie feels worn through, threadbare with waiting for whatever is coming. She knows something awful is on its way as surely as she knows her own name. Something. If this were a movie, the wind would be picking up, storm clouds would be moving in. Lizzie looks to the clear-blue sky. So much for Hollywood.

She wants to ask Sam where she's been, what's going on, but she can't. If she does, she will unleash the bad thing. If she pretends things are normal, she might be able to stave off whatever it is. Denial has served her well in the past.

The second tequila buffs Sam's edge. She relaxes into her chair, stretching her long legs straight. She pulls at the collar of her shirt trying to cool herself. She closes her eyes and massages them. They glow red when she is finished.

Their food is served and for the most part, they eat without speaking. Lizzie's mind wanders until she jerks to attention and asks Sam the date.

"July 29."

"It's my birthday one week from today." Lizzie grins. "I'm going to be eighteen."

"We have to celebrate. Let me take you out."

"That's okay. It's no big deal."

In Lizzie's family, birthdays had not been celebrated in many years, but her last had been a day to remember. More than a simple party, it was the event of the summer with a retro-fifties theme. Mama got the idea when she found a few yellowed magazines in Granny Gee's attic and tore out pictures of movie idols and popular singers to decorate the walls of the house. She borrowed her mother's old records and record player and served root beer floats and pigs-in-a-blanket. Lizzie's girlfriends raided second-hand shops and the closets of the town's seniors for crinolines and hoop skirts. Lizzie wore her hair in a ponytail tied with a scarf and Mama embroidered an L onto a pink sweater that Lizzie wore with the buttons in the back. Mama had even coloured the sides of a cheap pair of white tennis shoes to imitate the iconic black saddle.

Over the intervening years, whenever thoughts about what she had missed entered her head, Lizzie forced herself to remember that her parties had ended on a high note. "How could we have outdone that one?" she'd ask herself.

Lizzie is lying when she says her birthday is no big deal. Entering adulthood has great significance for her. Lizzie believes she will gain more rights, that she will be treated with more respect and that – and this is the most important thing – no social agency will have the right to take away her child.

"There's no one to take care of Sarah Jane."

"I could call Mickey. See if his daughter will do it."

"I don't know her. I wouldn't feel comfortable."

"Yeah, I get that. I tell you what. You leave it to me. I'll figure something out."

"Are you finished?" Sam checks her watch and yawns. "It's getting late. How about catching a movie on cable?"

"You're tired already? You're the night hawk."

"Taking a break. I'm beat."

Lizzie tips her head to the side, again wondering if something – or nothing – is wrong. Sam seems to have returned to normal. Maybe the gathering clouds are in her head. "No use worrying for worry's sake," Granny Gee would have told her.

They return home and Lizzie puts Sarah Jane to bed.

Sam motions Lizzie to sit beside her. They pick a movie and Lizzie lies down with her head on the couch next to Sam's lap. As Sam strokes Lizzie's hair, her hand movement becomes slower and then irregular and then stops. She begins to snore. Lizzie sits up. Sam's neck has fallen at an awkward angle. Lizzie rouses her and sends her off to bed.

She watches the movie almost to the end until she too is fighting to keep her eyes open. It requires some effort to pull away from the comfort of her position to walk all the way to her bedroom, but she does. Once she brushes her teeth and washes her face, she is less sleepy and lies in bed listening to Sam's snoring and Sarah Jane's periodic sighing.

The last time Lizzie checks her alarm clock it is two fifteen. She drifts into troubled sleep, resurfacing into consciousness throughout the night. Her mind whizzes around and around, wondering what secret Sam is hiding. For certainly she is hiding something.

As usual, Lizzie wakes before Sarah Jane makes her first morning sound. She is tired today and hopes a shower will get her going. The pulsating jet is invigorating although its restorative powers fade minutes later. Lizzie completes her morning routine without enthusiasm. She sets her daughter in her playpen and collapses onto the couch. She dozes, keeping an ear on alert for sounds of distress from Sarah Jane. When it is time for the infant's morning nap, Lizzie crawls back into bed and sleeps too.

At midday, they rise to find Sam gone. She is becoming as predictable in this mysterious new routine as she was in her old one.

The next days show no return to past domesticity. Sam comes and goes according to her whim and refuses to discuss her whereabouts.

Lizzie is near her breaking point and is determined to confront Sam the next time she sees her, which turns out to be that afternoon.

Sam wraps her arms around Lizzie and rocks them to and fro. "Be patient, little one. I'm doing this for you."

"If it's for me, why won't you talk to me? Why do I feel so bad?"

"I'm trying to be who you want. Aren't you happy about that?"

"I don't know what you're doing. I don't know what's going on. You don't have to change for me. "

"Exactly."

"I don't know—"

"I love you."

"You love me?" Lizzie looks into Sam's eyes. There is such sadness there, Lizzie's second of joy evaporates. "You don't love me."

"What other reason could I have?"

"For what, Sam? For what?" Lizzie cries in confusion.

"Be patient." Sam slips her arms from around Lizzie. Her face turns to stone as she withdraws to her room.

Lizzie's confusion is compounded the next day when Sam arrives carrying bags from Harry Rosen and Gotstyle. Overnight, Sam's stride has become manly; under a tailored shirt, her breasts take on the appearance of shapely pectorals. Her nails are clipped; her face is free of cosmetics and her heels are stowed away.

She has become a handsome man. A very handsome man and Lizzie can't deny the tug of attraction.

Despite the pull, Lizzie can't get rid of her sense of doom. It doesn't right, or even possible, that Sam's years of struggle to be recognized as a woman could be so quickly thrown aside. Could she have been wrong about her own identity? Could a person be wrong about a thing like that?

Lizzie misses the other Sam. The warmth she felt from her, the security she gave.

Days go by and as worried as she is, Lizzie's frustration grows. Sam is rarely home and offers no explanation of her extended absences. By Wednesday, with Sam missing yet again, Lizzie announces. "I am not spending another day waiting and fretting like a mother hen. We're going out, Miss Sarah Jane."

She revisits the Eaton Centre with renewed determination to find a job. This time she has a better plan in mind and gathers applications to complete at home.

"They aren't going to make me feel like dirt again," she mutters as she removes her daughter's cotton sunhat. Sarah Jane crows in response. "That's the spirit," Lizzie says.

Her confidence fades each time she asks to speak with a manager, but she carries on.

Who will take care of Sarah Jane? The thought nags at Lizzie. Without childcare, landing a job would be of no use.

Where do parents find such a person?

Next to the food court, Lizzie visits the women's room. She enters the larger handicapped stall to take Sarah Jane in with her. She slides the door lock into place and an answer comes to her as if on the wings of angels: Maria.

The Italian lady who fed her when she first arrived in the city. She had called someone about Lizzie. She must know about social services. She might know whom Lizzie should contact.

Lizzie hums as she finishes gathering job applications. This time, she doesn't care about the unkind comments and withering stares of the silly salesclerks. With her eighteenth birthday hours away, Lizzie believes she can reach out for help without fear. It is liberating.

She marches up Yonge Street and hops a streetcar to Maria's restaurant.

Chapter Twenty-Six

"You are back! And look at your daughter. She is so big." Maria marches to the stroller and lifts Sarah Jane out as if they are family. "You are a silly girl." She points a finger at Lizzie while she swings Sarah Jane into her arms. "Why you run away? You know how many times I wonder about you. I say to my husband, 'Massimo, I tried help that crazy girl but she run. This city no place for a child with a child.' Tsk."

Lizzie is abashed, yet heartened. Maria not only remembers her, she seems to care about her.

"You hungry? Want supper? Just a minute." Maria bustles away without waiting for an answer and Lizzie hears her call to the kitchen for some penne.

Lizzie is overwhelmed by Maria's rapid-fire patter. She tries to take Sarah Jane from Maria's arms, but the woman shoos her away. "I got her. First, you eat. Garlic good for the blood. You no run this time."

They sit at a table and Maria opens a bottle of wine. She pours a glass for herself and offers one to Lizzie. Lizzie declines but Maria pours her a small glass anyway. "It no hurt you."

The tantalizing smell of spices wafts toward Lizzie and her stomach growls. She remembers she hasn't eaten yet today and dives into the basic yet delicious bowl of spaghetti as soon as it's set before her.

She moans while she chews, sure that nothing she has eaten in her whole life has tasted this wonderful. Maria bounces Sarah Jane on her knees and the baby burbles as though she has found a new best friend.

When Lizzie is finished, she wipes her mouth and thanks Maria for her generosity. "I have a question to ask you."

"Go on."

"When I was here last time, you called someone. Were you calling child welfare on me?"

"Is that what you…? No, no no! I call my daughter. She work for the city.

I figure she might know how to help."

"Oh," Lizzie groans. "I thought I was in trouble."

"In trouble? Why?"

"I was underage. I thought I'd lose Sarah Jane." Lizzie doesn't share that she is also a runaway and thought Maria might have found out. She hadn't known whether there were news reports about her disappearance.

"Tsk. Nobody can take you baby. Silly girl. I'm Italian. We solve our own problems. Si?"

"I guess."

"So, is that you big question? Is that why you come here today?"

Lizzie shakes her head. "I'm looking for work and I figured that maybe you might know about daycare or babysitters or something like that."

"You need a job? Imagine that. I need help."

Lizzie is dumbstruck. She understands this to be untrue, that Maria is saying so only to be kind. "Thank you, but—"

"But? But what? You need job. I need help. What's but?"

"You don't have to do this for me…"

"Pffft. You don't tell me what I need, eh?"

Lizzie looks around the restaurant. While they have been talking, tables have filled. There remains only one empty. Two servers bustle about waiting on the patrons.

"What could I do with her?" Lizzie motions toward Sarah Jane.

"You know nothing of Italians, eh? You bring baby here. She okay for now. Maybe, if you want, my granddaughter can baby sit." Maria stands and places Sarah Jane in the stroller. "Look. I busy. You want to work here?"

Tears prick the backs of Lizzie's eyes. She nods and reaches for Maria's hand. "Why are you being so nice to me?"

"Now that's easy. I tell you. The night before you come that first day, I had a dream. I dream St. Gerard come and tell me somebody need me."

"St. Gerard?"

"Patron saint of mothers. Of course as soon you walk in here, I know. I know right away. God tell me to help you."

Lizzie only just manages not to roll her eyes. Religion is something she has done without. Where was the church, or this Saint Gerard for that matter, when she needed help? When her mother needed help? As far as Lizzie has been able to tell, Black River's faith community turned a blind eye and Lizzie did the same in return. But as she looks into the eyes of this kind, no-nonsense woman who believes she was directed by a heavenly power to help, she is humbled. Who is she to roll her eyes at the mention of a saint with a message of aid? Doesn't she pray to her Granny Gee?

She offers Maria her hand. "It's a deal then."

"Good. You start tomorrow. Dinner shift. Be here at three. I show you how we do things."

Maria rubs Sarah Jane's head, turns to the kitchen and calls to someone in Italian.

Lizzie catches the bus home. Happiness fills her and she grins with the obliviousness of an imbecile. She can't stop and for once she doesn't care. She has a job!

The moment she steps into the foyer of her home, she knows the house is empty. There is a hollow quality to a vacant place, a solitude that is quite different from a space that is merely quiet. It is, perhaps, the lack of animate energy that a person notices is lacking. It is, most definitely, palpable and gives Lizzie an echo-y feeling inside.

It is then that she remembers Sam's commitment to take her out for her birthday – tomorrow.

She writes Sam a note about her new job and slides it under the bedroom door, expecting that their paths will not cross before the planned and now-cancelled celebration. Lizzie tends to Sarah Jane then puts her to bed. She runs the shower to get the warm water flowing while she brushes her teeth.

She is going to have money of her very own.

This is exciting.

It also means she won't be here to cook suppers. She can pay rent instead. At least she hopes Sam will agree to this.

Days ago, Lizzie would have been sure that Sam would have welcomed her news. Tonight, she is not sure.

Lizzie doesn't know where she stands with Sam. Whether their friendship is intact or what Sam's declaration of love means. The anxiety crowds in once more. All she can be sure of is that she has a job and is no longer dependent on Sam's support.

She dries her mouth on a hand towel, acknowledging the one other thing of which she is also certain – that she misses Sam. Terribly.

When Lizzie fell for Sam, it was the truest thing she had ever felt, excepting her love for Sarah Jane. She'd had no thought of the difficulty it would cause. Of whether it was right or wrong. There was only the instant of recognition.

Afterward, the other repercussions dawned. Still, she held onto hope that they would be able to work things out. The details of how were sketchy, but she believed they could overcome whatever needed overcoming.

Now, things have taken a course Lizzie hadn't imagined. She is afraid she has destroyed Sam's faith in her. A trust given so rarely, it is like gossamer from a spider's web – complex, fragile and possibly irreparable.

Lizzie is in over her head.

She steps into the tub and the shower flows down her back like a warm caress. She would like to dawdle there, but washes quickly, in a hurry to call Sam who can't ignore her calls forever.

Yet when she calls, it seems Sam can.

Lizzie tries again.

Lizzie is frightened. And then she is angry. Angry at feeling frightened all the time. Like a little mouse in a tiger's cage or a bird with an injured wing.

She hits redial. This time she leaves a message. "Sam, I'm really worried. Please call and let me know you're okay. And talk to me tomorrow okay? I got a job. I wanted to tell you. I wish I knew you were all right."

She brings the handset with her and drags her feet to her bed.

She replays the events of the night of the jazz festival. She can feel the softness of Sam's lips against hers. Maybe it is her imagination, but she would swear that, for the briefest of moments, Sam had returned the kiss.

If this is the behind the change in Sam, Lizzie will not forgive herself. She should have known better. She did know better. She wasn't thinking and she had been so upset. The brush of lips wasn't malicious or selfish. It happened. They had been dancing. It was romantic. That's all.

That's all.

What if it wasn't? What if she did do it on purpose to force Sam's hand, to make Sam do something she didn't want to do? What if that's the real truth?

Chapter Twenty-Seven

Lizzie is again exhausted. She had just managed to fall asleep when Sam arrived home in the very early hours of morning. She debated whether to rouse herself to confront Sam until her sleepiness made the decision for her. Sam was at least home and safe. She would see Lizzie's note.

In the morning, Lizzie goes about her household tasks, foregoing the morning walk to catch Sam when she gets up. She is annoyed with herself for not speaking with Sam when she came home. Her impatience with waiting grows until, after tucking Sarah Jane into her crib for a nap, she marches to Sam's bedroom door and raps on it with force. There is no reply. She jiggles the knob. It is unlocked and she enters the dark room.

"Sam?" Lizzie pushes at her shoulder. Sam rolls over, still sleeping.

"Sam!" Lizzie shakes harder. Sam mumbles something unintelligible.

Lizzie flicks open the drapes and shouts, "Wake up! We're going to talk." She is emboldened by the sound of authority in her voice. "Now! Wake up now!" She pulls the pillow from under Sam's head.

Sam scowls, but opens her eyes.

"Come on, Sam. This has gone on long enough. A week. You haven't talked to me in a week. I'm freaking out."

Sam blinks and sighs in resignation. "Hand me my robe." Lizzie gives her the embroidered wrap and Sam motions for Lizzie to turn around.

Lizzie peeks into the mirror and sees Sam stand, naked. She cannot tear herself away from gawking. Sam looks like a mythical creature, perhaps a perfect one, half woman, half man. The human embodiment of yin and yang.

"Turn around."

Lizzie snaps her head away from the mirror, hoping Sam hasn't caught her peeking. She turns to face her, the image of Sam's naked body emblazoned on her brain. Soft and hard, nurturing and strong. Breasts and the barest beginning of hips. A thin layer of fat over her abdominals. A circumcised penis, flaccid, small yet manly against a hairless scrotum and strong thighs. Lean and muscled arms and calves.

Seconds pass before she can speak.

"We have to talk about what's going on between us," she repeats with difficulty.

"Go ahead." Sam slides back onto the bed and reclines sideways on an elbow. Her expression is one of amused disinterest. The corners of her mouth are arched upward ever so slightly, her eyes tired and half-closed.

Where can Lizzie begin this conversation? There is so much to say that she can't grasp just one thing, a central premise, to present in a sensible manner. She wants to rail, to declare her love and accuse Sam of rejecting her. She wants Sam to snap out of whatever funk she is in and return to being the Sam she admires. She wants passion and validation. She wants Sam to be in love with her.

She also believes that making any one of these statements will result in something she doesn't want at all – the end to their relationship. So she splutters, starting in one direction then another. Finally, she blurts, "I just want to know what's going on with you."

"With me?" Sam acts as if the question has taken her by complete surprise. As if being asked about the shift in her behaviour demonstrates an intellectual shortcoming on the part of the questioner. Lizzie watches her ennui fade and anger suffuse her face. "What the fuck do you mean by that?" She yanks herself into a sitting position. "What do you think is going on?"

Lizzie has gone too far and provoked the new Sam. Like poking a troll under a bridge. It is an irritation that, in Lizzie's recent past, would have had harsh repercussions. She shrinks away from the bed.

"What? Now you think I'm going to hit you? That's just great." Sam huffs in self-righteousness. She turns her gaze toward the window and then to Lizzie. "Maybe I'm getting tired of your little innocent act."

Lizzie's mouth drops open.

"That's right." Sam gathers steam. "You've made it pretty clear where you stand on me. I'm good enough if I stop here. Right?" Sam points to her groin area. "As long as I keep this, you're happy. As long as I have what you want. As long as I am not who I am, you're good with that."

"That's not true."

"Really?" Sarcasm pours from her tongue like lava searing Lizzie's heart.

"Is this about the other night? I wasn't thinking. I just reacted. And we didn't kiss. Not really. Can't we forget about it and go back to the way things were?"

Sam drops her glare and fiddles with the tie of her robe. Her fury is gone as quickly as it came. "It's not just that. It's everything. I'm tired." She rolls onto her back. "Just go away."

Lizzie wanders around the room, loathe to leave. She spots the note she'd left for Sam on the floor. "You didn't get my note. I wrote to tell you that I can't go to dinner with you tonight, if that's what we were going to do, you know, for my birthday? I got a job. I start tonight."

"Your birthday. That's today."

Lizzie remains silent.

"Happy birthday, then. I suppose you'll be leaving."

Lizzie can barely hear her. "What do you mean?"

"God, Milk Maid. What does this mean? What does that mean? Can't you let me rest? I said I'm tired."

"Stop calling me that! I hate it! I want you to stop that right now! "

"Then go. I don't want to get into this."

Tears fill Lizzie's eyes. She is empty, having arrived at the end of something that might have been grand, something she sat on the edge of, waiting and hoping to be allowed in. She doesn't know how to move on. She stands at the door, her hand on the knob and she sobs.

"Wait," Sam says. Lizzie turns and Sam is there, pity and grief etched on her face. She takes Lizzie into her arms. "I don't want you to go. Please stay with me."

"I don't understand—"

"You do. I know you do." Sam leans down and kisses Lizzie, her mouth soft and insistent.

From a pain-filled depth, Lizzie responds, the white light of colliding emotions explode in her brain. She throws her arms around Sam's neck and they kiss as if to stop means to die. Sam's robe drops away. She is crying. Lizzie rubs her tears with her cheeks. She is in a place without thought. A new territory of desire and desperation, of loss and redemption. A place where two lonely spirits are no longer lost.

They fall to the bed, crying and calling to one another in blind passion. Their bodies merge, atoms intermingle until Lizzie cannot distinguish where she ends and Sam begins. Lizzie opens herself, but Sam cannot enter. Her shrivelled penis does not respond.

Sam pulls away against Lizzie's protestations.

"It won't work." She's on her feet, reaching for her clothes.

"Wait. What are you doing?"

"I can't breathe. You're suffocating me. I can't do this." Sam strides across the room. "I'm sorry," she says, walking out the door.

Lizzie's heart breaks and she cries her pain into a pillow.

She curls into herself crying, unable to stop. She hyperventilates, her chest burns and her stomach twists and cramps. She races to the bathroom where she throws up until there is nothing left but hurt and heaving. She lies on the bathroom floor. The cold tiles soothe her fiery skin. Her head throbs.

Minutes pass.

Sarah Jane chirps and Lizzie must carry on in despair as best she can. She lumbers to the crib and lifts her daughter. She goes through her mothering duties by rote while tears trickle by.

She has a child. She can't afford to let grief stop her from doing what she must.

She prepares for her first day at work and when her crying has run its course, she applies a cold cloth to her face to take away the puffiness.

As the cold penetrates her skin, she is reminded of Mama and, for the second time, Lizzie understands how she was able to live the life she did. It is all about walking the road in front of you when you have no other options. Placing one foot in front of the other and carrying on.

I'll come and get you, Mama. Someday.

It gives Lizzie something to focus on. For better or worse. Something beyond Sam.

Chapter Twenty-Eight

At the restaurant, Lizzie finds Maria waiting for her; relief evident in the woman's face.

It's sweet that she worried. She must have thought I wouldn't come.

"What's the matter? You look like you got hit by a truck," Maria asks as she hauls Sarah Jane from her stroller and plunks her down into a half-sized play-pen set up next to the cash register. There is a high chair positioned next to it.

"Something like that." Lizzie shrugs, chagrined. How could she begin to explain?

"Eh, well. Never mind then. I get you fixed up and you forget about who-ever is bothering you."

Maria introduces Lizzie to the kitchen staff, led by her husband, Massimo. As they return to the front of the restaurant, Maria looks over her shoulder and says something to him in rapid-fire Italian.

Maria shows Lizzie how to work the cash and debit and charge machines. They are similar to the ones Lizzie used at the airport, giving her a boost of self-assurance, something she needs today. Maria explains the workings of the restaurant, tells her when to expect certain types of eaters throughout the day – working people who come for lunch and need to order, eat and finish within forty-five minutes, the suits who arrive after one o'clock to eat and talk deals, seniors who arrive about five and want the specials, and the theatre and movie goers on weekends who have to be finished before show times.

"Here." She hands Lizzie a leather bound menu. "Learn this from top to bottom."

Italian words float up from the laminated pages.

"English there." Maria points to the small lettering below the Italian names. "But you have to learn the Italian too. Customers order in both. Tonight you work the cash, clear the tables and make sure we have fresh coffee. When you not busy, you study the menu. Once you get the names, you see Massimo. He tell you how the dishes are made so when customers ask, you know the answer. And they ask all the time. Trust me."

"What about when I have to nurse my daughter?"

"You let me know or one of the other servers that you going to the back for a while. Use the kitchen or the office. That's all. Make sure somebody knows so the front is never empty. You got that?"

Lizzie nods.

"Now, I got to get the bank deposit ready. You stay here, read the menu and come get me if somebody comes in. Get them water first. Give them menus. Then you get me. Yes?"

Lizzie nods again.

"Adelina and Nico will be here before five. When it gets busy, I come serve too. Now, don't worry if you make a mistake. Just let me know if you do so I fix. Okay?"

"Okay."

Maria vanishes and Lizzie carries Sarah Jane to the window. She turns to face the room. "This is it, baby. This is part of our world now. I need you to be extra good. No crying or making noise. You've got to help me."

She examines the contents of the cupboards and shelves in the servers' area. Condiments, boxes of salt, bottles of peppercorns, oversized pepper mills and Parmesan graters, sweating pitchers of water covered with cling wrap. A small bar is stocked with soft drinks, beer, wine, a few spirits and liqueurs.

She straps Sarah Jane into the high chair, padding the spaces around her with blankets from the stroller to keep her upright. She clips a few toys to the tray.

Massimo trots to the front, carrying a plate of pasta with herbed chicken. "Here. Maria wants you to eat before the rush starts." He doesn't wait for her to comment or thank him before he bustles back to the kitchen.

Lizzie is just finishing her meal when the first customer arrives. She seats them and brings water and menus. As if on cue, Maria arrives.

"I was just going to get you," Lizzie stammers.

"I'm a witch. Maria always knows." Maria makes claws of her fingers and scratches at the air, laughing. She greets the customers by name; the couple stand and they exchange kisses. They chatter in Italian and Maria takes their order.

As she passes beside Lizzie on her way to give Massimo the order, she whispers, "Watch them. Make sure they get good service. They're family."

Lizzie puts on a pot of coffee as Maria returns to the table with a bottle of red wine.

The next customers arrive. A small elderly woman and a young man. Lizzie seats them and doles out menus and more water.

A young man and woman enter, say hello and walk into the kitchen. They aren't any older than Lizzie.

"Must be the other servers," she says to Sarah Jane. When they return, they are dressed in white tuxedo shirts and black slacks. They tie black aprons around their hips. Maria introduces Adelina and Nico as her niece and nephew.

The restaurant fills quickly and stays busy until near closing. Other than charging three customers for the wrong orders, the evening goes well. Adelina and Nico are friendly and stop by the desk to chat with her when they can.

"Tomorrow, you come at four to fill out all the paperwork. You will work till nine or ten o'clock. That will be your shift every day. Tuesday to Saturday. Yes?"

Lizzie opens her mouth to answer but she's too slow for Maria who is already flying out of the room. She shouts back at Lizzie, "You should be ready to serve in about a week. Till then, you take a menu home and learn it, eh? And don't forget the Italian!"

Adelina laughs at her aunt. "Nothing slows her down. She goes like that all the time. You should see when the family gets together at their house. We call her Generalissimo. She objects but, between you and me, I think she loves it. She knows we say it with affection."

Lizzie tucks her sleeping baby into the stroller and hopes that she will continue to sleep. "You did well tonight," Lizzie whispers.

They board a streetcar for home.

Work and being around other people has forced thoughts of Sam out of Lizzie's mind, but now she is unoccupied, the door is open and it is impossible for her to think of anything or anyone else. She replays the events of the day over and over, wondering how everything turned out so wrong. Her anxiety builds as she wonders what might be waiting for her at home.

Nothing, as out turns out. Home is still empty.

"Happy birthday to me," she gripes. "Well, I don't care anyway." She is lying to maintain her own sanity, knowing that she has to push love from her mind and get some rest or she will go crazy for sure. Mothers – especially single ones – can't afford that sort of thing.

On the way to her room, she raps on Sam's locked door to be sure she isn't in. There is no answer so, Lizzie pads down the hall, puts Sarah Jane to bed and, after a quick wash, does the same with herself.

Lizzie falls into a deep sleep until nearly eight o'clock. When she wakes, she feels momentary panic at having overslept. She leaps up to find Sarah Jane is wide-eyed and cooing.

"Well, Miss, you're in a good mood. How long have you been awake?" She stands waiting as if she might receive an answer. "Give me five minutes."

Lizzie rushes through her shower and pulls on a pair of shorts and a T-shirt. She nurses Sarah Jane and bathes her.

Lizzie rattles Sam's door on the way by. It is still locked so she has no idea of Sam is home or not. She fixes a pot of coffee, slices some cheese and adds them to a plastic bag filled nearly full with crackers. She pours coffee into a travel mug feeling that she needs a boost of caffeine. She heads off with Sarah Jane to the park.

"Just because Sam isn't here doesn't mean we aren't going to go out. Right?"

Sarah Jane waves her arms over her head in response. They travel to their favourite tree.

Sam is sitting there on a blanket. She is dressed as elegantly as always in capris and a sleeveless shirt. Gold earrings catch the rays of the sun that have filtered in through the trees. She has arranged a picnic breakfast and lifts metal covers off plates of pancakes. There is a pitcher of syrup and a pot of strawberry jam. There are insulated cups of orange juice and milk.

Sarah Jane squeals at a low-flying bird and tears sting Lizzie's eyes. She blinks away her fantasy and settles on the blanket with her crackers and cheese.

There's no harm in dreaming. Isn't that what Granny Gee used to say especially after Lizzie had had a run in with Papa? Sometimes dreams are all that get you through.

Granny Gee often followed this with, "I wish Doris'd leave that son of a bitch" and "I guess I wasn't much of an example, was I?"

Lizzie's heart aches with missing Granny Gee and Mama and with fear for Sam. She doesn't understand what's happening yet knows that whatever is, is at least partially her fault.

She finishes her simple breakfast and heads down a path to the shoreline. She wants to keep moving. Motion subdues the pain.

She replays her lovemaking with Sam. Was it wrong? Doesn't it prove that she loves Sam just as she is? So much has gone wrong in so short a time. Could it really have been only yesterday morning?

A squirrel soars from a tree onto the stroller, collapsing the sunshade. Lizzie shrieks and she yanks the stroller, scaring the flying rodent into the brush. Sarah Jane is flung against the restraining belt and starts to wail.

"Is everything in my life going to go wrong right now?" Lizzie yells. "Is it?" She frightens a sparrow that trills a warning as it takes to the air.

"Damn it all to hell! Now I'm scaring the wildlife." Lizzie beats a tattoo into the earth with her feet, pitching a small tantrum. "I don't know what to do. Granny Gee, help me. I need your steady hand."

A breeze blows past her and she catches her breath, inhaling deeply. She looks up, a glint of sun blinds her momentarily. It feels good on her skin. She forces herself to stay grounded, to feel the earth under her, to smell the warm air as it enters her nostrils, to feel the stroller grip in her hand, to hear Sarah Jane chatter. "I am here, world. Elizabeth Mathilde Valor is here."

It may be all she knows for sure, but it's something to hold onto.

They rest for a while until the lure of home pulls too strongly. Lizzie retraces her route and arrives at a still-empty house. She lays Sarah Jane down for her morning nap and walks to Sam's bedroom. She rests her forehead on the door and sighs.

Chapter Twenty-Nine

There was something Granny Gee used to say once Grandpa faded into his old age like a toothless tomcat. Lizzie racks her brain to come up with the right words. Something to do with karma. Granny Gee delighted in the notion that what went around would come around. She figured Grandpa was getting his and she was getting hers, and hers was by far the better deal.

Granny Gee was the toughest women on the planet as far as Lizzie was concerned. She hadn't faded as Mama had, but held on to her spark and spunk until she was able to enjoy it. She had known there would be such a time if only she could last long enough to get to it.

She was a fighter and gave as good as she got. Every scrap showed on her. She looked older than she was, a wizened apple doll with a gap where a canine tooth should be and a crook in her nose from a poor bone setting. Her hands were knotted and calloused from hard work, scarred from household accidents.

Lizzie could never figure why Mama hadn't moved in with Granny Gee after Grandpa died. There was room for her and Lizzie. She'd heard Granny Gee try to talk her into it time and again but Mama was steadfast. She wasn't moving. She'd made her bed, she said.

This made no sense to Lizzie at all. Mama had grown up with brutality. Why hadn't she run from it as soon as she could? In her adult years, she might have found peace in her childhood home.

The image of the landscape that appeared during her bus ride to the city comes to Lizzie again and she shudders. Something is there, something she is hiding from herself.

Try as she might, Lizzie can recall nothing more than that vista. Her sense of déjà vu could be imaginary for all she knows.

Missing Mama takes over and she wants so much to talk to her, to feel her hug. She has let Mama wait too long to hear from her. Then again, there is Papa. The fear of what he might do to her if he were to find her wraps around her head and pulls taut at her temples. A dull ache begins. Lizzie might be eighteen, but that isn't a shield against harm. If there is a safe way to let Mama know she is alive and doing well, she doesn't know what it is.

It seems to Lizzie that all she can do is wait and work and try to save some money for the day she might figure out how to get Mama to come to her.

Lizzie wonders how Mama would react to Sam. Sexuality and gender identification hadn't ever been topics of conversation. Lizzie wants to believe that with everything Mama has gone through, she'd be empathetic.

There had been one incident a few years before Lizzie attended Black River High.

A boy had been badly beaten after a football game, stripped and the word FAG sprayed with pink paint across his chest. Mama had been upset as much by what was done to the boy as by the knowledge that her own neighbours had raised children who could consider, let alone do, such a horrendous thing to another person.

The boy and his parents had moved away. Lizzie hopes he has recovered and has gone on to do well for himself. Those boys who'd beaten him hadn't amounted to much. Karma again?

Lizzie wiggles under a light blanket and plumps her pillow. She has completed her second shift at the restaurant and wants to sleep, to dream happy dreams but her troubled mind spins from one notion to the next. She feels rings darkening under her eyes.

Her thoughts turn, as they often do, to Sam. Dear Sam, who has been little more than a fleeting guest in her own home for what seems like ages. Lizzie has made attempts to talk about this chasm between them. She has tried to raise the issue of her new job and ability to pay rent, but Sam won't discuss their relationship and seems to believe that Lizzie's financial independence means she will want to leave.

Lizzie tosses about, trying to find a comfortable position for sleep when she hears the front door open and close, footsteps on the stairs and faint rap on her door. Seconds later, Sam crawls halfway up Lizzie's bed.

Lizzie is afraid. She hates admitting this is so but there is no way to deny it. She would never have had the slightest concern a month ago. But now? Sam has become so moody and unpredictable that Lizzie's old anxieties about violence have grown. She wishes this were not true; she hates feeling this way about the person she loves. This is Rue's gift to her.

Sam remains on top of the sheets. "Are you awake?"

Lizzie says nothing but Sam continues on. "I want us to try being a couple. I'm no good without you. Before you came, I was fine. My life was fine. I was on a certain track but now I've been derailed. All I think about is you."

Lizzie turns her bedside lamp on, better to see Sam utter the most amazing words. Is she dreaming again?

"When you came, things started going in another direction and I lost my way. I didn't know where I was headed and I need you, Lizzie. I need you by my side." Her face is sad and though her long legs hang off the end of the bed, she could be a four-year-old missing her mother. When Lizzie touches her face, it is too warm. Her eyes are too bright, her pupils are mere pinpricks in the light.

"You want to be with me?" If it sounds to good to be true, it probably is. Isn't that the way the old expression goes? Lizzie doesn't want to think that way. She wants magic to happen, to beat the odds. She feels her heart swell with hope. She searches Sam's face, wanting to see the truth of her feelings.

After weeks of silence, Sam can't seem to stop talking. "I don't want to be without you. It's been such a long time since I've felt love. I don't want to let it go. I can do this if you'll let me."

Something is wrong. Lizzie knows it, but she doesn't want to know it. She tells herself she is over-analyzing. When someone can't do without a person it means love. Yes, love. She takes Sam's hands between hers. "I love you."

Sam looks miserable and Lizzie's belief wavers. She tries to convince herself that all is well. "We can make this work."

Sam nods and Lizzie begins to weave a story, telling Sam about her dreams to be a wife and mother, about going to school and becoming a researcher, a fossil collector, a reporter of geographical history, about saving the planet.

"Maybe you could take something too. We could be students together."

Sam wipes her eyes, caught up in Lizzie's enthusiasm. "I could adopt Sarah Jane and we could be a real family."

At the mention of family, Lizzie sobers. Fighting and screaming and hurt travel to her over time and distance. Family. There is the fantasy and the reality. She shakes her head to erase the pictures like she would have done with her childhood Etch-A-Sketch. Turn the knobs and draw a new picture. Try to round the square edges. She wants the fantasy so terribly. People beat odds, don't they? They do, they do. All the time.

She cannot say all of this. It is too much for her to put into words. She settles for "I love you" and feels the inadequacy of it. These words that represent the single most important avowal, seems poor value for the feelings swirling inside her and piling on top of each other.

She traces Sam's head, running her fingers over the ridges of her ear, along the side of her regal neck, to the delicate indentation at the meeting of her breastbones. Her fingers rest there, feeling the beat of Sam's heart. "You are beautiful."

Sam pulls Lizzie close and Lizzie feels the heat radiating from Sam's body and inhales to smell her skin. She recoils; a tangy, unclean smell greets her and she lifts her head for cooler air. The odour is unexpected, as Sam is fanatical about cleanliness. It is an indication of just how difficult these past days have been for her.

"Will you move into my room?" Sam whispers.

Lizzie smiles. "Of course."

They lie in silence, Lizzie thinking about the comfort Sam gives her. It pulls her back to Mama and she tells Sam about the email that has been hanging over her head for weeks.

"You have to answer her." Sam is emphatic, sounding more like the old Sam than she has in a while. "We'll go to Mississauga or Belleville. Anywhere so long as you answer her." Her voice becomes peevish. "What if it was you waiting to hear from Sarah Jane? It'd tear you apart. You can't be so cruel to your mother." She pauses. "I'm surprised at you. Putting her through hell when it wasn't necessary."

"It's probably not even her," Lizzie snaps, stung by the accusation of cruelty. Her earlier recognition of something being not quite right returns. "And you don't tell me I'm cruel. You don't know what it was like back there. What I went through. To get caught and be dragged back into it with my daughter? That can't happen. No way."

There is a shift in Sam's demeanour. Her face softens. "I shouldn't have said that. I guess I was thinking about my mother. Maybe I was a little jealous. That mine wouldn't want to hear from me."

Lizzie stares hard, biting her trembling lips to still them. She doesn't know what to feel or how to react to Sam. What's niggling at her?

"Don't be angry with me. Not tonight." Sam touches Lizzie's arm. Her eyes are moist and when she kisses Lizzie, Lizzie feels like her heart might burst. "I missed your birthday."

Lizzie checks the clock. "Not by much."

Sam presents her with a little box. It holds a locket with a picture of Sam inside.

Lizzie leans over to kiss her and Sam wraps her hand around the nape of Lizzie's neck. Lizzie curls into Sam's embrace, fighting against the feeling that something is ending.

She hopes it is an end to their troubles, but at sunrise, she opens her eyes and, as she should have predicted, Sam is gone.

Again.

Chapter Thirty

A breaking heart, on its own, cannot be heard, seen or smelled. It cannot be tasted. And yet a breaking heart is not a metaphor for some intangible thing for there is nothing more keenly felt.

An injured heart leaves telltale signs. It makes pale skin paler; it darkens circles underneath swollen eyes. It etches lines onto a face like a hot wind carves a desert. It gives a voice melancholy and lends a body stillness. It scents skin with its own barrenness – the fusty smell of fruit withered and abandoned to winter, mixed with a touch of salt.

Lizzie wears her desolation heavily. She knows this because of the way Sarah Jane whines as if she understands she is not her mother's primary interest. The way the clerk at the mini-mart loads Lizzie's purchases into her cloth bag with tenderness, his furry, black eyebrows knotted in the face of her pain. The way Maria pats her shoulder and orders creamy gelato for Lizzie's dessert.

Two days after Sam's most recent departure, Lizzie is in the park under her tree, a finger hooked through the handle of a rattle, dangling it in front of Sarah Jane. There is no enthusiasm in Lizzie's play. Sarah Jane swings at the toy and taps it. Her face is filled with concentration. She is aiming and that is hard work.

Sam is the third person on the blanket. Her presence excruciatingly real to Lizzie who hums a desultory tune to fill the space around her.

She has been hurt before. Too many times to count. She has been frightened and alone and disillusioned. But she has never felt anything like this. Pain mixed with hope, despair and faith. In Lizzie's wounded psyche, there is still a shred of faith in Sam. A belief that she would not hurt Lizzie without causing harm to herself. A childlike trust in their bond. A sense that Sam is lost and will find her way home.

This faith does not dull the pain in Lizzie's chest or calm the fury in her head. The rejection is real. She wants an explanation. Something powerful enough to warrant her forgiveness.

She glances at her watch, grateful she has to work today. Something to do that involves other people and lets her put her own problems to the side. At least for a while. She tucks Sarah Jane into the stroller and gathers the blanket into a neat square. There is time for lunch and to put her baby down for a nap before work.

As she approaches home, she glimpses a familiar halo of red hair on a pedestrian far up the street. She cocks her head and squints. The person is too far away for confirmation, but Lizzie knows just who it is. Her mouth waters with the tinny taste of apprehension.

She rushes in the front door in time to catch Sam running downstairs toward her. They stop and stare at each other. Sam's look is one of guilt, as if she is a cheating wife discovered in the midst of a tryst.

Lizzie is frozen in the doorway; her heart pounds a tattoo against her ribcage. "What was she doing here?"

"Who?"

Lizzie refuses to answer. Sam knows damn well who.

Time seems to stand still while Lizzie waits for Sam to say something that will make things better.

Why won't you speak? Lizzie thinks. It would be so easy to do. To say something.

Sam sniffs and removes a tissue from her front pocket to dab at her nose. "Where were you?" she asks. It isn't a real question. Lizzie answers anyway. Her eyes narrow until she can barely see through their two angry slits. "Who was here?"

Sam shrugs. "You know who it was or you wouldn't be asking."

"Yes, but why? Why was she here?"

"I don't answer to you, Lizzie. This is my place, remember?" She is being dismissive. She fidgets from foot to foot, checks her watch and looks to the street beyond the front door.

Lizzie surrenders and she begs. "Sam, please. What's going on?"

Sam begins tapping the ends of her fingers against her thigh. Her eyes flit around Lizzie, hummingbirds unable to find a perch. She purses her lips and runs her hands over her hair.

"You didn't want to see me, did you? You were trying to get away before I got home." As the words sink in and Lizzie grasps the truth of it, she is stunned, the wind completely sucked from her. "Sam?" It is a plea to be told that this is not true.

Lizzie searches Sam's face. She takes in her sharp eyes and antsy demeanour, recalling the recent capriciousness and unforgivable lies. It's been staring her in the face for days. Weeks.

"Oh my god." She steadies herself with one hand against the doorjamb. Isn't this precisely how Sam herself had described ZoZo only weeks ago? "You're using. I don't believe it. You're doing drugs."

Sam crosses her arms across her chest. There is nothing feminine about her now. Her chest expands. She straightens her stance. She seems to inflate like a cobra before the strike.

Lizzie's bottom lip quivers. "What's wrong? You can tell me. I thought things were settled the other night and now… Didn't what we said, how we feel, doesn't that mean anything to you?"

"I was wrong. Just listen to yourself, Milk Maid. You come in here and I think this time I've found someone who can deal with me, but no. So you can just mind your own business and let me handle mine. I can deal. I've done it before and I can do it again."

This craziness makes Lizzie's head spin. "You're the one that came to me. Remember? Why are you doing this?"

"Think about it," Sam shouts at her. "This is all your fault. I was great before you came along."

Lizzie bursts into tears and Sarah Jane whimpers from her spot in the stroller. "I thought you loved me. You do love me. I know you do."

Lizzie's words hang in the air as Sam pushes past her and marches down the street, her long legs propelling her out of sight.

Chapter Thirty-One

When Lizzie moves out, there is no one to ask if she can take the crib or playpen but she does anyway. Everything Sam purchased for them is packed and loaded onto the family pickup by Maria's nephews. Lizzie doesn't know them. It doesn't matter. They are one of the tribe.

The boys joke with each other and it is halfway into the move when Lizzie realizes these boys, as she thinks of them, are probably older than she is. She feels middle-aged.

In less than an hour, everything is loaded and Lizzie crawls into the extended cab of the truck. The one called Nonno, Grandfather, – because of a predilection for wearing cardigans – hands Sarah Jane to her and Lizzie straps her daughter to the seat, wondering how safe this is. Whether she would be safer held on Lizzie's lap. There is no car seat.

"Don't tell the Generalissimo, eh?" Nonno asks. "She told me to get one but I forgot." He shrugs at his absent-mindedness and Lizzie is charmed, momentarily forgetting the reason for today's move.

Indeed, Nonno is a very good-looking boy. His black curls shine with the same intensity as his brown eyes. His eyelashes are as thick and long as any woman would want for herself. There is nothing at all grandfatherly about him.

Lizzie blushes and turns away.

Maria has given Lizzie the day off to get her apartment in order. Lizzie isn't sure she wants to be alone but she has learned that with Maria, it's best not to argue. As the boys unload her few possessions from the truck, she takes stock of her new home above the restaurant.

The bachelor apartment – depending upon how one wants to look at it – has housed one or another of Maria's family for almost forty years. It has been vacant since May when Massimo's youngest niece finished university and moved back to her parents' home in Montreal.

The apartment is cosy and furnished with second-hand goods from various relatives – rather lovely cast-offs, Lizzie thinks. Overall, the effect is eclectic rather than junkyard. There is a screened-off area for a bedroom and an island separates the kitchen from the sitting area. There is a comfortably sized bathroom and large closet in the back for storage.

Lizzie is lucky to be here. At seven hundred a month, the rent is affordable and she has only to walk down the stairs to get to work.

She begins by setting up the crib and change table then gives the bathroom a wipe down. It's more for form than necessity since the niece cleaned before leaving. Lizzie dusts the furniture and runs the vacuum over the rugs. She locates clean sheets and makes the bed, places clothes in drawers and the closet.

By the time she finishes, it's time for Sarah Jane's afternoon nap. Lizzie looks around her home. Although she has just moved in and little here belongs to her, she feels more at home than she did at Sam's. It could be because of the circumstances or maybe because this is her home alone. Well, hers and her daughter's. No one else will come in or out without her say so. No one will decide when she will clean or not clean. Only she will make the rules here.

Sure, she isn't completely independent. The apartment is more of Maria's do-gooding. But Lizzie is earning her keep and has rent to pay and a child to raise.

It's very nearly what she envisioned when she was planning her great escape.

If she weren't so unhappy.

She can't forget that she'd have none of this had it not been for Sam. She'd be in Rue's merciless arms, a prisoner in his house.

She owes Sam something. A measure of loyalty. Of friendship. She owes her some help. What?

Lizzie's stomach grumbles and she checks her watch. She has to buy groceries, but has to wait for Sarah Jane to get up from her nap. Lizzie grabs the baby monitor receiver and trots down to the restaurant. She returns minutes later with a dish of rigatoni, some antipasti and gelato.

She stashes the gelato in the freezer and the antipasti into the fridge for later and eats her pasta, staring out the window – her window – onto the street below. She has nothing to read. Nothing to watch. She can't afford cable for the television in the corner.

Below her, rush hour is underway and meter readers are handing out parking tickets to any vehicle taking up the outside lane. Horns honk. A man yells at someone. Lizzie can't make out what he has said. She is grateful that she relies on public transit and that Sam made her learn the bus routes. Manoeuvring through this traffic? Impossible.

She rinses her bowl in the sink and settles into a chair with nothing to do. She is sleepy and is just about to nod off when she hears a voice call her name. Lizzie jerks in her chair.

Mama?

It's a sign.

She checks her watch and decides Sarah Jane has slept long enough. It's time to pay a visit to somewhere she can access email.

Sam had mentioned the Go Train so Lizzie stops to ask Maria where to find the nearest station. Maria is about to phone Nonno to drive Lizzie to Union Station before Lizzie stops her. "I really prefer to do this alone."

The humidity of the street wraps around her like wet cotton batting. Ahead, the sidewalk shimmers. In the heat, Lizzie and Sarah Jane take their time walking to Spadina where they hop a streetcar south. Back to her old stomping grounds. It seems her fortunes will be forever tied to Union Station.

It looks so much different than it did when she first arrived. Smaller. Inextricably linked with Sam. Lizzie checks for her Amazon and even though she knows it's too early, is disappointed Sam isn't there.

Lizzie purchases a ticket and asks for a schedule of busses travelling from Northern Ontario, then finds the signs to the westbound train to Hamilton. She and her child round a corner and runs into a group of people facing the incoming train, their heads bowed as if in prayer. As they approaches, Lizzie notices their fingers move over the keys of their phones. Worship of a different sort.

They board one of the sleek green bullets. It travels quickly and within no time she is at the Hamilton station where they hop a bus to the nearest public library.

Lizzie logs on to an empty computer and accesses her email account. There is a response from the university. She has an appointment with someone named Taylor Norton in the admissions department next week. It's a miracle she hasn't missed the date. Another sign. She confirms that she will be there.

There is also a message from Mama. "I'm still here waiting. I'll keep checking." It is dated two weeks ago.

Lizzie's hands shake. She can't kick the feeling that, like Frodo, an evil eye is watching for her, ready to cause her harm.

She clears her throat, trying to banish her ridiculous case of nerves, and hits the reply key.

> Mama:
> I am sorry to have worried you, as I know I have. I hope you understand why I had to leave.
> I have a baby girl. Her name is Sarah Jane. She's beautiful and healthy.
> I also have a job and a place to stay. It's not much, but it's mine and there's room for you.
> I can't tell you where I am in case Papa finds out so I'm going to give you a place to meet me. That way I can make sure it's you coming and no one else.
> Meet me at the main bus terminal in Hamilton. On August 20 there's a bus from Sudbury that gets in at 5 p.m. There's a stopover in Toronto but don't worry about that. Stay on the train and when you get to Hamilton, I'll be waiting for you.
> Love,
> Your daughter,
> Lizzie
> xoxoxo

She hits send and leaps from her seat, adrenaline pumping as though she's had a fright. She logs out and pushes the stroller as quickly as she dares out into the evening sun. She can't get away fast enough.

On the way home, she stops for pop and chips, and a book of crossword puzzles. She picks up a few necessities like bread and toilet paper, and grabs a container of Ben & Jerry's Chocolate Chip Cookie Dough ice cream. Comfort eating was never so good as with a tub of Ben & Jerry's.

She feels drained, like sending an email was running a marathon. She puts Sarah Jane to bed and is soon bored with the magazine she purchased. She tries to sleep, but her brain will not shut off so she watches the numbers change, minute following minute, in the green glow of her alarm clock.

Too tired to read and too awake to sleep, she remembers the snacks in the kitchenette. She rises and grabs the bag of chips and the container of onion dip. Sitting in the dark, she scoops at the dip with chip after chip, trailing crumbs down her chest and onto her lap. She thinks about how Sam had helped her – saved her life really and not once but twice. Now Sam is the one needing saving and Lizzie has walked out. Not that moving was a bad idea. Drugs and babies shouldn't mix. Still, Sam is adrift and needs someone and, aside from Mickey, who else is there?

Lizzie checks her sleeping child, pulls on some clothes and runs down to the restaurant to use the phone. She dials Sam. Her hands shake.

As usual, there is no answer.

She waits a minute and redials but has no more luck than before.

Lizzie climbs the stairs to her apartment, feeling as wounded as ever, yet committed to keep trying.

Chapter Thirty-Two

The Valors live beside the Cousineaus. Mr. and Mrs. and six boys ranging in age from five to eighteen. The families had never been close, not the kind of neighbours who shared barbecues or chatted over the fence.

The Valors didn't have any friends. Lizzie had heard people whisper about her father. What could she say? The rumours were true. Over the years, the Valors' compatriots had abandoned them like rats with a sense of self-preservation.

Everyone except Mr. Cousineau. Every October, right after Thanksgiving, he and his brothers would take Papa moose hunting. It could be that he wanted to help the struggling family provision themselves or maybe it was an excuse for him to escape his own rowdy brood. Lizzie never really knew. It had never mattered. All that mattered was that Papa was away.

Whatever the men killed was shared among the families. They dressed the meat in the bush and carried it out as a team. With a bull weighing more than a metric tonne, it was a lot of work. Good work. Men's work.

Papa would be gone for a week and when he returned he'd be in such a good mood he became like the old Papa Lizzie knew when she was little. Apparently, he was handy with a high-powered rifle and got to show off at something he was good at.

Those were a few good days, but that week he was away — now, that was a great time.

Mama planned for it by setting a few dollars aside. She'd treat Lizzie to the things they couldn't afford all year. Things Papa considered frivolous. She'd take Lizzie out for pizza at a real pizza parlour or they'd order in rather than buying one from the frozen food section of the grocery store for $5.99. They would go to a movie with chocolate-covered almonds, their favourite, though these were purchased at No Frills where three or four times as many could be had for the price of a small box at the theatre's concession stand. Sneaking them into the theatre in Mama's purse was a thrill.

Lizzie and Mama's single most-special thing to do was to rent a bunch of movies – romantic comedies mainly – and stay up one whole night watching them and eating microwave popcorn and drinking Coca-Cola right out of the can instead of pouring it by the glassful from a two-litre bottle of the generic brand. They'd drag the mattress from Mama and Papa's bed into the living room and sleep there.

It was the best week of the year and it was their secret.

It wasn't just the fun food or the movies that made it so grand. It was knowing that for seven straight days, they got to do exactly as they wished. Six days, really, because on the seventh day they had to tidy before Papa came home. And they knew that when Papa got home, he'd be happy too. At least for a bit.

The week was filled with such small pleasures. It was enough to help them make it through the rest of the year.

Lizzie thinks of this as she travels back to Hamilton to check her inbox. Her stomach is in knots hoping for a message from Mama.

It is cooler today than it has been all summer. Like flipping a switch, mid August has brought some relief from the humidity and heat of July. Last night there was a cool breeze, perfect for sleeping and, with the temperature down by a few degrees, today seems less dusty, less suffocating. Heat always makes Lizzie think of dust regardless of the fact that it comes with so much moisture. It's just the way her mind works. She must have watched too many westerns when she was a kid.

Lizzie pushes Sarah Jane to the library and heads to the computers. She logs on with a mix of anticipation and anxiety.

She scrolls through her recent unopened messages, all of them junk. Her eyes run down the list three times thinking she may have missed something. But, no. Nothing.

She doesn't know what to make of this. Could be Mama has lost hope of contacting her daughter and has stopped checking messages. Could be she doesn't check every day.

Or it could be that Lizzie was right and Papa did set Mama up to do this and maybe Mama had to rush to delete the message so he wouldn't read it and maybe she is coming. There are a lot of maybes.

There is nothing for it but to head back to her apartment and get ready for work. She can return again tomorrow and the day after that and all the days until the twentieth, the day Mama is to arrive. And between now and then is her meeting at the university, another date for her to be nervous about.

Waiting and fretting will make the days drag, especially as she has no one with whom to share her worries. Lizzie hasn't discussed much about her life with Maria or anyone in Maria's family and they seem to have accepted her silence. If Maria is curious, she doesn't show it. She must have taken St. Gerard's message literally, checking regularly to see that Lizzie has what she needs. About the past or Lizzie's family, she asks nothing.

For her part, Lizzie doesn't want to tell her about Mama. She doesn't want to jinx Mama's trip or have Maria think less of Mama if she doesn't show up. A mother not rushing to the aid of her daughter is something Maria wouldn't understand.

Her boss has already noticed how distracted Lizzie has become. When asked about her absentmindedness, Lizzie explains she is simply getting used to her new living situation.

What she doesn't tell her is how much she misses living with Sam. She likes the idea of having her own place, but misses how close they had become – at least for a time.

Sam's obstinacy, if that's what it is, hurts Lizzie who fortifies herself with the knowledge that Sam is hurting too. She is steadfast in her daily calls, leaving the restaurant's phone number with each message. Lizzie imagines them deleted, unheard.

If this standoff is to be resolved, a bold move is in order. She will ask Maria to baby-sit while she pays Sam a visit.

Bold determination aside, Lizzie is nervous and takes pains with her appearance. She coils her hair into a long knot and clips it to the back of her head. She remembers Mama doing the same to tame her own curly mane before she went out to work everyday. How Mama had tried to banish the straightness Lizzie inherited from Papa. She wielded her curling iron with purpose, turning Lizzie's hair into corkscrews that sagged into a limp mess in minutes.

A home perm had been more disastrous. The top half of Lizzie's hair hadn't held though the bottom half had. For the first weeks of grade five, she looked like she was wearing a funnel hat made of hair. The straight top layer lay at a forty-five degree angle starting at a part at the top of her head and held aloft by the bush of frizz below. It lasted exactly two days when, unable to bear the teasing of her peers, Lizzie chopped away the curls with the kitchen shears, the resulting impression being that of a badly hacked hedge.

When Mama saw the job Lizzie had done, she broke down and gave her the money to go to a hairdresser who snipped and snipped until Lizzie looked like a little boy. "A pixie cut," the woman had called it. Lizzie loved her new style, which she gelled into spikes. She felt like a rock star. It was glorious. Her parents hated it, but said little. Hair grows, as did hers until it reached her waist where it remained healthy and strong thanks to Mama's regular trims.

Lizzie removes the clip and tries different styles, relishing the silky feel of her hair in her hands. It is her only vanity. She returns her hair to the clip, thinking the twist gives her an air of maturity. She needs whatever confidence she can muster to fortify herself against what is sure to be a chilly reception. If Sam is even home.

She alights from the bus a few stops early, her determination dissipated. She talks to Granny Gee as she walks to her previous home, asking for advice, for a sign that this is the right thing to do, for assurance that Sam still loves her. That true love doesn't vanish so quickly.

Her pace slows as she turns onto Sam's street, wanting to turn back.

She isn't sure she will be able to face rejection, if that is what she is travelling toward. Despite her self-assurances about the durability of love, Lizzie knows it isn't true. At least not always. Love can be weak. It can be destroyed.

She chastises herself for cowardice. Weakness isn't love. Being hurtful isn't love. It is hate. Or fear. Not love. And Sam loves her. She must hold on to this or everything she has worked to get beyond could be lost.

Her inner voice cannot still the trembling of her knees as her destination comes into view.

She takes a deep cleansing breath and knocks on the door.

As she raises her hand to knock again, the door opens and Sam stands before her. She is in her bathrobe and Lizzie wonders if the knocking has woken her up. She doesn't ask. It feels too trivial, too light-hearted a question.

They say nothing and stare at each other. Lizzie watches hurt and resentment flit across Sam's bloodshot eyes. Lizzie has to remind herself that it was Sam who spurned her.

Sam moves to the side to let Lizzie in and indicates with a wave of her hand that Lizzie may sit.

Lizzie's gaze wanders around the room, taking in the layer of dust on the furniture, the stale smell from the kitchen. She nibbles on the inside of her cheek. She isn't sure how to begin, what to say.

Sam glares at her. "What do you want?"

Lizzie's cheeks burn. Knowing Sam can see their colour only makes it worse. Words jam in her throat and her voice squeaks. She closes her eyes. Maybe if she doesn't look at Sam, she can say what she came to say. "I miss you. I want to know if you miss me. I want to know why you don't call me back." Her eyelids fly open. She hopes to catch Sam's unguarded expression but Sam has already assumed the cocky air of her alter ego.

"You miss me?" Sam chuckles. "Isn't that just swell?"

Lizzie wishes she could read Sam's thoughts. That she could be sure of whether to continue baring her soul or whether she should hold out a flag of surrender. She draws her spine straighter. "Yes. Yes, I do. And I don't understand why you said you loved me. Why you bothered to crawl into my bed and tell me you wanted to be with me, if you didn't." She blinks back tears, betrayed by them. "Why would you do that? To me?"

Sam seems to be debating her answer. Lizzie sees a new tremor as Sam runs her hands over her hair. She notices a new sharpness to Sam's cheekbones and a deeper hollow at the notch of her collarbone. Her skin has broken out in small patches of acne; dark circles rim her eyes.

Sam jerks out of her seat and begins to pace, her energy is jagged and bare like a live wire exposed. If it were a voice it would be high-pitched and desperate. "I…" she stops and shakes her head then scratches her cheek, her neck, her arms. She knits her fingers together then pulls them apart. She wrings her hands. Her eyes are moist. There is anguish in them.

Lizzie wants to reach for her, to hug her, but cannot. She waits for whatever is coming next. Please love me, she begs in silence.

Sam turns her back to Lizzie, pretending to examine a stack of unopened mail. When she speaks, her voice is a whisper. "I'm trying. To stay what you want me to be."

"But Sam! You don't have to do anything. You are who I want you to be already." She sees a flash of anger and Sam stands tall.

"Yes. Exactly." Sam faces her and her expression is cold, unyielding.

This takes Lizzie by surprise. She blinks as though she might be seeing something that isn't there. But no. There is no mistaking the clenched jaw, the narrowed eyes. "What did I say?" She hates the tremulousness in her voice, wishing, for once, to sound confident.

"You better leave."

"Sam. No. Please. You have to tell me what I've done wrong."

"I don't owe you anything. You're the one who started this beautiful ball rolling. Now you can deal with the consequences."

"Of what?" The conversation has become surreal. Doesn't everyone want someone to love her just as she is?

Sam heads for the staircase. "Lock up when you let yourself out."

The tears that threatened earlier now erupt, sending Lizzie to the bathroom for tissue. She sobs before the sink of the powder room for many, many minutes. Stop, she admonishes herself again and again but her command is unless. By the time she, exits the room, Sam has vanished and Lizzie doesn't have the strength to go upstairs to find her.

The tears continue to well on the ride home and throughout the evening. Maria sends Lizzie home within ten minutes of the start of her shift. "You look like somebody died. Customers don't want to see that." Lizzie knows the woman is annoyed with her and is right to be so. If there is one thing Maria doesn't have any patience for it is anyone who neglects her duties. Maria is big on duty.

"I'll make it up to you," Lizzie promises, squeezing Maria's hand. She knows Maria would listen to her tale of woe, but might not empathize. There are some things that could be considered too much for others' understanding.

How would she explain her feelings for Sam to anyone?

She snorts at this conceit. To whom? Her large group of friends whose number, without Sam, has shrunk to zero.

And she begins crying again.

Chapter Thirty-Three

Lizzie stands away from the entrance to the bus station, a floppy-brimmed sunhat hides her pinned up hair and sunglasses cover half her face. She sits on a bench under a flowered pergola for camouflage, watching buses come and go and checking her watch impatiently. She has arrived early to scope out her surroundings. Cops shows teach that sort of thing. She has more than an hour to wait and wishes she could focus on her paperback.

Sarah Jane stirs in her stroller but remains asleep, for which Lizzie is grateful. She doesn't think she would be the best sort of parent right now. She circles the bench to wear off some of her anxiety.

She has checked at the library for messages from Mama, but there have been none.

Will she come?

Once more, she recalls the rush of recognition she felt during the bus ride south. Emotion bursts out of her in a yip. She covers her mouth with her hand and looks around in embarrassment. No one is paying any attention to her.

What might Mama have done to support them had she left? And then: What had Papa done when he found her? What about this time? What if she comes and Papa follows her?

Lizzie forces herself to think of other things. Sarah Jane. Her job. Maria's stern kindness. She reads snippets of text from her book. It is Dickens. From the required reading list of the English course she might still be able to take this year.

It's hard to believe that university could be within reach. She had met with Her the dean of admissions at U of T and things had gone better than Lizzie could have hoped. Dean Nguyen listened to what she had to say, frowning and making notes while she told him of her life. She glossed over her relationship with Sam, but came clean about everything else. The dean promised to contact Mr. Patel and her high-school principal for an assessment of her. Teachers, he told her, could assign a final grade for her incomplete courses based on her previous performance. In the meantime, the university would hold a place for her. He suggested that things should work out just fine and sent her off to place her name on a waiting list for childcare.

She smiles at this unexpected victory; her heart beats a little faster.

Lizzie checks her watch. Five o'clock has arrived without the bus from Sudbury. Lizzie cannot enter the station to investigate the delay in case someone other than Mama catches her there. She drums her fingers on her book, wondering if the bus was cancelled. Or in an accident. What if her message pulled Mama into something as terrible as that?

Sarah Jane stretches her chubby arms over her head and blinks herself to wakefulness. She blows a bubble and giggles when it pops, pulling Lizzie away from distressing thoughts. Lizzie goes through the childcare routine: diaper changing and nursing. She holds Sarah Jane on her lap and explains that she is about to meet her grandmother. Hopefully.

Forty minutes later, the bus has yet to arrive and Lizzie can't wait any longer. She has to find out the reason.

Stop being so idiotic. What is anyone going to do to you? Kidnap you? You're an adult. You can live wherever you want. No one can make you go back.

Reason is fine in most situations, but it doesn't overcome deeply ingrained fear for long. Lizzie vibrates like a witching wand near water as she crosses the street and enters the station. She removes her glasses and her eyes adjust to the dim interior. She locates the information booth and waits in line for her turn.

As she inches toward the front, an announcement booms overhead. She can't make out the words as they echo off the plaster walls of the high-ceilinged chamber.

The woman ahead of her asks the attendant the same question Lizzie is waiting to pose. The explanation is mundane, nothing more exciting than a change in route not calculated into the arrival time.

Lizzie sighs with relief.

She scurries back to the bench outside to wait for the bus that should arrive in another ten minutes. As usual, her stomach is in turmoil. She swallows hard, jiggling Sarah Jane on her lap in an attempt to calm herself.

Ten minutes go by and Lizzie is tense with waiting and not knowing.

She wipes sweat from the bridge of her nose and there it is. A dust-encrusted bus with Sudbury-Toronto-Hamilton emblazoned across the top of the windshield in bold, black letters. She crosses her fingers, praying that Mama is on it.

"Oh my god." Lizzie places Sarah Jane into the stroller and shakes her hands, trying to release her nervousness. Should she go inside? Why didn't she tell Mama where to meet her? "Granny Gee, get me through this. Make it be her, only her, and everything will be all right from now on."

Why am I so frightened? No one can hurt me now.

With this, she pushes the stroller to the station. The passengers exit the bus at a snail's pace. The driver helps an elderly couple down the too-high steps of the bus. They thank him and move stiffly to the side to wait for their luggage. It has been a long ride for old joints.

Lizzie scans the faces of the passengers remaining inside. It is impossible to see enough detail to tell if Mama is among them.

And then, there she is, glancing outward from the top step.

Lizzie cries out and runs to her. Mama steps down and Lizzie grabs her to her, one hand holding the stroller. They cry and rock in place, blocking the flow of passengers, but Lizzie doesn't care. "You came. You came."

They pull apart and step out of the way. Mama grabs Lizzie's arm. "Sarah Jane." She stares at her granddaughter. "Oh my." She claps her hand over her mouth. "Oh, Lizzie. She's so precious."

Lizzie and Mama make their way – Lizzie clinging to Mama, Mama cradling Sarah Jane, the stroller loaded with Mama's belongings – to the train that will take them to Toronto and Lizzie's small apartment.

Lizzie is afraid to let Mama go, afraid she might evaporate, so she chatters, wanting to share every detail of every minute of their separation before she runs out of time. After a bit, she realizes that Mama isn't talking. "What is it?"

"I can't believe it."

"I know. Me too." They find a seat and Lizzie says, more to assure herself than Mama. "You're really here and you're really safe. The old life is over now. We get to start again."

Mama positions Sarah Jane on her lap and links a trembling arm through Lizzie's. Lizzie observes her as she tries to speak and fail. "It's okay, Mama. It'll take a bit of time to get used to this." And then, she remembers something. "Why didn't you answer me? Let me know you were coming?"

"I couldn't." Mama's voice is soft. "Like I would jinx it or that Papa might follow me and find out. I got Mr. Patel to help me delete that whole account before I left."

Lizzie pats Mama's leg. "That's okay. Everything's okay now."

She rests her head on Mama's shoulder, soaking up comfort, not wanting Mama to see her face and read the lie in it.

As the train whizzes along the tracks, Lizzie asks Mama the question that has been playing with her since her own bus ride south. The question about whether they had fled Papa years ago.

Mama bites a flake of chapped skin from her bottom lip. "That was a bad time, honey. I did try to get us out of that house. We didn't get far and that's all I want to say about it. Maybe later, but not today. Today's a good day. I want to take this in so I can remember it forever."

Lizzie squeezes Mama's arm. "How did you get away today?"

"It was easier this time. After you left, it was like he stopped caring. When he wasn't at work, he just sat in front of television, not really watching. I think when the town knew you'd gone, they stopped denying the rumours and they turned on him, shunned him."

"But the email. You said you couldn't answer me."

"I was still afraid of him. All those years of him… All I could think about were the what-ifs. The biggest being what if he found out and I lost you forever? If he, you know, came at me?" She leans forward and rubs her cheek on her granddaughter's head. "Like that other time. It was too much for me to risk. You said you'd be here and that's what I had to count on."

Lizzie turns in her seat and hugs Mama tight. She won't ask any more questions for now. She wants to be happy for a little while.

And then she wonders what Sam is doing.

Chapter Thirty-Four

Mama has signed up for a computer literacy program through social services that runs five mornings a week. For the first few days, Lizzie travels with her on the bus to and from the class until Mama's terror of the city subsides.

In no time, they develop their routine. After an early breakfast, Mama heads off to class while Lizzie tidies the apartment and plays with Sarah Jane. They eat a late lunch together before Lizzie heads downstairs for work, no longer having to take Sarah Jane with her.

It's true Lizzie feels a twinge of jealousy leaving her daughter in the loving care of someone else – even though that loving someone is Mama. She knows she'll get over it, that in time, she'll be happy for the extra freedom she has to come and go. In the meantime, she tries not to take her separation anxiety out on Mama. For that's what she's feeling she learns from her old resource: the parenting book from the Black River library.

It sounds right too. The way her mind flits to her daughter a million times a night. The way she watches for Mama to come in the front door of the restaurant so she can kiss Sarah Jane sweet dreams. The way she freezes in place if she hears a baby cry, holding her breath as she listens to determine whether it's Sarah Jane and if it is, whether the child settles quickly.

Lizzie will be glad when this phase is over. From feeling tied down to a house and a child only weeks ago, she now wishes she could be so again. The maternal call to care for her child pulls against her need and desire to work.

For Mama's part, she is like a tentative bud testing the air before unfurling its petals to the sun, readying to open wide. Peaking from beneath her lashes to gauge the pace and breadth of the city.

She'd been shy to begin a class, sure that she'd be the only dummy there, the only one unable to figure out how to format a document or search the Internet. It hadn't been true. After the first few days, how to use technology had made sense to her and she'd absorbed everything the instructor had thrown her way and come home thrilled with each accomplishment.

It isn't much, Mama acknowledged. Her first grasp of computers isn't much of anything at all. Yet, she'd heard there might be an opening for someone to do basic office work at a nearby women's shelter and if she can tackle one skill, she might convince them she would be easily trainable for anything else they'd need her to do. Her life experience would be invaluable to them, the social services woman had told her. Help clients feel understood.

As Mama walks through the door after class, Lizzie is laying slices of wholewheat bread on the counter for sandwiches. Lizzie turns to say hello, but there is something about the slope to Mama's shoulders that stops the words from coming out.

"I'm not good enough," Mama says. "That social worker was just trying to be kind, telling me I have a chance at that job. They'd never want someone like me. Someone who's only cleaned up other people's dirt for a living."

"Did something happen today?"

"My computer kept freezing and I couldn't keep up with the class. I missed so much." She pauses, her brow furrowed. Seconds tick passed. A look of determination sets her face and she straightens her back. "You never know though. I've done pretty well so far. Maybe I could help those women. Somehow." Mama's voice falters, trying hard to be positive.

"Are you kidding? You'd be so great, Mama. You're so good with people." A chill spreads over Lizzie. She has to put a stop to what's coming next although she can't say what it is.

Mama looks down. "Not with all people."

Lizzie is taken aback, confused until the recognition of what she was dreading dawns on her. "You mean Papa, don't you?"

Mama looks away.

"You can't mean that. That any of what went on was your fault. That's crazy talk."

"Maybe if I'd been different somehow. Maybe he wouldn't have changed so when the plant closed. You know. If I'd handled it differently."

"You can't—"

"I didn't take it seriously enough, I guess. I was sure it'd be back in business in no time. I never thought it'd be so long. That things would get so desperate."

"Now you listen here, Mama." Lizzie hands fly to her hips and she feels the heat inside her pump to the tips of her ears. "I don't want to hear that again. I can't believe you think like that. None if it was your fault. None of it. It's him that's got you thinking like this. Years of his brainwashing and bullying. You have to have some faith in yourself."

"Maybe…" Mama looks forlorn, her hands locked in supplication at her waist. "I've been thinking that maybe I should call him. Let him know I'm all right."

"He doesn't deserve to know how you are."

"He's my husband."

Lizzie's mouth falls open. "You didn't say that."

Mama's chin juts out. "We've been married for over twenty years, young lady. He wasn't always like he is now."

"But he is like this now, right? No matter what he was like before, how you were together, he is like this now."

"If only you'd seen him after you left. He was so hurt. I think he felt bad about how he'd behaved. Maybe things would be different now."

Lizzie sucks in wind. "You're thinking of going back to him, aren't you? Tell me you're not." She feels sick.

"I'm never going to get anywhere, Lizzie. I'm not that smart."

"What happened?" Tears choke her, making it hard to get the next words out. "You were doing so well."

"It'll take forever for me to learn anything that amounts to something. What's this one class going to do for me? Nobody gets a job just because they can find something on the Internet or set a margin."

"Oh my god!" The words hurl from Lizzie's mouth and her hands fly up to stop Mama from speaking. "You can't be serious. Everyone has to start somewhere. Everyone. I can't listen to this anymore. I just can't. You can't leave me." She darts around the tiny apartment gathering Sarah Jane's gear then grabs her daughter with one arm and the stroller with the other. "I've got to get out of here. I can't hear this. So many damn years of you letting him run all over you and me too."

She struggles down the stairs with her burdens, muttering as she goes. "I can't believe this. I can't. But I should have known she'd pick him over me. She always did and she always will. I was so stupid thinking she could change if she got away from him."

Lizzie hurries west and then south to a park, one of many scattered as verdant confetti throughout the city. When she arrives, she is too pent up to sit and keeps walking. Around and around the perimeter of the green space, her sense of abandonment burning her like a flame with its forked tongues.

Sarah Jane wriggles in her seat, thrusting her hips against the restraint. She whines and rubs her fists against her cheeks.

"I know just how you feel," Lizzie whispers to her, crouching in front of the stroller. "Well, you don't have a thing to worry about. I'll never ditch you for some horrible man."

Lizzie picks a spot away from the sunbathers and Frisbee-throwers, and they lie under the canopy of the trees, a comforting pose in its familiarity. Sarah Jane pushes her chest off the ground with her arms, looking with curiosity at the world around her. A breeze flutters her eyelashes, startling her.

"It's just the wind. Nothing to be afraid of."

Sarah Jane lowers herself and rolls onto her back, one hand reaches for a foot, the other pats her mouth as she sings a baby song, her voice rising and dipping to an unknown melody. "Unh unh unh unh."

Lizzie sighs, trying to relax in the peace of the shade.

Mama.

The word sets her jaw.

You can't stop her from being who she is, she tells herself. This has nothing to do with you.

But it does. Doesn't it? How can it not? There has been so much to overcome in the months since setting out from Black River. So much that she's had to face, to learn, to endure. Though some things have gone right, there has been much that has gone wrong. She doesn't want this to be one more bad thing.

She bites her bottom lip to stop herself from crying. There has been too much of that too. She can't let Mama, or anyone, make her cry anymore.

Maybe Mama's just having a bad day.

The understanding comes as a surprise, reminding her of her own bad days. The days when she didn't want to be a mother or the time she thought she'd have to go back to Rue. She can be generous to Mama, can't she? It must be hard for her too. Hard to give up the only home she's known, even if it scarred her. Hell on Earth, wasn't that the expression? Maybe Mama just needed some reassurance that no matter how long it took to get somewhere, achieve something worthwhile, it was better to spend her days at that than at anything else. Especially if the alternative meant a return to Black River and Papa.

Lizzie nurses Sarah Jane, cooing to her daughter and bracing herself to accept Mama's defencelessness. If Mama needed mothering so be it. Lizzie could take that on.

She gathers their things and places Sarah Jane into the stroller – the stroller Sam bought for her – and fights another wave of emotion.

Does it ever stop: this gut-wrenching crap that grabs you unawares at the smallest provocation?

"Toughen up!" she barks, trying to throw off thoughts of Sam, but the armour doesn't fit; Lizzie insides are soft.

She hasn't seen Sam in weeks. Lizzie has even stopped leaving messages for her to call – something she had sworn to continue forever if need be. Sadness weighs her down. She still misses her and wonders if she is missed in return. She shakes her head to erase her melancholy. There is a different battle she has to fight today.

Even with determination, her feelings for Sam are hard to ignore. Worry gnaws at her and by the time she arrives at her street, she has to force a smile of encouragement onto her face. Gloominess isn't going to help Mama feel hope for her future.

She reaches the door beside Maria's restaurant. The door that leads to the stairs to her tiny apartment. "C'mon,' she whispers. "You're a big girl. You can do this. Put a smile on."

She wrangles a squirming child from the stroller and climbs the steps as confidently as she knows how. Throwing the door open, she infuses happiness into her voice.

"Hey, Mama." She glances around, worry souring her gut until she hears the shower running. She knocks on the bathroom door. "Hey, Mama. We're home."

She can't make out Mama's response, but there is one, a fact she takes as a good sign. She makes sandwiches from the drying bread while she waits. Sarah Jane hops in her bouncy swing.

Mama enters the room, her face downcast. When she looks up, her eyes are red-rimmed. "I'm sorry."

Lizzie rushes over and wraps her arms around her. "No, I'm sorry. I shouldn't have run out on you like that. I know it's hard to get used to being here."

Mama shakes her head. "But you managed. I've got to find some backbone too."

"That's okay, Mama."

"No, it's not. But I'll get there if you'll just be patient with me. I'm so mad at myself. I didn't used to be like this, you know? So unsure of everything."

"I remember."

"You do?" Tears slide down Mama's face. "I've always been so afraid you'd forget how things used to be. I'm so glad you remember something good — something good about me. Before—"

"I remember lots of good things, Mama." She pats her back and pulls away, feeling a personal urgency to move from the past to the present. "Did you eat already? I made us some lunch."

As they eat, Lizzie chatters about the coming months and years, about education and work and about the two of them someday owning their own house and what they'd do to turn it into a home.

Mama smiles at first wanly, but then she joins in too, telling Lizzie that maybe she would be able to find something useful to do too. Lizzie can tell Mama doesn't believe her words, but the act of saying them, of vocalizing a future without Papa is a good thing. It's a promise that she means to make the attempt at a new life for herself.

Chapter Thirty-Five

The cell phone she purchased only this morning rings. In the dark, its trill is angry, a Morse-coded distress signal that wrenches Lizzie from sleep. Besides Mama, there are only two people who know her or have her number and Maria wouldn't call in the middle of the night.

These thoughts fly by in the time it takes her to race to where she's left it; the light of its screen is a beacon in the darkness.

"Hello?"

Music blares at the other end.

"Sam!" She shouts in an effort to be heard. There is a thump and something that sounds like "shit."

"Sam? Are you okay?"

The response is slurred and inaudible.

"Sam! Where are you?"

The phone goes dead.

With shaking hands and her heart pumping so fast she thinks she might be having a heart attack, Lizzie keys in Sam's number. The call goes directly to voice mail. Maybe Sam is trying to call her.

One second.

Two.

She imagines Sam at work and in danger.

She redials. "Come on, Sam. ANSWER THE FUCKING PHONE!"

"Lizzie. What is it?" Mama switches on a lamp from her side of their shared bed.

"It's Sam. She's hurt or something. I have to go." Lizzie pulls on her jeans and a sweatshirt as she tries to find a suitable explanation. Mama knows only of Sam as Lizzie's friend and Good Samaritan. "Watch the baby for me. I'll be back soon." Lizzie cannot know whether this will prove to be true and, as deep foreboding fills her, she remembers Mickey.

She grabs her purse from the floor by the door and searches for his business card. She dials the number to his personal phone and waits for him to answer while her mind spins over the events of past months. There is no answer.

To hell with waiting. She still has a key.

She calls a cab. Without traffic, she arrives at her destination in less than fifteen minutes. Lizzie pays the cabbie to wait. He shrugs as if to say that her wastefulness is his gain.

As soon as Lizzie opens the taxi door, she hears the deep sound of bass, pounding in the night air. Her hand shakes as she fights to angle the key into the lock.

"Sam?" she calls as she steps into the entranceway.

There is no one downstairs. Lizzie turns the stereo off then jogs up the familiar stairway to Sam's room. It too is empty. Her shoulders sag. As frightened as she was of finding Sam in a drug-induced stupor, the possibilities, she senses, are now worse.

She peaks into her old bedroom and draws a sharp breath. It is a disaster. Bed linens are strewn along the floor. The lamp is laying on its side, broken glass a spread in a halo around it. The nightstand is overturned. The pretty cushion from the rocking chair has been shredded. Its stuffing lays about the room.

Lizzie enters, frightened now and picking her way delicately over the debris. She is shaken by the devastation. Could Sam hate her this much? She makes her way to the bathroom to see what might be there.

That's where she finds Sam, sitting on the floor, her legs drawn to her chest. Her eyes wild and bulging, sweat trickling down her face. She pants like an overheated dog. Saliva, thick and white, billows in gummy threads between her lips.

Blood streams from a gash on her forehead. A puddle of vomit pools next to the toilet.

"Oh my god!" Lizzie rushes to Sam's side. "What's wrong? What happened?"

Sam's eyes roll back, exposing their whites and she slides, prostrate onto the floor. Her cell phone skitters from her lap over the white tiles.

Lizzie grabs a towel from the rack and rolls it into a cushion to place under Sam's head. She grabs her by a shoulder and shakes her roughly, shouting to wake her while she digs in her purse for her phone.

She calls for an ambulance then finds Mickey's card and leaves a message for him.

"Come on, Sam. Wake up! You can't leave me. Can you hear me? Wake up! What have you done?"

She wriggles in behind Sam, straddles her legs on either side of Sam's and pulls her upward into a seated position and into her arms.

Waiting for help to arrive, she continues calling for Sam to wake.

The paramedics burst through the door calling to locate their patient. They are firm, sure and practical. They check Sam's heart and blood pressure, peer into Sam's eyes and tell Lizzie to bring Sam's wallet for identification and health insurance. So matter-of-fact in the midst of crisis. They move Sam onto a stretcher, asking Lizzie questions about Sam's health and history of drug use. They talk to each other as though she isn't there, surmising a cocaine overdose.

Lizzie hovers near the taxi as Sam is loaded into the ambulance. Her attention is grabbed by blue and red flashing lights advancing down toward her, heralding the arrival of Mickey in an unmarked car.

The vehicle jerks to a stop as he throws it into park. He leaps from behind the wheel and runs to the paramedics, waving his badge at them. The three exchange words before Mickey bothers to look for Lizzie. He hollers at her to get into his car. She throws forty dollars into the open window of the cab, far more than the fare could be and darts to the passenger side of Mickey's car. She barely has time to slam shut her door before Mickey pulls away from the curb to follow the ambulance to the nearest emergency room; its lights and sirens are on all the way.

Entering the hospital, harsh overhead lights contrast with the soft rays of dawn outside. There is a flurry of activity around Sam who is whisked away without any explanation to Lizzie of what is happening or how Sam might fare. A paramedic returns from the beyond the "staff only" doors and tells Lizzie that Sam will be all right. Lizzie dissolves into tears not knowing if the statement will prove to be true or if it's been said to provide comfort.

The long wait begins.

Time moves slowly in the waiting room. Lizzie checks the clock on the wall at least twice a minute. She can't call Mama until the restaurant opens since there is no phone other than the mobile she has with her. She worries about Sarah Jane's morning nursing and tries to calm herself with the knowledge that Mama will figure something out. Get her some formula or something.

Mickey fields numerous calls from work and home. Lizzie envies this as a form of distraction she doesn't have. She's jealous of the fact that he spends so much time on the phone, that he has people to call him, people counting on him, family, friends. She is also grateful beyond telling that he stays here with her.

Lizzie studies the stark room. It's filled with those waiting to see a doctor and others like her, waiting to hear the fate of a loved one. There are the pacers, the fidgeters, the eaters and the performers – those who speak as loudly as possible either on their phones or to their friends so all can hear. There are the comedians, the souls who deal with problems through humour. Lizzie finds herself listening in on their conversations and wishing she could find it within her to laugh along with them. She isn't the funny sort, however, she falls into the pacer category so this is what she does.

Mickey finishes a call and motions for Lizzie to join him. She slides into a plastic chair, slouching and rests her head on the back.

"Sam'll be okay. You have no idea how tough she is. She'd have to be to get through the crap she's been through."

Lizzie glances at Mickey, curious about his relationship with Sam. "How come you were always okay with Sam. Back in school. When everyone else had problems with her."

Mickey grunts. "'Cause what the fuck business was it of mine or anyone else's what was under Sam's clothes or who she wanted to fuck. Man. That always pissed me off. And her parents. Jesus. What a couple of nuts. Now them, they need help, not Sam. Fucking hypocrites as far as I was concerned."

"What do you mean?"

"Church on Sunday, all that Christian love and then they treat Sam like she's a leper. Fuckin' with her head. I mean, what's that about? And you should see her old man. If he wasn't gay, I don't know who is. Took it all out on Sam." Mickey pauses. "Sam's better off without them. Not everyone who's blood is meant to be family, you know?

Lizzie nods. She does indeed know.

"She loves you though."

"No. No, she doesn't. She hates me."

Mickey looks at her, incredulous. "Are you fuckin' nuts? What the fuck do you think this is all about?" He circles his arm in front of them.

Lizzie is taken aback at the emotion in Mickey's voice. She sits straight in her seat.

"Don't tell me you don't know how fucked up Sam is because of you. The only thing that makes you moderately okay by me is your intention. I know you never intended to hurt Sam. But don't tell me you don't know that you did."

"But I didn't do anything." Lizzie's defences rear up at the unfairness of Mickey's words. "I'm in love with her. That's right. Me with her. What do you know about it anyway?"

"I know a lot. I know that Sam tried to kill herself once over her gender. And now she's tried it again only this time it's over you." Mickey's phone rings and he swears as he checks the incoming number. "You wait right here," he barks. "I gotta take this."

"Where have I got to go?" Lizzie snarls at Mickey's back as he walks to a private corner to take the call.

When he returns, Lizzie is ready to explode. She launches into him the second he sits.

"I love Sam, but I can't live with someone doing drugs. I've got a baby. You of all people should know what happens to kids that grow up in a home where there are drugs. I told Sam how I felt about her. How easy was that for me, do you figure? Falling for a woman? But it didn't matter to me. Okay. I admit, somewhere inside me I hoped she wouldn't go ahead with the operation. I admit that I hoped maybe she'd be okay to stay just as she was. But I accepted what she had to do—"

Mickey interjects. "Does Sam know that? That you'd still love her if she went through with the sex change?"

Lizzie's anger evaporates, her voice less sure. "I… I'm sure she does. I told her. I'm sure I told her."

"Maybe she didn't hear you."

"I just wanted to be with her. She's the only person I've ever truly loved. This can't be my fault. You don't even know that Sam tried to kill herself. It has to be an accident."

Mickey throws an arm over Lizzie's shoulder and pulls her close. "Okay, kid. Maybe you're right." He holds her against him and tells her about Sam's struggle with drugs, her search for love and her determination to find her own identity.

By the time he is finished, Lizzie is crying. Mickey gives her a gentle hug then walks to the nurses' station. He shows his badge and speaks with one of the triage staff who picks up a phone and talks with someone. After he hangs up, he says a few words to Mickey. Mickey salutes a thank you and returns to Lizzie's side.

"Sam's stable. Someone'll be out to see us soon."

They settle as best they can on the hard chairs. Lizzie leans her head on the wall behind her. She yearns to sleep for even a few minutes but cannot. She is stretched thin. Electrons spark and scratch under her skin and her head lurches forward. Eventually, she rests against Mickey's shoulder, not caring if he minds or not.

She closes her eyes, trying to sleep for even a few minutes. Pictures of Sam come to her. Sam as she was the night they met, Sam as she was when they walked in the park, Sam protective, Sam gentle, Sam sad, Sam lonely. This is how Lizzie thinks of her now, very alone. Traveling solo, despised and discarded by many, through her journey to complete womanhood.

Where had things gone so wrong between them?

Surely, Lizzie isn't wrong about the closeness they had developed. About their ease with each other. Lizzie had felt that together they could tackle the world.

Hadn't Sam seen that too?

All Lizzie wanted — no, wants — is to be a family. The three of them. With Mama. She has pictured this many times. Grocery shopping, meeting Sarah Jane's future teachers, sharing dinner and late night movies, growing older. She has pictured her future with Sam.

Even when she knew she had to leave, to separate herself from Sam's self-destruction, she had believed their problems would be resolved, that they would be together.

This, Lizzie must confess, if only to herself, hasn't been all that she has imagined. There has been a part of her that hoped Sam wouldn't proceed with her reassignment surgery. In her desire to have the love she wanted, she may have pushed Sam to deny her own longing. Her own identity.

Lizzie has tried to cover this up, to gloss over it but as of today, she cannot. If she is to have any sense of personal redemption, she must own up to her role in Sam's downfall. She saw Sam's attempt to deny her womanhood. She saw the change in behaviour, the change of clothes. She saw the agony she had caused and she turned away from it.

Lonely, wonderful Sam had been nearly killed by Lizzie's childish wants.

It must have been torment for her to have fallen in love with Lizzie, for what other than love could have forced Sam to attempt to please her so? After years of solitude, Sam must have felt desperate at the possibility of losing the love and affection Lizzie offered.

While Lizzie waits to know the outcome of her terrible work, she offers her soul for the taking if Sam will be all right.

She has gone beyond her confused feelings about Sam's gender and her longing for a male counterpart. She can picture herself without a man. She can't picture herself without Sam.

A long hour later, they are summoned to Sam's recovery room and once he checks to see that his long-time friend is indeed on the mend, Mickey leaves for work, promising to return before the day ends. Lizzie watches Sam's statistics on the monitor that hangs on the wall next to the bed. Sam has been given drugs to counter the effects of her overdose. These and the physical and mental strains of her ordeal have sent her to sleep.

Lizzie leans forward and places her head next to one of Sam's powerful hands. She takes it in hers and strokes it, hoping to soothe Sam in her dreams. She contemplates what Mickey has told her about Sam's addiction during her late teens. About how she got herself clean as she came to terms with herself and her gender. About how her previous drug use created an environment for a new addiction to develop quickly.

Lizzie is hungry, but the pain in her stomach feels good, a justifiable punishment.

Chapter Thirty-Five

Lizzie and Sam smile at each other. The smiles are tentative, scouts sent to get a feel for unknown territory.

Lizzie's chin quivers with emotion. She wants so much for this to go well.

"Don't. You'll make me start too," Sam croaks. Her throat is dry from the intubation.

Lizzie hands her a glass of water and a pudding cup left over from the lunch she purchased in the cafeteria.

"There is so much I have to say to you." Lizzie wants to throw herself on the floor, to beg forgiveness, to be denied, to suffer.

A nurse bustles in to check Sam's temperature and blood pressure. "A doctor will be in to see you shortly. He's making his rounds as we speak. He'll want to talk with you about what to do from here." The nurse makes a few notes on his clipboard and slips behind the curtain of the next patient.

The intrusion brings Sam and Lizzie back to the reason they are in the hospital and makes them self-conscious. They smile at each other then look away, unsure of how to proceed.

Lizzie clears her throat. She has to jump. There is a knot in her stomach. "I love you." She can't bear to look at Sam even as she wants to see her reaction. "But I haven't been acting like I do." She reaches for Sam's hand, the tips of their fingers touch before Lizzie jerks her hand away. She has no right to presume this familiarity. "I don't have the words to tell you how sorry I am, how much I hate myself for leading you to this."

Lizzie begins to cry. Sam tells her to hush but Lizzie tells her she must go on.

"Here's the thing of it. I love you. The person you are, the person you want to be. I wish I had figured this out sooner."

Silence falls between them. Lizzie stares at nothing, trying to find the right words that will make life right. Sam closes her eyes. The voices of other patients in the room and the noise of hallway traffic fill the space between them.

When Lizzie speaks, her voice is faraway. "What I want is for you to have everything you want for yourself."

Sam's stillness intimidates Lizzie who doesn't know if it indicates acceptance or anger.

"Mickey and I figured out a way to help you get what you want." Now Lizzie looks squarely at Sam, intent that there be no misunderstanding between them. "Mickey will write a letter and provide whatever paperwork is necessary to say that you've been working for him for a year as his nanny. His female nanny."

Sam says nothing.

"That's the last piece, right? That's all you need for the surgery?" Lizzie stammers. This isn't going at all how she planned. Why isn't Sam speaking? She takes a deep breath. "You can file an income tax return to make it official." She pauses, puzzled by Sam's lack of response. "I thought this would make you happy."

Sam's composure crumples. Tears tumble, dropping onto her hospital shirt. She holds her arms out and Lizzie thrusts herself into the embrace.

Lizzie is the first to pull away. "There is more. I have to tell you something more."

Sam grabs tissues from the side table and wipes her face. "I'm not sure I can take more. I feel so… I feel like I've been through the fire and I'm afraid that if I believe what you're telling me, I'll crash right back into the flames."

"I have to tell you and then, if you want me to, I'll leave."

Lizzie watches Sam restore her face to its usual expression of wary detachment. While she prepares for the worst, Lizzie braces herself to do the right thing.

"I want you to know that I'll be here when you get back from Montreal. That I'll wait for you, and I'll help out while you recover. I realize that I've hurt you." Lizzie begins to cry afresh, but carries on. "I'm so sorry for that. The only excuse I have is ignorance. I couldn't have known that my… my…" She trails off, trying to find her way. "I want you to know that I can love you as a woman. Gender doesn't matter. Not to me. Not anymore. Maybe it never did. I don't know. Maybe, after what I've lived through, it's even better this way. But that doesn't matter to me either. You're all that matters to me. That and whether you think that you can be with me."

Sam clasps her hands together. Her forehead is drawn tight in concentration. She moves her mouth as if to speak but stops. She tries again, her voice cracks.

"I'm really fucked up right now, Lizzie. I want to say yes, to live happily ever after, but I can't do that from today. I've got a stint at rehab waiting for me and, if what you say is true, an operation that's going to change my life. Forever."

Lizzie sees fear in Sam's eyes. She reaches for her hand.

"I love you more than I've imagined loving somebody. That messed me up really bad. I started thinking that everything I'd been through was for nothing. Why change my body to be a woman only to fall in love with a woman? I never saw myself that way. Until you. I wish I could but I can't make any promises. I don't know who I'll be at the end of it all."

"I do," Lizzie wants to tell her. "I know who you'll still be." Instead, she nods. Sam's words aren't the ones she wants to hear but they are honest. Lizzie will have to be patient. Maybe that's what love is. Having the patience to let your love just be without a requirement for anything in return.

Sam isn't the only one with changes on the horizon. Lizzie has her own path to hack out of the wilderness. She has her next appointment with admissions tomorrow. Who knows where she'll be six months from now?

Still she has hope.

Lizzie leans forward and they kiss in a gesture of consolation and love, of tenderness and longing, of endings and beginnings.

A doctor enters the room and Lizzie excuses herself.

At the door she turns and smiles and waves. "I'll be back."

About the Author

Colleen Gareau is the author of *My Mother's Summer Vacations* and *Sam(uel)*. She lives in Kingston, Ontario, Canada and has worked in public relations for 20 years. Colleen enjoys literary fiction, especially CanLit and the work of Southern authors. She periodically needs a nature-fix to keep her sane.